LOOKING FOR LIFE

A COLLECTION OF SCIENCE FICTION SHORT STORIES

D1715152

CLAYTON GRAHAM

CONTENTS

ALSO BY CLAYTON GRAHAM

<u>MILIJUN</u>

A tangled web of alien intrigue descends upon an unsuspecting Earth...

"Take a deep breath and dive into the future, with contact and much more with ET. From the very start this superb novel takes you on a journey you won't forget."

— Kay Mack

<u>SAVING PALUDIS</u>

An alien revolution centuries in the making will change mankind's future forever...

"Saving Paludis is a wonderfully intelligent, creative and superbly written book. The author is clearly highly skilled in bringing alien races, otherworldly technology and distant planets to life with such clarity that the reader cannot fail to be impressed."

— Lynne Barnes

<u>SILENTLY IN THE NIGHT</u>

A collection of tantalizing tales with more twists than braided hair.

"Just when you think you have figured everything out ... nothing is as it seems."

— Deborah Lavery

AMIDST ALIEN STARS

They awoke surrounded by alien stars...

"Admirable world-building and the unsurpassable, indefatigable, drive of the human Spirit to not just survive, but to thrive, power this engrossing sequel to the author's debut science fiction novel, MILIJUN"

— Mallory A Haws

WAITING FOR WATER

Maria Kerr puckered her brow and focused tired eyes on the horizon, trying to make out the camel's hump that was officially known as Uluru and what she called *The Rock*. These days, this was as far away from the homestead as she wandered; her world consisted of maize and desert—and, of course, the irrigation canal.

The canal ran straight as a die from Uluru, which in the year 2175 gathered its fair share of rain in the summer months, and ended up at the broad fields of the station. Adjacent to the station, dwarfing the homestead in its mechanical glory, a huge red mobile bore machine stood like a sentinel, ready to spring into action at the drop of a hat. The machine did not belong to Maria or her partner, Karl. It was a government machine, to be used only to suck the underground aquifers dry should surface water disappear.

But there was a problem. The canal was practically empty, and the aquifers had not been replenished in over two years.

Following a succession of dry summers, rain was out of fashion in Maria's part of the world.

The only devices currently functioning were the ninety thousand square metres of solar arrays and the planting drones that lay idle in the barn. What was the use of sowing seed on parched land?

Karl had once claimed, not that many years ago, that they could get an additional two acres of crops from their water supply. But all the water was up in the sky now, and a long time coming.

She smiled as her husband's image ghosted through her mind, shimmering in the heat haze. He was usually out in the fields or tinkering with the drones or checking out the Kantju Gorge for signs of new water. But today he had gone to what remained of Tennant Creek, driven up, not flown. Nobody flew anymore. He had gone to plead their case for an extension of their lease, water or no water.

She thumped her thigh in frustration. There was such an investment here; but what good is an investment if nature is not with you?

Two hundred years ago, she mused, it was a different world—and a different rest of the world. Now, war and pestilence were over and could be no more, at least not for her and the next generation to come. Cities were not what they had been, solely inhabited by individuals who scavenged and preyed upon their neighbours among what remained of the once-proud buildings. Fertile soil had turned barren, leaving only untouched desert to provide nourishment for her fellow countrymen, such as they were—a mere handful compared to what once had been.

But she and Karl were alive and now, by government edict, servicing those demanding survivors who had somehow risen from the ashes.

Maria sighed. She was twenty-five, yet felt like forty. She was happily married, yet lonely. *In fact we are both lonely. This place is so isolated.* The one and only consolation was the regular government payment that slipped into their Alice Springs bank account.

And how long was that going to last, now that the water was almost gone?

The Rock caught her eye once more. It must be millions of years old. A tear caught her by surprise, and her hand leapt to her cheek. *Why do old things make me cry?*

She walked a little and saw a roo bouncing over the stubble. A survivor, if ever there was one. It stopped to sniff the air in her direction, gave her a haughty glance, and was gone, the breeze seemingly catching unseen sails and lifting it to almost the height of her head.

With two hours left until sunset, Maria decided to check the canal. She knew it would be dry, but it was part of her world and held fond memories. Two years ago, such a walk would have been rewarded with a swim.

Under golden skies, she would run to the silver channel and let the waters cool her sun-kissed legs. Then she would swim, strong strokes taking her towards The Rock. Over on her back, shielding her face from the sun, she would watch for wedge-tail eagles in the sky.

The stillness had been overpowering. Often a roo would dip its muzzle into the water, ears held high. Craving fun, she would dive, drift silently, and surface under its nose, a metre from the browsing head.

On occasion, the animal would remain where it was and not turn tail, staring at her as if she were the trespasser. Which, of course, she was. Had those indomitable creatures known of the impending drought?

The world was darker now, subdued; a world of less hope. A world that had turned against nature, as nature had now turned against it.

So there it was — the canal of survival. Despairingly empty now, devoid of water and devoid of roos. It ran like a rail-less train line, straight to Uluru, no stopping it, its two-metre high sides cracked and worn like a saddle that had never been oiled.

Maria turned back. The food drone would be here soon, and maybe there would be some mail, maybe a bank statement. What was it like before the wars, she wondered, having mail delivered straight into your home, and delivered as soon as it was sent at that. Now she and Karl had a food and mail delivery once a week, dropped by a drone, and if there was mail, it was usually at least two weeks old.

The sight of the homestead cheered her up, but Karl would not be there. It would be at least another day before he returned. And, in all likelihood, he would be the bearer of bad news. There would be no more farming, no more government cheques. No more future life, really.

The last of the crop had been taken three months ago, what there was of it, and no more had been sown. The bulk container had dropped from the sky, and within hours the fruits of their labours had disappeared, the sweat of their brows sucked up and diminished to a figure in their bank account.

Sowing came just before or at the beginning of rain — a frenetic exercise, full of energy and promise. Undertaken by their team of automatic drones, the task would be completed in a day. Now the flying machines stood idle in the barn, row upon row, looking dejected and sorry for themselves. If they had been human, they would have been declared redundant and put out to pasture, if there were pasture to be found.

Maria heard a siren sound, a galah screeching a sad and forlorn reply, and saw the drone descend as she approached the homestead's front door. It was down and gone in a flash, a fleeting contact with whatever authorities now ruled her world. She walked over to the delivery box.

The usual food parcel and one red-lined envelope, contents unknown.

The envelope's contents gave her cause for both joy and despair; there were no in-betweens, no grey areas that could be subject to misinterpretation.

The letter was from the government overseers, and it read:

Dear Karl and Maria,

We understand you are struggling, and have struggled, to maintain your crop yield to the requisite quota. We also understand that this is through no fault of your own, either through mismanagement or lack of effort.

It is therefore with great pleasure that we inform you that you have been chosen for a pilot cloud seeding project to assist your rainfall metrics. Please understand that you must trigger the orbital seeding drones yourself by simply transmitting the code at the top of this communication.

This means, of course, that you must choose the correct meteorological conditions for the seeding, which will be undertaken by the drones within thirty minutes of your signal.

Please note that this assistance must be triggered within one month from the date of this letter. There are other properties on the seeding waiting list.

Failure to trigger the seeding, or failure of triggered seeding to produce rain, will unfortunately result in cancellation of your management permit and you will be required to leave your holding forthwith, as it will be deemed unsustainable.

We trust you understand the principles behind this notification as we all struggle to maintain our food supplies.

There was no signature at the bottom, just the government logo.

Maria was stunned. *Lack of effort! One month!* Her hands were shaking; tears were in her eyes. She cast a glance at the sky. Not much point in seeding that!

This meant they would be studying the sky every day. Not just the sky: the humidity, the wind direction, condensation patterns. But weren't they doing that already?

But this was different. This time it was their livelihoods.

She wondered whether Karl knew. She wanted him back now. They needed to talk. They needed to do something.

* * *

Two days later, Karl returned. A junior bureaucrat in Tennant Creek had told him about the offer in an attempt to ease his troubled mind. It hadn't worked.

"I got as far as the controller's door," he explained angrily. "But no further."

Maria studied his face. He had not shaved on his trip, and

a not unattractive greyish stubble had sprouted on his sun-tanned face. Strong, piercing blue eyes stared at Maria.

"They don't care. Nobody cares," Karl continued. He waved the government missive as if trying to attract attention from a passing ship. "And this is BS. It's not rained for two years. What are the odds on rainclouds in the next few weeks?"

"Perhaps we should leave now," Maria suggested tentatively, her heartbeat clicking up a notch at the thought. She knew he would not dream of leaving, knew he would want to see this through. All the same, she felt obliged to mention the possibility of deserting the holding.

Karl shook his head. "No. But we should do something."

Maria pursed her lips. There was nothing they *could* do except wait for clouds. "Perhaps," she said, "we could send the signal on the last day anyway—if it doesn't rain, I mean. Just to show we understand." She looked at him with tears welling. "Just before we leave."

Karl stepped forward and took her in his arms. "We've been here ten years, Maria. Farming regeneratively, replenishing the soil with carbon, feeding conflict survivors like there's no tomorrow." He gazed into her eyes. "I'm going back to Tennant Creek to ask for another holding. Even if I have to break the bloody door down."

"Then I'm coming with you," Maria responded.

Karl shook his head. "You can't. What if it looks like rain? Who'll send the drone code?"

Maria took a deep breath. More loneliness, stretching ahead, teasing her with its presence.

Karl kissed her gently on the lips. "We're a good team. Even when we're apart—we're a good team."

Maria nodded. The uncertainty of the future was killing

her. Or maybe it wasn't that uncertain. Maybe they were destined to leave and join the hopeless, desperate masses in the city; to pursue a life of dog eat dog, government ration books, and life among the rubble. She would hate that, and she would not survive it.

"Tomorrow," Karl was saying. "I'll go straight back tomorrow. I'll see the controller, even if I have to use our credit to do it."

Maria should have felt shock. Their credits were the only thing they really owned. But this was a life-or-death scenario. She nodded. "Let's go to bed."

* * *

Karl stood in front of the controller's door.

He had left his vehicle in the old car park, noting that there were hardly any other vehicles there. Either people didn't come here, or very few had their own transport anymore.

He had got past the first two officials with talk, and the last two with cash. On all four occasions, he had been met with acerbity and false smiles. The last two officials, in particular, had exuded a total lack of cooperation, initially suggesting that he was wasting his and their time, at least until Karl offered them sufficient monetary inducement to change their minds.

His and Maria's account had been halved, but now it was done. He had left the last bureaucrat, walked down a characterless corridor, entered a small grey foyer, and now stood awaiting entrance to the controller's office.

Karl didn't know exactly what he was going to say. Would he plead for patience or for another holding where rain was more plentiful? Or would he tell the controller where he could stick his letter, turn tail, and walk away from the entire system?

A buzzer sounded in the foyer, and Karl heard the controller's door click open. Taking a deep breath, he walked through.

The room was empty. No furniture, not even a chair. Not a single decoration adorned the bland, white walls. The ceiling was green; the floor appeared to be solid concrete. There were no windows and no other doors.

The entry door shut behind him, and he heard the lock slide home.

Alarm bells rang, and he turned to seek escape. The door wouldn't budge. He was trapped. His heartbeat increased, and he found himself fighting uninvited panic: a mind-devouring flood of grand proportions, to be beaten off at the source of entry before it crippled his mind.

"Karl Kerr. You are welcome." The voice came out of the wall on all sides, a quadraphonic sound that did little to ease his fears.

"Where are you?" Karl's voice was shaky, coming as it did through a dry mouth and a tight throat.

"I am all around you," came the answer.

"Where's the controller?" Karl asked.

"I am the controller," the voice bounced back.

Karl's mind raced. Who was he talking to? Why was the controller hidden behind an insipid, featureless wall?

"Come out so I can see you," Karl demanded.

"You can see me. I am all around you," the controller responded.

The penny dropped. Karl realised that he was talking to a machine: a machine that was running the whole bloody enterprise.

Sweat sprang to his temples, coated the palm of his hands. There was no way he was going to be aggressive here. There was no way he would win this battle.

"Can you help me?" he asked.

"I have every one of you within me," the controller answered. "I have all your inputs and your outputs. I have your body signals and your mental signals. I make decisions to help the whole, not the individual. Do you understand, Karl Kerr?"

Karl nodded, cleared his throat, said, "Yes."

"Your holding is dry, but I have given you a second chance. Be grateful. Some do not get a second chance. Some are instantly removed."

Karl pondered that for a few seconds. It really was a fearful statement, a totally undisguised threat. It was, he realised, the response of a machine. "So a month is all we get?"

"Yes. A month is all the system can afford."

Changing tack, Karl asked, "Can you calculate the future? Can you predict the weather and all its interactions? Will we survive? Will humans survive?"

"You care about the others?"

"Without the others, we are nothing," Karl answered. "We toil for nothing."

There was a silence for a moment, as if the machine was actually digesting his words. "You have reduced your credit in order to speak to me," the controller said eventually.

"I did," Karl replied. There was no point in denying it.

"That is appreciated," the controller said. "You show initiative."

Karl played along. "Thank you," he said.

"You can have an extra week," the controller announced. "If there is no water on your holding by that time, you will be removed."

Karl did not doubt the words. "Thank you. And thank you for the cloud seeding drones."

"Two additional weeks," the controller rejoined. "Not many humans say thank you anymore. It is wearisome."

The entry door clicked open.

"But no more than that," the controller added.

As he walked down the corridor, Karl summoned a smile on his face, especially for the bureaucrats in the outer offices. "Thank you," he said to each of them as he made his way out. "Thank you so very much."

* * *

Maria counted down the days, marking them on the wall as if she was a prisoner in a medieval prison cell. She didn't understand how things had got to the stage they had: how their livelihood, perhaps even the survival of their state and country, had fallen into the hands of a computer, albeit one of great capacity. But she believed Karl when he said he had done the best he could. Only time would tell whether it would be good enough.

A month passed from the date of the letter. There was no rain.

"We've two weeks more," Karl insisted. "We still have a chance."

It was agony. Every day they searched the sky. Not just for clouds, but for signs of a drone bearing bad tidings. Every day took a further bite from their nerve bank. With only two days to go, they were hardly talking to each other, both being solely focused on what seemed like more important matters.

Sleep was out of the question now. Karl spent his time

checking the seeding drones, praying that they would soon be needed.

The two days passed, and though there were no clouds in the sky, there were plenty in their hearts.

Maria ticked off the forty-fifth day. One month and two weeks. Tomorrow they would receive their eviction notice. She idly wondered whether the robot controller held any remorse for its actions, how many other families had been treated as they had.

They held each other close that night, seeking solace in the warmth of their bodies.

"We'll be okay," Karl whispered. "We're survivors. Somehow we will survive."

* * *

The next morning came with a distinct lack of sunshine endeavouring to break through the window. Maria rose and ran outside, still dressed in her nightdress. There were clouds over Uluru, not dark and foreboding, but subtle and promising.

"Bloody hell!" she cried. "It's too late." She raised her head to the sky and screamed. Karl came racing past her.

"I've sent the code!" he yelled.

She shook her head. "Too late. We're past the deadline." Tears were falling down her face.

Karl took her in his arms, brushed away the tears. "Like you said before, no harm in trying. Let's just wait."

Thirty minutes later, they saw a swarm of dark shadows drop from orbit and head towards Uluru. *The cloud seeding drones.*

Maria could not believe her eyes. She sank to the ground,

crumbling the dry soil between her fingertips. Karl joined her, both of them watching in awe as the drones went about their business high above The Rock.

The same dreadful thought occupied both their minds. They were past the revised deadline. Would the new managers of the holding benefit from the seeding? Would they soon get their eviction notice?

A drop of rain fell on Maria's hand, then more on her head. She looked up. It was going to rain: at long last, it was going to rain.

For a full hour, Maria and Karl sat on the steps of the veranda, watching the water fall, waiting to be evicted. They dreaded the arrival of a messenger drone. The darkening sky filled their vision and their thoughts. Melancholy enveloped them, as if they were surrounded by a sudden mist somehow conjured from the dry desert dust.

The siren sounded, and a drone dropped from the sky. Both of them froze. The terrible news had arrived. Karl walked over slowly, the rain suddenly becoming heavier, as if mocking his every step.

He retrieved the mail as the drone climbed into the heavy sky. A red-lined envelope!

Maria joined him, and they both stood leaning on each other, getting soaked. Karl protected the letter under his shirt, grabbed Maria's hand, and tugged her back to the shelter of the veranda.

"This is criminal. Surely we don't have to go," Maria whispered. "It's raining, for God's sake."

Karl still had the letter beneath his shirt. He held his hand over his eyes, gazing in the direction of Tennant Creek, expecting to see a police car throttling down the road.

Maria could bear it no longer. "Open the damn thing," she

said vehemently.

With shaking hands, Karl opened the envelope and read the letter out loud:

Dear Karl and Maria,

We congratulate you on the launching of the seeding drones.

Our sensors tell us rain is falling on your holding, and as this is within the prescribed timescale, including the allocation of your additional period for politeness, you are now free to pursue your next crop.

We wish you all the best for the future.

Thank you.

PS. I added one more day to cover the inconvenience of your journeys to see me.

Maria shrieked, grabbed the letter, and read it for herself.

"Bloody hell," Karl said. "Who said machines don't have a heart."

He grabbed Maria and planted a huge, sloppy kiss on her lips. "Don't just stand there, girl," he said. "Let's go get the planting drones ready."

LOOKING FOR LIFE

Confusion reigned for several seconds, ably reinforced by a dull ache inside his skull that seemed to ricochet in slow motion from ear to ear. He swivelled his eyes and surveyed the interior of his enclosure, pausing here and there to review an unfamiliar object. Where the hell was he? And why did he feel like crap?

As his eyes turned, there was a whirring sound; when they stopped—silence.

Charles Edgar Fantom, he thought, *retired astronaut of distinction.*

He shook his head. He had asked where he was, not who he was. He felt dopey, drugged. A hint of fear threatened rational thought.

Recovering from an operation? The room was white, brightly lit. It could be a theatre. But there were twinkling lights all around him, as if he had been thrown into the middle of a star field.

Far-flung Fantom they had called him, with Saturn, Neptune, and Pluto safely tucked under his belt. An astronaut, yes, *but where am I now?*

He raised his eyes to the ceiling and once again heard the whirring sound. Should he try to stand? The room was becoming clearer as he gradually adjusted to the various depths of field, and he felt an abrupt urge to explore. *Old habits die hard.*

He decided to stand but found he couldn't. Nothing happened. He tried to call out; no sound found its way to his ears.

Fantom's eyes turned, and he caught his reflection in a shiny console. A sinister numbness seized his mind, but there was no nerve-tingling shock. But hell, there should have been! The reflection did not show a human face, but the unemotional features of a robotic head.

Two large lenses stared back at him. A rectangular mouth used for God knows what sat beneath the artificial eyes. He glanced at his body, finding nothing but a black metallic box, the underside of which was hidden from view.

He wanted to scream, but he had nothing to scream with.

A screen suddenly lit up in front of him, and he found a morsel of relief as he realised he could read the words:

Hello Charles
This is your LFL computer
Glad to see you have awoken safely

Fantom watched, his robotic eyes slightly glazed, his mind still cold and blank. Was he dead or in a living hell—or was he perhaps dreaming? He tried to pinch himself, but, of course, he failed.

The screen went blank, and then more words came into focus:

Please watch carefully
On July 17 2231
You, Charles Edgar Fantom, passed from Earth's life

There! He had it. He *was* dead. Yet here he was actually watching and thinking. Or maybe he was a computer aligned to the thoughts of the late version of himself.

Your brain was saved and linked to the prototype of the machine you now inhabit

Fantom mentally wiped his brow. So, he was alive after all.

The year is now 2381, and you are in deep space
You have been in effective suspended animation inside this spacecraft

Fantom blinked, the process itself just a surge of electrons. Unbelievable! *Far-flung* was not the word. For the past 150 years, he had been dead to the universe!

The screen blinked out again for several seconds, as if giving him time to digest the enormity of his situation.

In five seconds, your body will receive full power
5, 4, 3, 2, 1—

Fantom braced for the shock but was surprised to encounter only a slight tingle in the bodily zones below his head.

You are now on full capability
You can move, talk, smell, and hear and have two operational
hands

He automatically glanced downwards. The screen flickered.

You are capable of withstanding intense extremes
Both pressure and temperature
You are now ready for your mission

Mission! *Here comes the catch,* he thought. He ordered his brain
to extend his right arm, watching in fascination as a jointed
cylindrical tube—attached to which was a beautiful replica of
a human hand—came into view. He waggled the fingers play-
fully.

"*When you are ready.*"

He actually heard the words this time, gobbled up by his
electronic ears.

"*Here begins your mission.*"

The screen was abruptly filled by the head and shoulders
of a man. He was tanned with short grey hair, strong blue
eyes, and an aquiline nose. The face was full, set above a large
square jaw, and it carried a look of determination.

"*You don't know me, Charlie, but I sure know you. You must
be the oldest human alive.*" Fantom stared at the screen, totally
intrigued. The face broke into a grin. "*Let me introduce myself.
My name's Jamie Alexander, and I'm the head of the World Federa-
tion for Space Exploration and Utilisation.*

"*You, Charlie, as you will recall, have a unique record in space,
and that is why you were chosen in 2231 to undertake this mission.*"
The face grew serious. "*Your assignment is to bring life back from
another world. Nothing big, just life forms your new body can carry.*

Please note you have no weapons. It is not that kind of mission.

"No human body could live long enough to complete this mission, yet alone withstand the traumas of space. So you have a new body, Charlie." The face creased into a grin. "*And you get a bonus—one hell of an extended life.*"

"What happened to my old body?" A fair question, Fantom thought, considering the circumstances.

"*You wish to know?*"

The recording was obviously primed to recognise possible questions. "Yes, I bloody well do."

The screen lit up and showed a death certificate: his death certificate. He saw his name, the date, and the cause—automobile accident. He had to laugh. After all those years in space, he had met his end in a car crash.

But now he had a new body, apparently supremely equipped for life among the stars. He required neither food nor water and was totally self-reliant.

The image of Jamie Alexander filled the screen again.

"*Now Charlie,*" Alexander said, "*you may wonder why you have been awoken at this particular point in time. I don't know when it is—it could be a hundred or a thousand years from when I made this recording. Little matter. Your on-board Looking For Life computer is keeping Earth time.*"

Fantom decided to answer. "It's plus 150 years."

Predictably, the image before him never flinched.

"*The fact is, your ship has detected life on a nearby planet. And you are now zeroing in on that life. Everything has been automated.*" Alexander leaned further into the screen. "*But once you hit that planet, Charlie, you are in charge. You go out there and explore, and capture something living for us.*"

Alexander's face relaxed. "*So that's it, Charlie. By the time you hear this, I will be long gone. One word of warning, though.*"

Your ship takes off exactly three months after landing, no matter what, and retraces its way back to Earth. Make sure you are on board. If you want to leave earlier, that's fine—but definitely no later." The image on the screen gave a small wave. *"Best of luck, Charlie."*

The screen went blank, then lit up again.

"End recording. For time to life, press button one two."

Fantom's right arm shifted, and he pressed the appropriate button with his robotic index finger.

"Time to life: one week, two days, two hours, three minutes, five seconds. There is a spacecraft manual in locker A. Advise study."

Do you indeed, Fantom mused. He commanded his body to move towards the series of lockers located against the right wall of the cabin. The movement was smooth and effortless, like the glide of a swan. He found locker A readily enough and, opening it carefully, took out the manual.

For days on end, he read and re-read the instructions.

There was a layout of the ship that located the computer control complex, the nuclear motors, the energy cells, and the specially quarantined hibernation headquarters for extraterrestrial life of any shape or form. There were also hints on how to capture live animals.

Fantom's excitement grew. He felt like a big-game hunter about to explore a dark and unknown continent, with the additional advantage of possessing an invincible body.

He found the control for the external cameras and for the first time saw his target. With only a few days to go, it took up a good portion of the screen.

His dexterous fingers typed a series of questions to the central computer, and the console screen lit up with information:

Diameter: ten thousand kilometres
No moons of any significance (whatever that meant)
A day of 28.13 Earth hours

Not unlike Earth, Fantom mused. That was good.

He glanced at the camera screen again. The planet had a greenish hue with dark brown patches at both poles. Grey, fluffy patches were prominent around the equator, presumably clouds of some kind, but not necessarily water.

It wasn't until the penultimate day that Fantom started to think seriously about his mission. What kind of life could he expect to find on the planet? Was he supposed to capture anything dangerous? How the hell was he going to go about it?

For the first time he felt unhappy about his situation. He also felt tired, suddenly realising he had gone several days without sleeping. *Do I sleep? Or am I too much of a machine?* His body may not need sleep, but his mind most certainly did.

He pressed button one two.

"Time to life: one day, two hours, forty three minutes, seventeen seconds." Even the ship's voice was starting to sound weary.

"I'm going to sleep," Fantom announced. "Wake me up when I need to wake up." He didn't want to see the approach of the planet; he had seen enough of those. He just wanted to be on its surface.

* * *

There was a bell ringing. Fantom slowly opened his eyes. A voice echoed around the cabin.

"Landing imminent. Landing imminent."

He glanced at the console screen. Numbers were scrolling, too quick even for his new eyes.

21

"Secure all loose objects."

His awakening mind recalled the section in the manual on landing procedure. He pressed button one nine and immediately sensed a drift over to the centre of the floor. There was a click, and he found himself held from beneath, almost as if he were a prisoner anchored to the cobbled flags of a medieval prison cell.

"Passenger secure. Landing imminent. One minute, three seconds."

Imminent indeed! Fantom recalled similar landings back in the solar system, where he had been supported within the arms of a comfortable G-couch. This time he felt as if his mind was held in a block of ice. But it still held thought. At the end of the ship's manual, there had been a bit of history; he was familiar with most of it, but by no means all.

*Ages ago, when scientists first evolved the idea of the Looking For Life spacecraft and its ground-breaking occupant, there had been much bitter argument centred on the design of the life-detector. After all, life could be detected in many ways: respiration, conversion of energy, reproduction, bio signatures, to name but a few. However, it was the old school that emerged the victors, the school that had wanted **real** life. And that required major translation—the ability to move from one place to another based on reasoning and thought and, of course, the means to do it. And maybe also the sign of dwellings—intelligently created habitats. Naturally, that meant that planets supporting some kind of bacterial or basic plant life would be bypassed. But the main purpose of LFL was to find animal life—animal life that seemingly moved at random over periods of time.*

Fantom saw clouds on the screen. And then they were

through them, and he noticed a cloud of dust pirouetting against a blue-green sky. A tornado! The craft banked away, and a rocky plateau bathed in light by a faraway sun came into view, mountains in the distance seeming impossibly high. Then what may have been an ocean, glinting in the sunlight, with rolling waves but no sign of life upon its surface.

The ship's voice took him by surprise. *"Approaching landing site. Earth date July 16, 2381. External temperature seven degrees Centigrade, external pressure 1.4 atmospheres, gravity 1.18g. Time of day dusk. Atmospheric percentage content oxygen 20, nitrogen 40, hydrogen 12, carbon dioxide 26."*

Fantom was trying to absorb all that information when the floor suddenly shook and the lights flickered. Then everything became still as the roar of the engines died. He glanced at the screen. It depicted what he presumed was the immediate external view: a brown rocky surface spreading to distant hills turned purple by the setting sun. To the right there was a stand of what looked like trees—life, in other words. *If I had a heart,* Fantom thought, *it would be beating madly.*

"Passenger release imminent."

A click from beneath and he sensed his freedom, yet he was scared to move. The screen started to pan around.

The ship had chosen the landing site well. The ground underneath appeared firm and flat, the sun revealing only a few long shadows treading the plain. Other than the trees, there was no other vegetation as far as he could see, and certainly no higher life forms darting around. Still, early days.

The terrain stretched away in a mixture of greys and browns, eventually merging with uneven craggy hills on all sides. *The ship has probably landed in an ancient crater,* he thought.

He admitted to feeling disappointed. He had not expected

babbling brooks, birds in the sky, animals roaming over grassy plains, but he had expected more than he could currently see. He hoped the computer had not made a mistake. Perhaps it would look more promising in full daylight; most things did.

It would be dark soon. *Should I take a quick look outside before the light fades?* At least he would get a better view of what the ship looked like. He propelled himself over to the elevator and one minute later was pressing the switch to operate the external ramp.

On reaching ground level there was a hum, and he started to hover. Even though he had read that his body could operate hoverjets once outside the ship, the feeling took him completely by surprise. Evidently, his body possessed some kind of automatic anti-gravity mechanism, likely kicked in by the perceived terrain. It was a good feeling, as if the shackles had finally been removed.

Fantom made out the first of the stars as he moved a few metres away from the ship. He could almost feel the alien soil beneath his feet. He turned back to look at the spacecraft.

She towered above him, bigger than he had expected. And she had a shiny white surface that reflected the sunset: three spheres joined together, the largest at the bottom, the smallest at the top. Beautiful, he thought, as beautiful as any ship he had ever flown. Sitting proudly on three wide circular feet, each at least three metres across, the spacecraft towered to the sky like some kind of omnipotent Earthly cathedral.

The sun was now hiding behind the distant mountains, having given birth to a green afterglow that bathed the top of their peaks. Light was fading, and he suddenly noticed something tracking across the sky. What was that? A bird, a satellite, a vapour trail, a sign of life? Or maybe just a meteorite.

Whatever it was disappeared behind the hills and left the sky as naked as it had been when he had initially disembarked. Fantom found himself shuddering, or at least his mind gave him that impression.

Surprisingly, he wasn't afraid, but that somehow felt wrong. There should have been at least a modicum of fear pulling on the reins of his excitement. No doubt it was because he lacked nerves and hormones, his mental processes seemingly subject to the limitations of his robotic body.

It was strange, he thought, that he was alone on an alien planet that apparently supported life, hostile or otherwise, and he felt nothing but pleasure at being there. Somebody had tinkered with his brain cells, or their electronic equivalent.

There was a wind from somewhere—his sensors could feel it—but there was no sound to accompany its veiled motion. Green-lined clouds appeared, scudding over the far mountains, moving quite quickly in his direction. They looked menacing, as if herded by an unseen intelligent hand: withholding their presence for as long as possible, then suddenly leaping out to surprise any weary traveller on the plain below.

He looked back at the ship again—his home for the next few days, maybe months. Time to get back on board.

He didn't have to do anything! He abruptly found himself speeding up the ramp and entering the elevator.

What the—!

Fantom tried to stop the movement, but nothing happened. Damn it. What was going on? He entered the control room, saw the clouds much nearer on the screen. Then came the familiar click from beneath. He was a prisoner once more, and he began to realise he was not in sole charge of the mission.

"Passenger secure," the ship barked. *"All power minimised."*

Fantom fumed. Could he still talk? "What's happening?" Thank God!

"Electrostatic storm approaching. All unnecessary power severed."

For his own protection, power had been diminished. Whoever had designed the systems had evidently not trusted the occupant of the spacecraft to make his own decisions.

Everything was in darkness now. The cabin lighting and the camera screen had been the last to lose energy, and Fantom could not see the approach of the storm.

Outside, the sky was threatening, full of lightning. Green and purple, black and silver, decorated the heavens. The planet was angry. Fantom slept.

* * *

He awoke with all power restored. The screen showed much the same view as yesterday, except he could now see the ship's shadow stretching a good distance along the ground. The daylight of dawn, he presumed. Things certainly looked a lot brighter in the aftermath of the storm: beautiful in a weird, alien way and quite peaceful.

And then he detected movement. He checked it out again, zooming the screen in closer. Something was on the plain, something he was sure hadn't been there yesterday. A shape, with a shadow. Yellow in colour, a single brown stripe running along the top, a slug-shaped body, incredibly large. It was hard to determine how long the body was. A single tentacle grew from one end and waved towards the ship.

He focused the camera even closer, converging on the tentacle. It was mounted on top of what he presumed was the

26

head, and below it he could make out some kind of mouth: a long, prominent slit about three-quarters of the way down the front. There were no eyes. Fantom presumed there was one at the end of the tentacle, that it was, in fact, an optical stalk.

The body flexed and shifted. The creature was moving. Fantom drew the camera back and caught further movement. Another one! He scanned around. More of them. All waving their appendage at the ship. He wondered whether it was some kind of greeting or something more sinister.

His surge of excitement could not be quelled. All around him, alien life was stirring. He zoomed in on another of the creatures. Much the same, perhaps larger, though it was diffi-cult to tell. He tried another, and another. All alike. And all moving towards the ship.

Okay. So let them. He debated his next move, deciding he would go outside and take a closer look. But he didn't want to lower the ramp and wondered whether he could hover down from the ramp door. He asked the question.

"That is possible, but it will use up more energy. I will bring you back before it gets too low."

So that was it then. The plan was made. In fact, he would keep a steady height above the aliens. For all he knew, the ten-tacle could be used as a weapon.

* * *

It was a strange feeling, hovering in the sky. There was no doubt they could see him; every tentacle followed his move-ment as he slowly passed over them. He gained a bit more height, leaving a good four metres between his body and the tip of the probing alien stalks.

Fantom looked for a good spot to land in order to save

27

power: a position that would allow him to assess the situation. He could now see a pattern developing below. About half the aliens were continuing towards the ship, the rest were changing direction and sticking with him.

Thwack! Thwack! Thwack!

What the—!

Three of the tentacles had stretched skywards and attached themselves to his body.

Mistake number one! The appendages were much more than an optical stalk!

He felt his body being dragged downwards.

"Get me out of here!" he yelled at the ship.

There was a momentary surge upwards, but it only seemed to encourage the aliens to pull harder. Fantom could actually feel part of his body beginning to overheat with the effort.

"That is not possible," the ship replied. *"I will look for another way."*

Thwack! Another stalk joined the attack.

There was no resisting this time. Fantom was drawn down to the planet's surface. He counted twelve of the slug-like creatures around him. The four that had brought him down maintained their hold. The other eight waved their tentacles in his direction. Despite his predicament, Fantom found time to study his adversaries.

They were quite big, perhaps four metres long, one metre high, the surfaces of their yellow and brown bodies rippling with what he assumed were muscles. The mouth, if it was a mouth, consisted of a pair of long lips that parted intermittently as if the creature was breathing.

Mistake number two! They had not provided him with a weapon!

"Can you fire at them?" Fantom asked the ship.

"We are forbidden to take alien life," the ship responded, *"so we are not armed. It is against the directive."*

Fantom groaned, racked his electronic brain for a way out. But there wasn't one. The only way was up, and currently that was not possible.

Back at the ship, something was moving. Fantom looked across in disbelief. The ramp was lowering. What the hell was the good of that!

"What d'you think you're doing?" he called out angrily.

"Just wait," was the only response.

One of the sluglike creatures paused at the base of the ship's entry ramp, then slowly made its way upwards. In less than a minute, it was inside. *Oh, marvellous,* Fantom thought, *we have an alien.*

The ship obviously thought the same thing. The ramp raised, the door closed.

"What're you doing?" Fantom's voice was barely a whisper.

Mistake number three! He had trusted the ship.

The rockets fired, and his way back home leapt into the sky.

"Mission accomplished, Charlie. Well done."

Fantom could not even weep. He just wasn't capable. He watched the flare of the rockets until they disappeared. He was quite capable of expletives, though, and several soared into the heavens chasing the wake of the ship.

The other aliens, the ones that had been approaching the ship, were now sidling towards him, and he wasn't going anywhere.

After ten more minutes, Fantom deduced that the aliens did not know what to do with him. One had approached and

29

tested its lips against his body, shrinking away in obvious disgust. So what now? Would they go away?

He wondered how long his power would last. Quite a while, he thought. And he did have a solar array. Perhaps things weren't so bad after all. Perhaps he could survive for years on this planet.

A streak of light crossed the sky. Was the ship returning?

A dark silhouette dropped towards the plain. God! Definitely not the ship. It looked like a giant bird, and it was massive. It soared in circles above them, wings, legs, and neck outstretched, and Fantom began to feel vulnerable. The grip on his body ceased, and the slugs were moving away. He got the impression that they were traveling as fast as they could. But it wasn't fast enough.

The bird swooped and was upon them, picking them up and flinging them towards the horizon with a flick of its long neck. They went in all directions. It didn't appear to be swallowing any, but that could have been mistake number four.

Fantom wanted to run, get out of there, but he was actually entranced.

Work done, the bird settled down some thirty metres away, dust rising beneath its huge feet and dancing among its long legs. It was indeed enormous, standing some ten metres high, long wings settled onto the ground on each side of its substantial body, two eyes staring at him balefully from a head that must have been at least four metres across. The beak, now dormant, hung below like the ripened seed of some giant Terran tree.

Am I to be its next plaything?

The eyes flickered, and something moved within them. Fantom jerked, zoomed in, couldn't believe his eyes.

There appeared to be people moving around inside the

eyes. He tried to zoom in closer, but the view became blurry.

He turned his attention to the wings. There were certainly no feathers: in fact, the surface appeared to be moulded in one piece. How the hell did they flex? The body was the same, smooth and glossy. There didn't seem to be any joints anywhere.

The bird took two steps towards him, moving like a vulture approaching its prey. A strange hopping gait, awkward. He could make out the tail, held erect in the air, bobbing with the motion.

He looked at the eyes again, but they were empty this time. Nothing stirred behind their vacant gaze.

Something dropped to the ground. An egg! Or at least an egglike object. It rose and hovered in the air, rotated its pointy end towards him. Fantom felt a shiver run down his non-existent spine. Time to get out of here!

But then he was hit by a beam of light, and he couldn't move. The light disappeared, but he was still paralysed. The egg grew closer and settled on the ground six metres away.

Two humanoid figures emerged from the egg. They were small, not much over a metre high, and they wore tight purple one-piece suits, or maybe that was their skin, some kind of alien epidermis. The bird, Fantom realised, was an alien aircraft. Sure, it resembled a bird, but the eyes were twin cockpits.

The aliens walked over to him, one head, two arms, two legs, just like him—or at least what he had been. He zoomed in on their faces before they got too close. Not human, more like deer, long snout and big eyes. Still, pleasant enough.

They started to walk back to their transport. Were they leaving? No such luck. The light beam hit him again, and his body rose and floated towards the huge birdlike machine.

They took him inside, the door closed, and all became dark.

* * *

Light returned out of the blue. Fantom looked around. He was in a small room, and four of the purple aliens stood two metres away, observing him with their large brown eyes. Now and again, their snouts would lift as if they were trying to detect an aroma from his body. Maybe they were. Maybe smell was their strongest sense.

A screen lit up on one of the walls, and Fantom saw stars: a galaxy, he presumed.

"Home?"

He froze. The word had entered his mind out of nowhere. Surely these people could not speak Earth languages. He noticed that a cord ran from his chest to the floor. What the hell was that? And then even darker thoughts. *How long have I been here? Have they accessed the inner workings of my brain?*

"Home?"

There it was again. He looked at the stars on the wall. Nothing he recognised. He replied. *No.* It was the only thing he could do.

The stars changed. *Home? No.* This was ridiculous. There were billions of known galaxies. The stars on the wall changed again. Same routine. They started to cycle faster. One every ten seconds, then every second, then a tenth of a second interlude, and then every millisecond. Even as Fantom surveyed the rapidly switching images, he was calculating how long it would take. Galaxies shown in one hour would be 3,600,000. Galaxies shown in one year: 31,536,000,000. The time to show 200 billion galaxies was well over six years.

He wanted it to stop. But it didn't. He thought he would

get tired. But he didn't.

They were priming him through the cable, nourishing his battery and his circuits. Clever bastards.

His life just consisted of remaining stationary, viewing images, saying *No, No, No.*

If he were human, he would be dead. Long-time dead.

Yes. There it was. The Milky Way. Galaxy number 6,307,231,407. *Yes.*

Only 2.4 months. Relief swamped his mind as the Milky Way remained on the wall. It could have been a lot worse. Maybe they had searched the nearest galaxies first. He didn't care. The probing had stopped.

But what now?

* * *

Fantom was in a different room, wondering what they would do with the information he had given them. Not much they could do, he thought. The Milky Way was huge. But he knew what was coming next. How many solar systems in the Milky Way? Around 100 billion, he reckoned.

Here we go again, he thought, as a picture flashed up on the wall.

It didn't take as long this time. Fantom assumed they had weeded out solar systems where the planets were unviable for life.

And there was home: the solar system, *his* solar system. *Yes.*

Oh well. He'd told them where Earth was. Would they go there? He did not give a damn. After what had happened, he did not owe Earth anything, not a darned thing.

So what now?

* * *

Fantom gazed around. He was aboard one of their ships, attached to the floor inside one of the eyes, his umbilical cord running to an adjacent cabinet.

He hadn't expected this. They were taking him with them. On board one of their bird machines, one of hundreds. It seemed he had seeded an invasion. It was about now he started to regret his actions. But, of course, it was far too late. The stars were flashing by, lines of light like they used to show in the old movies heaven knows how many centuries ago.

He had hardly seen the aliens. It seemed they could put him to sleep at will, only rousing him when they wanted to move his position.

But he was awake now, which, he supposed, probably meant they were at the end of their journey.

Speed was slowing. The stars became more like stars, huddling together like a huge herd of sheep, yet with light years between them.

Home: Red dwarf, three planets. Fantom looked eagerly out of the spacecraft's eye.

He recognised the sun and the position of the planets. But it didn't feel like home.

They moved closer in.

Home?

Yes. This was home. He stared through the window, stared at the planet below, stared at the sky. It seemed full of ships. Definitely an invasion fleet!

Home?

Yes. Damn you.

They were dropping lower, entering clouds. He could see buildings, but they looked strange to him.

The coin dropped! *Wrong system.* This was not his birth planet—his artificial memory had been uploaded with a completely different solar system: a safety device installed by his creators. He had an inkling where he was, but he didn't really care anymore. This was crazy. It was all going haywire.

Not home?

They had cottoned on. He could only respond the way he had done before.

Why hadn't these stupid creatures followed his own ship? Maybe they couldn't. Maybe they were not ready. Maybe there was not enough time.

Lights were coming up from the planet. Missiles? Human-launched missiles? Probably. Otherwise, Earth would have labelled this planet as supporting alien life.

All hell was let loose. The ships around him were catching fire. They were returning the missile assault with balls of vibrant energy that swept downwards like jet-propelled snowballs. There was screaming light everywhere, painful to behold.

A purple-skinned alien entered the deck, removed Fantom's battery, and unplugged his umbilical.

Everything went black, and he was glad.

THE COMEDIAN

T he sound of applause. *The silly creatures.*
Applause. I hate it, but I can't do without it. Like most entertainers, I need it. It's like a drug. It's the only way I can exist. I tell jokes. I know nothing else. There is nothing else I can do. I cannot do mechanical things, nor can I understand how this world's system works. It is too complicated for me, too haphazard, much too severe.

I was introduced to this world by accident, a big accident. It took all my guile and energy to survive. I used to mingle in pubs and clubs, trying to be inconspicuous, picking up the odd joke, some good apparently, some not so good. I got quite a collection, and I needed them, believe me. I was on my last legs, so to speak.

So I became a comedian.

Applause feeds me and gives me enough energy to survive. Just.

36

I live in a shed. I call it *my* shed, but it isn't really. It belongs to one of the creatures I followed from the pub. Heaven sent, it stood there in the moonlight, a home from home.

Can a kangaroo jump higher than a house? Of course, a house doesn't jump at all.

Laughter. Applause.

There's not much in the shed. A few old things. Not as old as me, though. And spiders. Quite a few spiders. Webs in the corners. That kind of thing. I don't sleep much, but I don't really need to. I just rest — recover from my comedic exertions. Telling jokes takes a lot out of me, but it's good to be appreciated.

What is the difference between a snowman and a snowwoman? Snowballs.

Laughter. Applause.

I don't really understand that one. It doesn't make sense at all. But the people in the audience like it, that's the main thing. So I keep telling it.

I look down at my suit. I made it myself from stuff in the shed and what I found on one of my midnight walks. Stuff they hang on horizontal lines, fluttering in the breeze. They'd call it stealing, I guess. The jacket is yellow with black spots I put on myself. It makes them laugh. When I walk on the stage, they laugh. I think that is good.

I have to keep in shape, though. It takes so much energy, this keeping in shape. More energy than I thought I possessed. But I manage. I have to. There's no alternative. Jokes, and lots of them. Telling them once a week. Keep in shape to tell the jokes, to survive in this crazy world.

But it gets to me, not knowing what else to do. It breaks my heart, or it would do if I had one.

I dreamed I was forced to eat a giant marshmallow. When I woke up, my pillow was gone.

Groans.

Oh no! They didn't laugh at that one. This is serious. I'll try another.

A man asks a farmer near a field, "Sorry, sir, would you mind if I crossed your field instead of going around it? You see, I have to catch the 4:23 train." The farmer says, "Sure, go right ahead. And if my bull sees you, you'll even catch the 4:11 one."

Titters. Not laughs. No applause.

Try again

I tried to remarry my ex-wife. But she figured out I was only after my money.

A few laughs. Scattered applause.

This is no good. I feel unwell. I look to the stage door, wanting to make an escape, but the boss is there, the man who hired me. I'm losing strength. My shape is going. I look down at my body. The suit jacket looks like it's going to burst.

Huge applause. Lots of claps.

They think it's part of the act. My jacket and pants are lying on the floor. The clapping is starting to stop. I hear a scream. Someone actually screamed. I look at my body. It's yellow with brown spots—and it's growing, growing, and growing. Rounder and rounder.

I hear lots of screams now, and people are falling over each other to get out of the building. And all the time, I'm still growing. Two old people on the front row aren't moving. They're mesmerised, eyes agape. My body absorbs them.

I hear a siren. Now I feel better. I have more energy. I am getting into shape again. But I have no clothes. The boss is gone. I make for the stage door.

Out into the night. I'll just have to try another town. They won't come here again. It'll be in their heads, what happened tonight. Another town is needed. Another place.

Another interview. I'm in full shape now. Absorbing people is better than absorbing applause.

Next town. I'll have them rolling in the aisles. I'll slay them.

THE SCORCHED GARDEN

Jay Svenson stepped from his two-man orbital shuttle and dropped gingerly onto Umbriel's hard and unforgiving rocky surface. Lifting his helmet's visor and looking around, he could only see an abundance of small grey rocks and some larger black and purple boulders. And numerous impact craters that had mocked him with their ancientness as he'd made the swift descent to the moon's surface.

If he was not mistaken, the ice was returning, faster than predicted. He could see crystals forming on the rocks, on the ground, on nearby hills. The oxygen, of course, was long gone. The universe was reclaiming its own: rocky core, icy mantle, just as it had been.

This barren world had recently been his home. Humans had vanquished its meagre carbon dioxide, added a gravitational network, and, over hundreds of years, successfully terraformed this small third moon of the outer planet Uranus—a piece of ambitious cosmic engineering unlikely to be ever repeated.

Jay sought the horizon, curved and jagged against a black sky littered with the pinpricks of countless yet barely visible stars. Glancing up, he made out his spacecraft twinkling in a synchronous orbit. And close by, in a more distant orbit, he made out what was the nuclear-powered artificial sun—not shining now, just a dead thing, devoid of purpose. Much like himself.

As always, as he stood in this place, he was overwhelmed by a feeling of extreme solitude. Nonetheless, he was effectively returning home. The war had finished a year ago. *And that is exactly how long the precious process will have taken.*

Umbriel, once the shining light of humankind's terraforming endeavours, had been devastated by the Ring War, and desolation was returning, had for the most part returned; a desolation not too far removed from the moon's initial state when discovered in 1851, by William Lassell.

And that is why he now wore a spacesuit, where once he had roamed free.

Jay glanced up at pale Uranus, then searched the sky for his new home—Ariel, just another moon, another barren rock, another Alexander Pope name, and another of Lassell's discoveries. But Ariel did not look or feel like his home. It was too early, too soon after the war. And too soon after the event that had changed his life forever.

He had brought the shuttle down on the summit of a ridge so he could walk down into Zlyden, or what was left of it. From where he stood, he could view the devastation caused by the missiles and energy beams: craters, scars, the ruins of old buildings. His buildings! His farm. His and Debb's.

Hundreds of years of work destroyed in less than a year. Atmosphere gone, gravity gone, sunlight gone. Why did the human race insist on degrading the work of others of its kind? Why did it have the insatiable need to dominate others with its political creed or religion or lifestyle? Why could humans not just concentrate on their own lives? Why did they impose?

There had been no logical reason to destroy Umbriel. The few settlers here were pioneers, struggling to live on a moon that needed more support than other terraformed worlds. It was so far from the sun, so far from Earth.

Jay inhaled deeply. He needed to focus on his current task. And that made him nervous.

For a moment, he closed his eyes and sought treasured memories.

* * *

Jay and Debb looked out of the window, staring at the rain. They had been settled less than an Earth month, and the first clouds were shedding huge tears onto Umbriel's precious new soil. It had taken over two hundred years to make it happen, and they felt privileged to be among the first people to witness the water's fall. Before the showers had started, they had been admiring the distant heights of Zlyden Crater, but now the view was completely hidden behind a veil of mist. Never mind, the rain is better, *Jay thought.* It's a miracle.

He marvelled that although Umbriel's gravity was only around one-sixth of that of Earth's moon, the gravitational network over the small moon's surface ensured rain would fall, although at a lower rate than it would on Earth.

They were pioneers, he supposed. Stretching the limits of man's expertise to the farthest reaches of the solar system. Living a dream that few others shared.

Yet they were simple farmers. The vast fields he saw through the window had just been robotically sown. Soon, when the time came, the crop would be harvested, processed, and sold to the new breed of interstellar explorers who were stationed on Ariel, the second closest moon to Uranus. And, of course, their own supplies would be restocked.

He had no wish to venture beyond the solar system. That was for others. He was content to live with Debb and someday have children. If that made him reclusive, so be it. His life adventure would be here, on this small moon, with the woman he loved.

Jay sneaked an arm around Debb's waist and breathed on her neck.

She giggled and said, "Let's go outside."

Jay laughed. "But we'll get soaked to the skin." His face broke into a huge grin. Debb was only wearing a thin cotton top and leggings.

She span around, long blonde hair whirling in the artificial gravity, blue eyes sparkling, kissed him briefly on the lips, and was gone. He saw her outside, breathing fresh air, raising her arms to the sky as if she had made the rain herself.

It was amazing, Jay reflected, how Umbriel had been terraformed, how they had come to be here to see the first rains. It was amazing how Debb kept on loving him. He stared at her, his heart full. She was dancing now, soaked to the skin and loving it.

* * *

Jay was halfway down the scree, halfway to the underground shaft. Below, to his left, were the ruins of their cabin; farther across, the scorched remains of their garden and fields. That powerful view held memories that tore him apart. He and Debb had watched the automated sowing with their hearts in their mouths, praying that nothing would go wrong. They need not have worried. The machines had been programmed to perfection, each seed inserted at the prescribed distance apart and at the correct depth.

There had been six machines in all, each allocated their acreage, each dedicated and purposeful. And they had toiled for Umbriel day upon Umbriel day, each day four Earth days long, never complaining, never even stopping until their allocation was completed. They were gone now, of course, dissipated to the stars like so much unwanted debris.

Jay paused to rest, laboured breaths grating through his suit helmet like a rasp on bare metal. His heart was beating faster now, more from nervousness than exhaustion. *Is this insane? Am I mad to have done it?*

He looked to the right, away from his old home, and saw a few of the cloud-making towers still stretching high into the sky. Many others lay bent and broken, listless things against a lifeless landscape. They looked like broken windmills, sails akimbo, reaching out from ancient history, searching for some kind of resurrection. Beyond them, Uranus hovered like a doting and mournful mother.

There was no way he was going to stop now. No way.

* * *

They were in the garden breathing the cool air and watching Uranus rise, the planet, powered by unseen universal forces, gently lifting over the rim of Zlyden Crater. Tears were in Debb's eyes, not flowing, just holding there as if reluctant to leave.

"I don't believe it," she said, turning to look at Jay with sorrow tarnishing her beautiful face. "Could there be war, after all this time? It's not possible. There must be some mistake."

"Earth won't see reason," Jay stated sadly. "And Mars wants her share of the Uranus moons and rings. This system is a stepping stone to the stars. It's critical to further outward missions."

"Then they should share it," Debb said. "Peacefully. I don't care who we grow food for."

Jay slung his arm over her shoulders. "Neither do I, Debb."

They were just sitting there, observing their own bit of the cosmos: their fields blossoming, green growth everywhere, and the sky so serene and so quiet. She turned to him, and his heart sank to see the misery on her face. "If the moons and rings belong to anybody, they are surely ours, the people of this part of the system."

Jay shrugged. "We can't fight them, Debb. We're too small."

They lapsed into silence and watched the heavens bathe the faint rings of their planet. Jay wondered whether the sky would soon be lit up by bright explosions. Much too early yet, he reasoned. Both Earth and Mars would still be preparing for conflict. Diplomats would be trying to ease the situation. That was not even a hope, more like a prayer.

Jay suddenly reached out and grabbed her hand. "I've been talking to people on Ariel. I've a proposition to make."

She stared at him, open-mouthed, her expression wary, full of confusion. "What?" she said, her voice small, almost inaudible.

He smiled at her, trying to imbue love and confidence into the only person he had ever truly loved.

"It's for us," he said. "To help us survive."

* * *

There were the remains of a small building above the shaft: half-broken walls and no roof. At least they had used conventional missiles and lasers, not anything that would have left a more deadly legacy. Jay approached and looked over the

45

nearest collapsed wall.

Among the rubble, he made out what remained of the opening to the elevator shaft. It looked accessible, only partially damaged, certainly good enough to make a descent.

A white-suited invader among dark, timeless terrain, he carefully made his way to the entrance. Once there, he negated the gravity cells that he'd activated following touchdown—Umbriel's own network now being defunct—turned on his helmet lights, took a step forward, and dropped into the void.

It was as if he had lost his voice, floating aimlessly and living someone else's nightmare. He could not even begin to describe how he felt. *I am so close now, so close.* Desperate memories hit him out of the blue: an avalanche of raw emotions that dragged his thoughts into a quagmire of despair.

Immediately after talking with Debb, he had spent some hours on Ariel before the first hint of war threatened the rings. Even though it had been a fleeting visit, they were nervous hours, for always at the back of his mind had been the threat of being unable to return. But it had been an essential trip—if his plans were to reach fruition.

Fallout Technologies had been supportive: the science was well-proven; the transport of equipment to Umbriel, easier than he had expected. It could all be arranged in a matter of days. At a cost, of course. But what cost was greater than not having a future?

They had asked why not build on Ariel, but that would have been a betrayal of his and Debb's dreams, and who could say whether Ariel would be any safer than Umbriel? His plans were, in any case, a last resort.

The shaft and the underground rooms—a haven from future aggression—were mostly built by androids and AI machines. They were here one minute, gone the next—like most of his credit—or so it seemed. And amidst all the mechanical efficiency, the dust and the noise, he and Debb watched for signs of violence in the surrounding skies.

He took meagre comfort from the fact that Ariel was functioning normally.

Jay descended slowly under Umbriel's weak natural pull until his boots eventually found solid ground. He reset his gravity, took a deep breath, and played his lights around.

The place was much as he recollected. He was in a circular chamber some five metres across, and there were a couple of man-high rounded archways leading to other rooms. Dust from the surface had found its way down to the polished rock floor, and cracks ran around the edges of both arches. *None of that matters,* Jay thought. *What matters is that the area is still intact.*

Approaching one of the portals, he opened the door and passed through into a small room filled with dim white light. The indistinct hum of a working battery broke the silence. A few digits raced across a small screen set within the top of the battery's console. As he stood there, he could feel Debb's spirit swimming all around him, hear her voice, concerned and frightened.

He returned to the main chamber. The other door was different: locked and sturdy, as if knowing it held his future behind its solidity. Taking a sonic pass from his suit pocket, he pushed it into a round slot. Once more, memories flooded his mind.

* * *

They were holding hands in the garden, just outside the entrance to their home. Bright lights flashed in the sky around the rings. Debb was white with fear, and the grip on Jay's hand tightened.

"It's started," she whispered.

"Yes," Jay whispered back.

Something soared through the air close by, and Jay felt his stomach churn. Dreadful sounds, carried by Umbriel's newly fashioned atmosphere, fell upon their ears. "Oh, Jay," Debb said, turning to him, eyes heavy with tears. "They're attacking us."

It was true. The military drones, for that's what they were, were turning their attention to Umbriel.

They went inside, shut the door, and turned on the comms screen. There was nothing but crackling, shapeless static. Why are they attacking us? Jay thought. What's the point? We're just simple farmers.

Through the window, they saw a beam drop from the sky and ravage the garden, turning everything in its path to a burnt, dry powder. It went away, a rampaging beast, leaving destruction in its wake. It was no consolation that the beam came from a computer-driven machine. In fact, it made it worse. Everything seemed out of control.

The ground suddenly shook, and Jay wondered whether the whole moon would split asunder. The sky darkened. Rain fell. Umbriel is so new. How can it survive this?

Far away across the fields, their neighbour's house caught fire, and as they gazed outside, it looked like the end of the world. Two tremors hit their room, and cracks appeared in the wall. Something landed on the roof with a thud, and Debb screamed. They ran through the door into the scorched garden. Behind them, an entire wall fell outwards, dust rising in choking clouds.

They ran for the shaft, their last refuge, the way to a possible new future. The rings were alive with fire now, a burning arc in the sky. More tremors ran beneath their feet. Poor Umbriel, to be created for this.

They ran away from their dream. Away from the house that was crumbling behind them.

And then for Jay the nightmare was complete as the hateful beam returned and dropped and raced towards them. So swift, so deadly, it took Debb in its path and raced away uncaringly. Jay stopped in his tracks. She was gone, turned from a living being to millions of useless particles of airborne dust.

Jay dropped to his knees, raged at the sky, clawed at the scorched ground, and wept.

* * *

The airlock door beeped three times and slid open. Jay stepped through. The door closed behind him, and the one ahead opened. The humming was louder now. He walked through, and the inner door sealed. Across the room there were two spacesuits hanging on the wall and, nearby, the bodies: the clones that he and Debb had created, each held vertically in its own gravitational field.

Sweat sprang to his forehead, threatening to run into his eyes. He checked the room stats on the wall screen, took off his helmet, and wiped his brow. The irony of it all was that the warring parties had ultimately agreed with Debb. The moons and rings had been returned to the stakeholders. Those who were left, anyway. Tears sprang to Jay's eyes. *Bitter* was not the word. There just wasn't a word.

Even as he approached, he could hear Debb's remonstrations as he had explained the final part of his scheme: "Oh, Jay, we cannot do this. It's illegal. Even war cannot make it legal. If either of us is killed, then let it be so." And her large blue eyes were staring into his, full of fear, full of portent, as though she had known that if the step were taken, it would be tempting fate.

He approached his own replica first and switched off the field. The body slumped, but on the screen the heartbeat laboured on. Almost in a frenzy, he turned everything off until seemingly a cold hand gripped his own heart. Life ebbed from his clone, and he looked away as the chest stilled and the eyes glazed.

He turned towards his wife's clone.

This Debb was dressed in a white gown, so lovely, so peaceful. He turned on the activation switch and watched with wonder as she slowly stretched her limbs. Then she shook free of the gravity field and stepped forward.

She paused in front of him. "Oh, Jay," she said. "We cannot do this. If either of us is killed, then let it be so." Her voice was strange, dreamlike, staccato. And so saying she smiled at him, swept her hand to her mouth, and fell to the floor.

For a moment, Jay stood paralysed, then he fell to his knees, cradling the motionless body in his arms, willing life back into it. He breathed into her mouth, frantically pumped her chest. But she was gone, dead by some mysterious self-inflicted means, a victim of her own reluctance to flout society's laws, laws that had been broken countless times in a meaningless war. And so the cloning had failed; somehow her own resilient thoughts had defeated her body's will to live.

He held her body tighter. It would not end here, he vowed. The process would be repeated, and repeated, and repeated again if necessary. He had all the genetic material he needed in his arms.

Next time he would be ready for her. He would intervene before she could utter a word, before her thoughts could force her mind to shut her body down. It would take time, but he had plenty of that. He would return to Ariel, seek advice, return and tweak the cloning system. He would create space tracks between Umbriel and Ariel until the real Debb was back in his arms.

But he could not prevent a small voice from torturing his mind. *Is that what Debb would really want?* He flung the thought away. There had been a war, and there would be a future. Even if it took forever. And that future would be for both of them.

MOTHER

Mother turned her face into the breeze and wrinkled her nose. No doubt she could smell dingoes, Elyon thought, a large pack judging by the time she spent with her head held high. She stopped sniffing and said as much.

"Oooh," Elyon replied. "Do you think they're after us, Mother?"

Mother clicked her tongue. "I sincerely hope not."

Elyon nestled further into the pouch. The eleven-year-old was as brown as the nearby river with short-cropped blond hair and stunning green eyes that complemented his round, smooth face.

They didn't move yet; Mother was still testing the wind and resting on her muscular tail. Over the rim of Mother's warm pouch, Elyon could see the settlement, marvelling, as usual, at its symmetry. Beyond the buildings, he could make out the snakelike river, nearby hills rising, scatterings of granite boulders, and, to his left, a glimpse of the sea on the horizon, far away and flat and blue.

In the centre of the village stood the rotunda and its gathering space, where day by day the five elders would take turns at reading the rules of the settlement. Across from the rotunda stood the assembly hall and the elders' building, edifices of authority among their community.

Surrounding this pivotal zone were many smaller buildings, each identical, radiating outwards along lines that resembled the spokes of a giant wheel. And on top of these houses were the sun panels that provided the meagre energy requirements of the settlement.

This was his home, and he loved it.

The rim of the wheel was green, a verdant strip where several large roos could be seen grazing. Even from this distance, Elyon could tell that several of the roos were much larger than Mother, some of the females no doubt carrying a newborn child in their pouch.

Elyon had only been in the rotunda once, and then only to see the collection of ancient writings and pictures that adorned its walls. He had found the experience more puzzling than inspiring. There had been faded pictures of strange people mounted on creatures that the elders called horses. Actually sitting on their backs—how awkward must that have been? The horses looked ugly, with no fur to speak of at all.

Elyon had concluded that there must not have been any roos in those long-ago days.

There were many other pictures in the rotunda, but none attracted Elyon more than the horses. There were ancient artefacts, too, like the computer—a rectangle with a screen that had, so the elders said, contained moving pictures. Needless to say, they didn't work now. They were too old, the elders said; they had tried the sun power, but the artefacts were broken.

Or the elders were not clever enough to make them work, Elyon mused.

The elders were the rule-makers of their settlement. They did not have children and did not involve themselves in roo training. Elyon had already decided that he did not want to be an elder, although the images and artefacts in the rotunda did interest him.

Mother made her first jump, disturbing Elyon's reflections. He urged his carrier home, and the giant roo took huge bounds down into the valley, snakes and birds fleeing from beneath her descending feet. Each leap was at least eight elders long and two elders high, yet Elyon felt little disturbance inside the pouch. So much better than horses. And Mother could also talk!

* * *

That night there was a tremendous storm. The sky became alive with water and noise and flashes of light. It was as if the heavens were plummeting to earth—like the clouds were falling upon their heads. And in the morning, the river was twice the width of the previous day, hostile and waved, flowing faster underneath a leaden sky.

Light fell across Elyon's eyes as someone drew back his curtain. The excited face of Effy, his sister, filled his vision.

"Come see what the river brought us," she cried.

Elyon yawned and stretched, but made no effort to leave his bed. Effy began pulling at the furs. "Come on," she insisted. "It's bigger than anything before."

Elyon looked at his sister through sleepy eyes. It was like looking at himself in the waters of a lake when the day was warm and the wind a mere whisper. She was two years older, a little taller, and her fair hair was longer and cut level with the top of her ears; her green eyes were shining with the excitement of a new day.

With a grunt, Elyon rose and dressed swiftly, choosing a tunic with deep pockets, then they left their dwelling and walked side by side through the green area towards the river. Mother grazed nearby and lifted her head slightly as they passed. Not for the first time, Elyon wondered about his and Effy's parents, both lost after such a storm a few years ago. He had been eight years old at the time, Effy ten, and they had clung to each other as if they were sharing the same skin. And even now, years later, they shared everything, even Mother.

Many of the female roos were chosen to look after the settlement's children, even while they still crawled about inside their own mother's pouch. And over the subsequent months they were taught the people's language, a slow and laborious process, but one which Elyon often participated in himself. He loved the roos, and he loved Mother. Adults in their village had no time to rear children. They were too busy making, building, repairing, tilling, and reaping. And so, he believed, it had always been.

There were many people already gathered at the river, some other children too, but mostly adults, and the air was full of anticipation. Two of the elders stood on the riverbank dressed in the ceremonial robes that marked this as an important occasion. Next to them was a large box, at least an elder long and half an elder square at the ends. Brought by the river, Elyon discerned, caught in the crook of its arm as it meandered past the village, as many artefacts were, especially after a storm.

The crowd, many hundreds in number, gathered in a half circle around the elders. They were clad in knee-length tunics of various pastel hues, held at the waists by roughly knotted twine. They did not all look the same. Some were as pale as ghosts under a strong morning sun. Some were as dark as the night sky when covered with seamless clouds; others were brown, like Elyon and Effy, the colour of the tannin water that fed the river. But as one, they were all excited.

There were markings on the box, but only the two elders would understand their meaning—and they did not inform the crowd.

One of the elders held up his arms. "Kinsfolk," he said, "the storm has brought us another gift from the hills. We will take it to the rotunda and open it there." A murmur of disappointment echoed around the assembled group. "Do not fear," the elder added. "You will eventually see its contents in the display areas."

The box was duly loaded onto a cart and towed by a walking roo back to the village. The creature was smaller than Mother, and did not hop, having been trained from birth to walk, to put one foot in front of the other in imitation of its owners. Elyon thought it looked rather sad, as if it wanted to discard its harness and hop away. He supposed a horse would have done a better job.

* * *

Five days later, the people had still not seen what was in the box.

"It is difficult to open," one elder said.

"There is some kind of hard inner lining," remarked

another.

Yet another had just shrugged. "The fates are against us," she had said.

And even as they spoke these words, the box lay open in the rotunda's inner sanctum, lid off and contents revealed.

After a further five days, as midnight grew close, Elyon and Effy cautiously approached the rotunda under a full moon and a cloudless sky. The streets were deserted, and only a small breeze ruffled their tunics.

They passed through the main portal, Elyon lit his torch, and they tiptoed around the wide outer passage to the next inner door, for once oblivious of the pictures and strange glyphs that decorated the walls. They passed through the door and repeated the procedure twice more—until they arrived at the entrance to the inner sanctum.

The escapade was Effy's suggestion, of course. An adventure, a challenge to the elders, *a quest for knowledge!* Whatever other excuse they could come up with if they were caught.

Inevitably, the door was locked. Effy held her finger to her lips. "Shush," she whispered fiercely. They both stood there, the only light coming from Elyon's small, flickering torch. They held their breath.

The humming was very faint, barely noticeable, but they could hear it in what should have been absolute silence.

"Something hums," Elyon said. "Like this." He echoed the sound with his lips clamped tightly together.

Effy tried the door again and again. There was no way in.

Elyon gazed upwards. There was a narrow gap between the top of the mud brick wall and the heavy bracken ceiling. He may be able to squeeze through if Effy hoisted him up.

His sister had seen his glance. "Let me try," she said. "Lift me up."

Elyon looked uncertain. "You won't be able to see. And if you can't unlock the door, you'll be trapped."

Effy shook her head. "I know how the lock works. It's a bar that I can easily lift from the other side—I can open the door." She looked earnestly at him. "Honestly. Put the beacon down and lift me up."

Elyon did as requested, the flickering flames casting weird shadows on the walls, a tapestry of unworldly creatures cavorting to some strange, unheard music.

Effy scrambled up and, with an immense effort accompanied by a series of unbecoming grunts, hooked one leg over the top of the wall. Elyon could see that her back was starting to push tightly against the bracken ceiling.

"I can't get through," she hissed.

"Come back down then," Elyon replied, picking up the beacon.

"No. Wait." Effy pushed up against the ceiling, and Elyon saw the dense covering give slightly. She pushed again, wriggling sideways. Bracken was tearing at her tunic. Then she was gone, and a thump and a cry of pain came from the other side of the wall.

"Effy," Elyon cried anxiously. "Are you alright?"

For a moment there was no reply, and Elyon's heart quickened with fear. Then there came a faint voice: "Yes. I'm fine. Just bruised, I think. Shine your light under the door so I can find it."

Once more, Elyon did as directed. A loud clunk echoed around the corridor, and the door opened outwards. Effy stood there with a wry grin on her face.

"Well done," Elyon said, nodding his approval, happy to see his sister was apparently unharmed.

Holding the beacon before him, Elyon led the way into

the inner sanctum. Some kind of contraption stood on the table, presumably the contents of the box. He held the torch closer so the flame shed more light on the newly arrived enigma.

There was a screen, like the ancient computer thing in the outer display area, but it was more elongated in shape. A series of wires led up a pole and out through the ceiling. Sun power recently rigged, Elyon thought, presumably by the elders.

A small green light shone from one corner of the cabinet that held the screen. Elyon touched it with a finger and watched in fascination as his fingernail turned the colour of a leaf. He walked around the room, light dancing hypnotically from the walls. He found the box from the river, running his fingers over the plaque he located on its side. There were words that he couldn't read, but he knew they meant something important.

Enticed by the humming, Effie was playing with the cabinet: pushing her fingers into recesses, running her hand across the monitor, pressing buttons.

The screen suddenly sprang to life. Symbols raced across it, and then a face materialised—a strange face with fur on its chin.

Words came out of the box. The unusual face was actually speaking. Elyon and Effy stood entranced. The language was not known to them, and they could not understand the words, but it was obvious that the speaker was under severe stress.

And then horrifying images replaced the speaker's face. Bombs were falling everywhere; huge flashes of light filled the screen. They saw tall buildings being destroyed, huge waves overwhelming shorelines, thousands of people running in mad panic. Not their people: people of some other race. The people of the man on the screen!

More pictures: plumes of smoke towering skywards, strange flying vehicles hurtling through the sky. And when it all subsided, there seemed to be nothing standing, nothing running, nothing walking or even crawling.

"Who was that person?" Effy whispered.

She was looking at Elyon with tears in her eyes. He did not know what to say.

The screen suddenly flickered, and the face returned. It was the same face, but it looked more haggard than before, as if it was carrying the weight of an entire world upon its shoulders.

Bitter words issued forth, but they were unintelligible to Elyon and Effy. And then a terrifying thing happened. The man held up a picture and tore it into pieces, his expression filled with hate.

Elyon and Effy stared in horror. For the picture had shown one of their own kind. It had resembled one of the elders, an adult of their own race. The bizarre person on the screen was obviously saying they were responsible for the destruction they had just witnessed.

Elyon shook his head. "But we do not have the weapons, or the flying machines," he said. "It cannot be true."

"There's one way to find out," Effy said.

Elyon stared at his sister. The look on her face made him nervous. "Talk to the elders?" he suggested.

Effy shook her head vehemently. "We need to find the truth, not the elders' version of the truth."

Elyon kept staring, but said nothing else.

"We must follow the river upstream," Effy continued. "We must find the source of the artefacts."

"But that is not allowed. The elders—"

"May or may not be keeping a terrible secret."

They left the room and closed the door firmly behind them. The lock engaged with a satisfying clunk. As they weaved their way out of the building, Elyon asked, "Could the elders have translated what we heard in there?"

Effy nodded. "I believe so. I am sure they have decoded many things from the river."

"But why would they not tell our people? All we have in the rotunda is stuff we cannot understand."

"Maybe they are afraid of how we would react. Maybe one day they will tell us," Effy responded. "Or maybe not."

They left two days later at sunrise, before the village rose for daily work. Mother saw them and followed, and before long they were snuggled inside her pouch. Once they left the settlement behind, she took huge bounds up the gently sloping hillside, tracking the course of the meandering river.

* * *

Elyon and Effy had never strayed far from the village in the past, for they were forbidden to do so by the elders. "There is much to fear," the elders proclaimed. "Dingoes and giant snakes and scorpions as big as your heads. Better to stay in the sanctuary of the village."

They stood side by side in the pouch, peering out in fascination at the scenery. There were mostly head-high bushes, but a few tall silver trees dotted the landscape, and they could see that the terrain got steeper up ahead.

"Mother, you must stop when you get tired," Effy said.

"I will stop every hundred leaps," Mother replied. "You will need to stretch your legs in any case."

After four brief stops, they had a prolonged rest, and

61

Elyon and Effy ate the food they had brought with them, whilst Mother browsed the grass beneath their feet. Eventually, Mother sat back on her tail, held her paw to her eyes, and squinted ahead.

"The river is narrowing but is fast," she said. "The way ahead is steepening. You will have to go on foot from now on. What you seek may not be far."

Elyon nodded. "Will you go home?" he asked.

"No. I will wait here for you next to the river. There is good water and plentiful food."

"Thank you, Mother," Effy said. "You made it so much easier for us."

"Be careful," Mother said. "The way forward is unknown."

As Elyon and Effy climbed, the ground became significantly rockier and much more difficult to traverse. They saw two more boxes in the water, snagged on the rocks. "Leave them," Effy said. "They will find their way to the village sooner or later."

Looking up ahead, Elyon declared, "I'm not sure we can go much farther. There seems to be a cliff face."

Effy followed his gaze. "I think there may be a waterfall," she said. Then after a few moments, she added: "But the artefacts cannot be coming from beyond the top of it—they'd be smashed to pieces on their descent."

Elyon sighed. She was right, of course. They must be nearing the source of the storm-gifted ancient relics. If that's what they truly were. He started to feel the first hint of fear. What if the people up here were still alive?

After less than a hundred further steps, they could hear the sound of the falls. And then, rounding a bend, they paused to wonder at its frenzied drop down the face of a towering and glistening escarpment.

The waterfall was as tall as the silver trees, stretching high into the sky, and the sound it made was thunderous. The water fell into a large pool before cascading down the hillside, and the pool was quite deep. But the markings on the surrounding rocks showed Elyon that it could become much deeper yet.

Effy grabbed his arm, pointing at the lichen-covered rock wall just to the right of the falls. There appeared to be a cave at water level. "We need to get into there," she proclaimed excitedly.

Elyon grimaced. The cave looked dark and forbidding. And the only way in was through the water. He shook his head. "I don't like swimming."

"It'll be fine," Effy responded. "It's away from the falls and quite calm. And it's only a few strokes."

"Only a few to the entrance," Elyon replied. "Maybe a lot more inside if there's no path or place to emerge."

"There must be," Effy said, logic working overtime again. "Otherwise where are the artefacts coming from?"

Elyon looked at the water. It looked cold, probably was.

"I'll go first," Effy said, and with that, she was in the water and powerfully stroking towards the cave. She disappeared inside, and Elyon felt a surge of panic. He was suddenly on his own in the middle of nowhere, his only company the sound of roaring water. And scorpions the size of his head! What he would give to be back inside Mother's pouch.

"There's a path by the water," Effy called back. "Come on, it's easy."

Elyon took a deep breath and entered the water carefully. Taking a look towards the cave, summoning courage from somewhere, he took the plunge.

He counted over twenty strokes to get to the cave—no doubt twice as many as it had taken his sister, who was by far the better swimmer. Raising his head from the water, he saw Effy on what seemed to be a small path. He swam over, and she helped him out.

"Well done," she said. "Look. The path goes farther in."

"It'll be dark," Elyon said.

"No," Effy responded. "It actually gets brighter. There must be light coming from somewhere."

That didn't make Elyon feel any better. Light may mean people.

The surface of the water was an arm's length below the path, but the top of the bank was still damp from the cave's flooding during the recent storm. The certainty that the water level had recently been much higher dented Elyon's confidence even further.

Effy was correct about the visibility. As they walked along the path, the cave, which was really a tunnel, actually became brighter. Before too many steps, they came to where the passageway opened out and became an extensive and totally enclosed cavern. The water formed a large pool, and the path continued all the way round to the other side. Overhead, they could see the source of light; a large hole in the cavern's ceiling, which served as a natural open skylight to the terrain above. Through the rocky aperture, they could see the welcome sight of the sky. The sun must have been almost directly above, for the underground grotto was extremely well illuminated—well-lit enough for them to see the pile of boxes on the far side and the entrance to another cave further around the path. Not just an entrance, but one with an open door!

"There may be someone in there," Elyon whispered anxiously.

Effy shook her head. "I don't think so. Not anymore."

They walked cautiously around the path. There must have been hundreds of boxes, some submerged, some entrapped and floating, and some riding on the back of others. The water was dark around them, as if harbouring secrets from some bygone age.

"The source of our artefacts," Effy remarked. "When the water rises after heavy rain, some escape, while others change position, ready for next time."

Many of the boxes carried similar markings to those seen in the village. Indecipherable, but meaning something to someone, in the past at least.

They looked at each other. "The door," Effy said.

They took careful steps around the edge of the pool. The door seemed to be constructed of brown metal and hung half-open, as though uncertain whether to grant them access. They went through without touching it, pausing just inside. The air smelled musty, and there was a heavy tang of decay.

"Hello," Elyon said nervously. "Anyone here?"

Effy gave him a scornful look. "Not anymore," she said again.

The light from the door was the only source of illumination, but they could see that the room was small. Effy turned around and pushed the door open as far as it would go. It creaked, but it moved. Light rushed into the room and visibility improved significantly.

"Over there," Effy said. "There's something on the floor."

As they slowly approached, both of them suddenly stopped. The *something* was a skeleton, person-shaped but not person-sized. The skeletal frame was around half as tall again as an elder. Remnants of clothes cloaked the bones; a piece of equipment was clamped around the skull.

Elyon grabbed Effy's arm. "There's another over there," he said hoarsely.

A chair and desk supported another assembly of bones, not as clearly defined as those on the floor and more widely dispersed. There was also a familiar-looking screen thing toppled over on the desk; other desks with strange pieces of equipment ran around the walls of the room.

"What is this place?" Elyon whispered. He was beginning to feel sick and longed to return to the fresh air.

"A final refuge for them," Effy replied. "A historical storage place for their race." She looked at Elyon sadly. "A last stand." She wandered around the room, picking up objects from the desks, thrusting some smaller ones into the pockets of her tunic.

Elyon looked at her with wide eyes. "A last stand from what?"

"Unfortunately, I believe from us. A last stand from us."

Elyon shook his head. "We could not have fought these people. They are huge. And we do not have the weapons shown on that screen in the pergola. It's not possible."

Effy shrugged. "Maybe it is. A long time ago, maybe." Her eyes were scanning the room, looking for something else of interest.

One last item appeared to catch her attention, something lying on the desk where the bones rested: a screen like the one in the inner sanctum, but this one was only hand-sized. She picked it up, blew away the dust, turned it over in her hands, shrugged, and handed it to Elyon. "Put it in your pocket," she said.

Elyon handled the item as if it were scalding hot. "Does it work?"

"Maybe in the village. If we hook it up." She gave a final

look around, perhaps debating whether to take one of the bones, deciding against it. They knew where they were now, Elyon mused. They could always come back.

Leaving the door wide open, they made their way out of the cavern and down the tunnel. Elyon eyed the water with distaste, not relishing another swim.

"Wait," Effy said. "Give me the artefact back. I don't want it to get wet. I can manage to swim one-handed." She took the object and entered the water, kicked over to the bank with one hand holding the relic high in the air. Elyon took a brief look back at the tunnel and followed in her wake.

Mother was grazing peacefully where they had left her. As she heard them approach, she lifted her head, ears high in the air and swivelling in their direction. "Well?" she said.

Effy told her about the inner cave, the skeletons, and the artefacts in the pool.

Mother nodded twice. "Mmm, humans," she said.

Effy and Elyon stared at her, eyes wide and mouths open.

"What are hu...manz?" Elyon asked.

"You know about them?" Effy queried, looking sharply at the roo.

Mother stood to her full height. "Did you find anything?" she asked.

Effy nodded. "Many more artefacts. Another screen, like in the inner sanctum."

Mother clicked her tongue. "You need to be told, but I will only tell it once," she stated. "We must go back to the settlement, talk to the elders, talk to the people. See what happens."

"See what happens?" Effy and Elyon said together.

"Mmm," Mother responded. "It will not be easy, but it is time it was done."

* * *

In the elders' building near the rotunda, Effy and Elyon stood nervously before three of the elders. They had told them everything, which was what Mother had advised, but it would be fair to say that the elders were not pleased.

"You have disobeyed the rules of the village," one said, anger written all over his face. "Broken into the inner sanctum and ventured into the hills."

"And you must be punished," added another.

"But there are dead people in the hills," Effy remonstrated. "Where the artefacts come from."

"You must be banished," the first elder said.

Effy dug deep into her pockets and produced the small screen she had picked up in the cave. "We think this carries a message like the one in the sanctum," she said. "What does it mean?"

"The message is nonsense," the third elder proclaimed. "And whatever is inside that thing will also be nonsense."

"The pictures we saw were not nonsense," Elyon ventured. He did not want to be banished, and he did not want to leave without answers. Confusion flooded his mind.

"We must show the people," Effy said.

"That is not necessary," the second elder stated. "You will leave the artefacts you found in the hills, and you will leave the village, never to return."

"I demand that you power up this screen," Effy cried, waving the screen in the air.

The first elder grabbed it from her grasp and smashed it against the wall.

"Now you have nothing," he said.

"You are afraid," Effy claimed, every fibre of her body

tense with anger. "You are afraid of showing the people the images."

"Effy and Elyon," the second elder stated solemnly. "You have broken the law and must go into exile. You must never return. We will accompany you to the edge of the hills, and you will go from this place of your birth."

Two of the elders grabbed Effy and Elyon and marched them to the door. But they did not get far.

The entire village was gathered outside, including the two remaining elders. And with them, all the roos from the green verge. And the young that they carried.

The first elder stepped forward, bristling with rage, but also showing fear. "What is the meaning of this? Return to your work."

It wasn't a person that stepped forward; it was a roo. It was Mother.

"It is time for the truth," Mother said. "All the people deserve to know the truth."

"What truth?" the second elder countered, an unpleasant smirk upon his face. "The truth of a roo?"

"There are remains of people in the nearby hills!" Effy yelled. "We have seen them and their artefacts. You, yourselves, have seen some of their artefacts, stored in the rotunda. Innocuous objects, if you would believe the elders, brought by the river." She looked at the three elders, then back at the crowd. "And you must see the remains. They are not our people: they are different."

Elyon blinked. He wasn't even sure what *innocuous* meant. "They were called hu...manz," he added forcefully.

Mother faced the elders, rising to her full height. "You flatter yourselves that you taught us your language. But we could speak the language of the dead people in the hills long before your arrival, long before you eradicated them from this world. We were bred by the humans for companion tasks, much like the ones you have us undertaking for your young. And they helped us to talk, so we could help each other."

"Lies!" the third elder cried. "It is not true. There are no humans."

"There are no humans *now*," Mother retorted. "But there *were* humans." She turned to the crowd. "Are there six volunteers to see the image-artefact in the rotunda? Who wishes to find out the truth?"

Everyone in the crowd was looking at the three elders. Nobody came forward. They were afraid, Elyon realised. The elders had too much power.

"See," the first elder proclaimed triumphantly. "They do not believe you."

Elyon stepped forward. "Effy and I will take you," he said. "You must know what happened."

Two young people stepped forward, then three adults. Then ten more, then fifty, amongst them the two remaining elders. Elyon heaved a sigh of relief. The spell of the elders was broken.

"That is good," Mother announced to the gathering. "But all five of the elders must remain here, otherwise they may damage the sun power to the artefact in the inner sanctum." She looked around. "Who will stay with them?"

Most of the people and all the roos held up their arms. Mother nodded sagely.

"After we see the images," she added, addressing those in the crowd who had volunteered to go to the rotunda, "we will bring the artefact to the assembly hall and give it power. Then you can all see what it shows. I will tell you the words that the artefact communicates. After that, the elders will speak to us." She looked at the three elders outside the rotunda and the other two elders in the audience. "Is that not so?"

There was no reaction from the elders until one of the two in the crowd yelled out, "The artefacts must be destroyed!"

"No!" thundered Mother. "In the past, you had no choice but to keep them, for most of them were found by the people, even by the children. If they had been destroyed, questions would have been asked, suspicions aroused." She glared angrily at the first elder. "But now it is time for everyone to know where they came from and who really made them."

"Who made them?" one person in the crowd questioned, and the refrain was taken up by others, the chant even echoing within the walls of the elders' building.

"Hold the elders inside their building, now and overnight," Mother cried. "We will go to the rotunda." She looked at the first elder. "Will you give us the key to the inner sanctum? The people will thank you for it."

The elder looked at his colleagues, undecided, looking for another way. They all held their heads to the ground. Eventually, he shrugged. "It is in the box on the table." Elyon ran inside the building, emerging with a triumphant look upon his face and holding the key on high.

"Let us go. It is getting late," Mother said, and a clamour of excitement rang around the gathering space.

* * *

The following day, everyone in the village gathered inside the great circular assembly hall. They were seated in four concentric, tiered circles, and all eyes were focused on the central dais. Effy had hooked up the newly acquired inner sanctum artefact to the building's sun power source and arranged for the screen to rotate slowly so all would see at least a portion of the images. The screen was too small to let them all view it simultaneously, but it mattered not: they would all get to see it close up when time permitted.

Those who had seen the images in the inner sanctum had spread the word, and the building was buzzing with anticipation. The five elders were on the front tier; they had been held comfortably but securely overnight and were now effectively corralled by the throng around them. Effy, Elyon, and Mother stood next to the dais with one eye on the elders. They were fully aware that this was a crucial moment.

And now Mother was about to speak. Effy turned on the artefact's power, and Mother's voice rang forth, loud enough to be heard above the human's voice emanating from the screen.

"This is what the images are saying," Mother began. "This is what the human says:

"*This message is being recorded in the year 2537, December 12. It is being made before our final destruction by the enemy. The bombs have fallen everywhere, even in the desert. The air is rank with radiation, and thousands upon thousands have been killed, are being killed at this very moment. Our once proud cities are destroyed, and there are few outposts left standing and able to resist. Yet resist we must, for surrender is worse than death against this enemy.*"

The face on the screen screwed up in anguish, and the watching crowd gasped as they witnessed the images. "*Sometimes the devastation is such that it is hard to accept it is real,*" Mother continued. She paused, letting the images on the screen strike home in the hearts of the people.

As if in a final, futile gesture the face appeared again: "*The enemy is unseen, and his weapons reach us from afar, from places unknown. We stood and now we fall, unaided, alone and finished,"* Mother translated.

And then the final words and images brought forth cries of horror from the assembled people.

"We have a small victory," Mother related. *"We have captured the image of one of the enemy. Look into his eyes, I beseech you, and hold no truck with his race. God bless you."*

Effy froze the image on the screen, the image showing the face of one of their own—the face that looked like an elder. And now, as the image slowly rotated, everyone saw it and explored its countenance.

The assembly hall was filled with more strange cries. This could not be true. It just could not be true.

Effy stood to face the people. "Who are we?" she asked. "Where are we from?" And to the group of elders. "How did we get here? Why are we here?"

"Preposterous," an elder cried. "There are no humans. This is a trick."

Mother rounded on the elder. "You are the tricksters. You are the fable makers."

The elders shook their heads, but said nothing.

Effy walked across to a bag that was placed near the dais. She took out what was inside and held it high above her head.

Elyon was totally astonished—for Effy held up the skull of a human. Had she returned to the cave in the dead of night? Swam across that cold pool again? How would she have been able to see? Any torch would have been extinguished in the water. He watched in awe as his indomitable sister addressed the gathering.

"This is a skull of a human from the cave in the hills," Effy said. "This is the head of one of the people we crushed."

There were no cries this time, the people were hushed into silence. They were, in fact, shocked beyond belief. They were a peaceful village. They lived off the land. They had no weapons. No flying vehicles. No bombs. They had no malice in their hearts.

"One of the elders will now address us," Mother announced, lifting her head and throwing a challenging gaze at the group of five. "Who shall tell us the truth?"

All eyes turned to the elders. No one moved. No one said a word. Silence hung over the assembly hall, as if the very presence of sound had been magically removed.

"We wait," Mother said.

One of the female elders stepped forward. "I will speak," she said.

Effy and Elyon looked at her nervously. Would she tell the truth? Or would there be more lies? Effy recalled the elder's name: Syra, the youngest and hopefully the most truthful.

Two of the other elders grabbed Syra's arms in a futile attempt at stopping her. She shrugged them off, mounted the dais.

"You will be punished," one of the other elders hissed. "When they return."

Effy and Elyon watched the protesting elder warily. Mother sat back on her tail, ears fully erect.

"People," Syra began, "I will tell you the truth as I have been told it, as the other elders have been told it. We are a pioneer settlement for our people—the only one on this planet. We are a trial, a survival experiment." She looked directly at Effy, Elyon, and Mother. "The humans were already dying when we came here, but yes, we had to defeat what survivors there were. We had weapons and bombs and flying machines that came out of our spacecraft."

"Why did we not help them? Try to talk to them?" Elyon cried.

Syra looked sad. "We were afraid of their strength, their size, their aggressiveness. We did not believe friendly communion would work. We did the only thing we could do—we eliminated them."

There is conflict in those words, Elyon thought, *for we were the aggressors.*

"Where are we from?" somebody shouted from the audience.

"It matters not, for we will never return," Syra replied, "but we are from a faraway star. A long voyage away."

"Why do we not remember?" another voice asked.

"This is a pioneer settlement: a test," Syra reiterated. "Only elders are granted the retention of ancestral memory: otherwise you would all yearn to return home. The memories of your forefathers who were first in this settlement were erased, and so too, by birth, were yours, their descendants." She scanned the audience, turning full circle. "It is the same on all our settled planets. The same procedure."

Elyon blinked. This was so hard to take in. His kind were on other worlds, in other villages! The truth was beginning to hurt. Did that mean that people from other worlds had been erased also?

"But elders have died, and others have taken their place," Effy asserted.

"That is true," Syra responded. "But their knowledge is only passed to one person, their chosen successor. It is passed in a ceremony known only to the elders. And the new elder is guided by the other elders."

Restrained, Elyon thought. That would be a better word.

Kept within the circle.

"And why are we here?" Another shout from the audience.

Syra held her arms out, palms upwards. "To populate this world. To spread our people far and wide."

"That's ridiculous," Effy cried. "We are not even allowed to leave this village."

"When the time is right, when our numbers are large enough, then some will leave and explore this world."

"Our people have spacecraft and weapons and bombs," Effy stated. "But here we have nothing: just sun power and basic technologies. And we scrape a living off the land, and gaze in wonder at alien artefacts that arrive by the river's flow."

Syra smiled. "And that is how it has to be. If we are to survive, if the experiment is to succeed, then we must learn to live with what this damaged planet offers and nothing more."

Effy turned to Mother. "Is what she says the truth?"

Mother looked at Syra with her large brown eyes. "Will your spacecraft return?"

"It will," Syra replied. "But only to observe. It will not interfere. And it could be a long time in coming."

Mother stood high. "At least now you all know about the humans, the people who were here before you. It is true that they struggled to make this world work. They had many problems. And they fought amongst themselves. I wish you a better future than your predecessors." She looked at the elders. "I hope you can help your people—and that your people can help you."

* * *

Three days later, Elyon and Effy left the settlement at the crack of dawn.

The people of the village did not seem to trust them. It was as if everyone held some kind of grudge—as if Syra's revelations had induced some kind of mass trauma.

Elyon suspected the hand of the elders in play. It was as though the people did not wish to believe what they had witnessed and preferred to ignore what they had heard. And maybe that was a natural reaction, Elyon thought.

But, of course, Syra may not have spoken the truth. However, they had no reason not to believe her.

They had talked to Syra, and they had decided to become the first of the pioneers to leave the settlement, to explore this new world. As Syra said: "You have already done so." Elyon thought she was glad to see them go.

Mother was with them, of course. It had been she who had returned to the cave and taken the skull, safely carrying it back to the village in her pouch. "Roos are good swimmers," she had told Elyon, "and we see well at night." She had clicked her tongue. "But we are not good walkers, and the cave path was not comfortable. And my head was too near the tunnel ceiling."

Elyon had smiled and nodded.

"Where shall we go?" he asked. They were in the foothills now, letting the rising sun warm their bodies.

Mother twitched her ears. "Water," she said. "Always follow the water."

She looked at Elyon and Effy. "There will be more artefacts to find."

"Oh, there will," Effy said, withdrawing a piece of paper from her pocket.

She unfolded the parchment and showed Elyon and

Mother.

"A map," Elyon cried.

"From the cave," Effy said. "From our visit. It got wet, but dried easily enough in the sun. Look. There are marks to follow."

Elyon had a sudden thought. "What if there are still some hu...manz alive?"

They both looked at Mother. "Then we will cross that bridge when we come to it," she said. "Come. The world is our oyster."

"Sometimes, Mother, you speak in riddles," Effy said.

"Human riddles," Mother said. "Maybe I can teach you a few."

DESPERATE TIMES

The strange machine glinted under the subdued glow of fluorescent lighting as if it were the psychedelic creation of some artistic genius with a flair for the macabre. It was, for all its warped geometry and irregular construction, the culmination of man's dreams ever since he had first wondered about the passing of a day, or the revolution of the sun.

It had taken many years to build, many more to design: years of frustration and dead ends, of ignoble blaspheming and vicious argument. But now it hummed with life, even if the designers did not fully understand to the nth degree how it worked. They were restricted by Einstein, and Einstein, from wherever he was now, did not budge an inch. They had thought outside the box, but the box always drew them back inside, as if it contained a strong magnet that persistently attracted their desperate thoughts.

None of this mattered to Phillip M Wells as he sat in the cockpit of the machine, staring at the four simple buttons that would decide his future: *Forward, Backward, Stop,* and *Home.* That was it, those innocent switches and the date clock on the console above them: a clock depicting the targeted year as well as month, hour, and minute.

Dressed in a blue jumpsuit and sturdy black boots, he primed his mind for a change in circumstances; a massive change in circumstances, come to that. *Everything is thoroughly tested, everything is fine. Will be fine, will be.*

He convinced himself he was in complete command even though this was the first manned mission, the first with a human payload. Technically nothing could go wrong. Historically, socially, physically, there was lots of scope for error. But he could always return of his own free will, which was good to know.

The red light that indicated the time machine was still tuning in to the appropriate space-time vector was still flashing; the console clock still chuntering backwards.

When he'd been chosen for the mission, his mind had spun with the burden of responsibility. Not that there hadn't been fear lurking there, but as always duty pushed it into the background. The decision to undertake the manned mission had been made after the animals came back alive, their hearts racing and noses twitching—much the same as when they had left, really. They had been on automatic return, but he would choose his own moment to press the *Home* button. That way he would not be stranded in the middle of surveillance or data collection.

"Two minutes, Phil." Control's voice, echoing around the cockpit, interrupting his train of thought. As a trained astronaut, he had flown to the moon and to Mars, but he had never even considered for one moment flying through time—until the offer came.

"One minute. Don't forget—just five seconds after pressing *Home* you'll be back."

Phil took a deep breath. There was still time to bail out. Make a desperate run to the restroom.

"Ten seconds." There was no countdown. No point really.

There were faint echoes of *good luck* from the assembled crew.

And the clock stopped turning. A quick glance: *200, 7, 13, 0.* Roman Britain: Britannia Inferior.

He was suddenly tumbling in a rainbow of colours, head over heels in a seething world of numerous dimensions. Stars appeared and disappeared. Worlds, different to the Earth he knew, came and went. Then calm took over, and he was surrounded by a golden haze until, minutes later, the space around him cleared.

Phil focused his eyes on the clock. The numbers looked strange but were still there: *200, 7, 13, 1,* but the surrounding screen was now green. If everything had gone to plan, he was in the summer of the year 200, in the exact position he had started from: around twenty miles out of what was now the city of York in the north of England.

There was no room, of course, for there was no building to create a room in. Looking beyond his cockpit to the outside world, he saw lush meadows and hills beneath a grey sky. There was no sign of life, no sign of any movement. Not even many trees. He recalled that the recent Iron Age had quite a voracious appetite for trees.

He now had a choice to make. Press *Home* or disembark.

But that soon became a difficult choice. He couldn't understand the damned buttons. He couldn't bloody well read them. Or more accurately, they had become meaningless to him. There were letters there, but they were nonsense, at least to him.

He vaguely recollected what they were: *Home, Backward, Stop,* and *Forward.* But he didn't know which was what. Something had happened to his mind! And he had a one in four chance of getting back to base!

Why the hell wasn't there a *Go* button, and the ability to just set the clock to his exact time of departure? Then he realised he didn't recall the year when he left, never mind the month, hour, and minute—maybe that's why they just had a *home* button, in case he did forget. Or did they suspect his mind may be affected? He cursed; cursed them all.

Was there a recall from base, like the animals had? No, there bloody wasn't. He was on his own. That was the point of it all. He was a pioneer, a solo explorer of time—and he was in control. Even if his mind now said otherwise.

Maybe he was just dazed, a little concussed. He shook his head savagely. Nothing changed. Time to get out then. If he could recall the release procedure.

There was only one lever in the machine. One pull and it worked.

His nostrils flared as they caught clean air. Phil scrambled outside and stood tall, looked all around. He was in a valley and could hear water running nearby.

Turning, he stared with puzzlement at the strange contraption that had brought him here. Much bigger than a chariot. Too big for horses to pull. Unfamiliar materials catching the sunlight as the clouds briefly parted.

Something niggled at his mind. Get the hell out of here. Go back inside. Press the button.

Which button?

He started to walk over the lush grass towards a rise, stopped to look back. The machine was still there. For some reason, he had expected it to disappear. It didn't look right, didn't belong, even if it was his.

Phil topped the rise and saw a small fort in the distance with a narrow road leading to its entrance. Two figures were at the top of the tower, with quite a few more gathered around the base. Going down the other side of the mound, he suddenly stopped. He had lost sight of the machine. Panic rose in his chest. He was suddenly struggling to recognise the connection of the machine to himself. Then he realised that he had to find his tribe, find his family. But where were they?

He sat down, his back against a boulder, and watched the people at the fort. They showed no sign of seeing him, or were not concerned if they did. Something about their clothes looked familiar, but he had to stretch his mind to the future. They carried weapons, though, as plain as day: short swords, shields. They wore helmets and upper body armour.

I should have a weapon.

There was something at his waist, something in a pouch. He retrieved it carefully. It didn't look threatening, just an odd piece of bent metal. He put it back. He dare not go any further. He might lose his way. And there were too many of the invaders. *Invaders? Romans?*

Phil rose and turned, retraced his steps. The horseless chariot was still there. He knew it was his, but he didn't know how to ride it. *Press the button.* Bollocks!

His mind was reeling from successive assaults of past and future. He reached the door, looked inside. The seat looked comfortable enough. But the four buttons looked as if they had been designed to torment his agitated mind.

He sat in the seat, gazed at the obscure letters, summoning

some kind of logic from his addled 200 AD brain. There were four, he surmised, counting on his fingers, so he would press them one by one, starting on the left and working his way across. Find out which was the *Stop* button.

If he pressed the one on the left and he didn't move, it would be that one. If he crossed time again, he would wait six seconds and, if not *home*, quickly (very quickly) press the others in turn until he stopped. He would know from the time clock whether he had gone forward or backward in time. Either way, at least he'd be left with a reduced choice for *home*. Then he could repeat the process with more confidence.

It's haphazard. Is that the best I can do? Problem was, if he went too far back, his mind would likely become mush; he would likely possess a pre-historic caveman's intelligence. His hands were shaking. They did not, in fact, want to press anything.

How had the scientists not predicted this? Why had they not worked out that if you went back in time, your brain-power would revert to that time period's level of intellect? He shook his head vigorously, as if trying to jiggle loose some of his dormant acumen. Right now, he understood what the buttons did, but he did not comprehend the language written upon them. If he went further back, he would probably not even know what buttons were!

And if he went forward? He would be okay, he reckoned. As long as language had not changed a great deal. He guessed that depended on how far he went. Speed was of the essence. No matter which way he went, he did not want to travel far.

With a prayer on his lips, he made a choice and pressed the left-hand button.

The rainbow was back, and his thoughts were tumbling. As before stars came and went. He strained his eyes and attempted to press the buttons one after the other: second left, third left.

On pressing the second button, the rainbow colours started to run together, as in a child's watercolour painting, red into yellow, indigo into violet, smudging and swirling in a meaningless mess. His seat vibrated beneath him. His eyes lost focus. He felt for the next button and pressed. He didn't get to the fourth. Everything stopped.

Phil sat there until his vision cleared. Eventually, through bleary eyes, he looked outside. He wasn't home, that was for sure.

He looked at the screen. It was green. At least he hadn't stuffed up the system. Gradually the numbers became clear: *4193, 1, 8, 12.*

He had to let that sink in for a moment. January 4193 AD. Just after eight in the morning. He was cold, and his heart was racing. His hand crept to his side, felt for the firearm, gained some reassurance in its cold, metallic touch.

Phil checked out the buttons. The lettering appeared somewhat different to before, but at least he could decipher the damn things. His brain tried to analyse the subtle differences in the words and could only deduce that in two thousand years, language had evolved. *Why is it not the same?* But it didn't really matter, he mused; the one on the right was the *Home* button—the one he hadn't got round to pressing.

All he had to do now was push it.

But he should have a quick look outside first. This was his chance to get a glimpse into the future. He raised the door and scrambled out.

He trod on yellow grass and found himself on the edge of a huge crater that was almost completely shaded in darkness: *meteor impact* or *large bomb* ran through his head. The air was warm, not overbearingly so, but unusually warm for January. The sun was only just scraping above the horizon, and most of the sky was still dark and leaden.

He suddenly gasped, a small sound in the early morning silence. To his right, the heavens were aflame. At first he reasoned it was due to some kind of disastrous fire, some man-made catastrophe, but then he realised what it was: the *aurora borealis*, the northern lights. But how could he be seeing them on a future Yorkshire moor?

His astronaut training had told him about the flipping of the Earth's magnetic poles—a sluggish event, not an abrupt one. He reckoned that the flip must have happened. He was witnessing what none of his colleagues would ever see. For some minutes, he just stood there and watched, enchanted by the colourful display that was now beginning to fade as the sun slowly made its presence felt.

When Phil diverted his eyes from the sky, he got the shock of his life. A man stood a few paces away, staring straight at him. He was wearing a silver protective suit and a helmet that covered his entire head. He was also carrying some kind of firearm, currently pointing at the ground.

Initially, Phil didn't say anything, and neither did the intruder. Eventually the stranger said, "Ooyu."

To Phil it sounded like "who are you," so he replied, "Phil. My name's Phil."

His suit-clad visitor raised his weapon in an obvious threat, and Phil drew his pistol and fired. He was a useless shot, but as luck would have it, he hit the chest of his target, who collapsed like a rag doll. An unearthly shriek sounded, and Phil kept his pistol on guard as he stepped nearer the prone figure. *Have I killed him?*

He carefully knelt down, trying not to look at the huge

hole in the man's chest where his laser had left nothing in doubt as to its intent. He checked out the helmet's joining mechanism—not too much different from his old spacesuits—and tentatively removed it from the lifeless head.

Except there wasn't a head, at least not a human one. Where the head should have been, there was an array of fine wires and what looked like small circuit boards embedded in a substantial mass of black, synthetic matter. No eyes, no ears, no mouth, no nose.

Dumbfounded, Phil abruptly jumped up and looked at the chest wound. There was no blood, just a jagged hole where small sparks were jumping around like demented fleas. Some kind of robot, he assumed: an automaton roaming the Yorkshire moors. It was two thousand years on. He should have expected as much.

His eyes ranged over the robot's weapon. Definitely something he didn't understand, but not a laser. Also, he noticed, it was at one with the arm, a natural part of the android's upper appendage, fired presumably with a command from the artificial brain.

Phil stepped back and looked around.

The terrain had changed significantly from what he remembered. Crisp, pale yellow grass edged the crater, which was littered with various sized boulders; gritstone, he presumed. In the far distance he made out shadowy hills. As the sun rose a little further, quite a few buildings revealed themselves in the base of the crater, their rooftops just starting to glow orange. Several of the silver-suited figures were moving among them. There was also a central tower reaching high into the sky.

So where are the people? Should I find out, or should I return to my vehicle and press the fourth button?

Curiosity won out, of course. Problem was, there was no cover. They would see him approaching. He was as smart as the people of this age, he knew that, but was he smarter than their robotic servants?

Something left the top of the tower and headed straight for him.

Taking no chances, Phil entered the cockpit but left the hatch open. He sat with his finger poised over the right-hand button. At the faintest sign of aggression he would leave.

A small open-cabined helicopter landed next to the prone figure of the robot, and the sole pilot swung down to the ground. She, and there was no doubting it was a she, was covered in a body-hugging black suit that followed the contours of her body as if it had been sprayed on. Her head was covered by what resembled a black goldfish bowl with two lens-covered eyeholes to enable the wearer to see the external world. She looked like a cross between an early scuba diver and a deep-sea diver.

Walking over to the robot, she picked it up effortlessly in both arms, carried it back to her aircraft, and placed it gently in the passenger seat.

Phil watched carefully as she turned back and approached his machine. There was no sign of any weapon.

"You be?" Concise, clipped tones, somewhat aggressive.

Phil considered leaving his seat, getting out, but thought better of it.

"My name's Phil."

"Fil." She looked at him through the peepholes in her helmet. "You kill bot."

"It pointed its weapon at me."

"It thought you invader."

"Invader?"

She waved at the rising sun. "You need protect. From sun."

"Radiation?"

"Yes, rad."

Phil endeavoured to process the information gained from the brief encounter. Were these people wearing a protective layer to protect them from bursts of solar radiation? Was the robot some kind of guard?

She stepped closer and tapped Phil's machine. "Where from?"

Phil decided to tell the truth. After all, he was well in the future; time machines may very well be on production lines in 4193. "The past," he said. "This is a time machine."

She pointed at the sun. "Not work anymore."

Phil started to sweat, and not just because of the rising sun. Not work! What the hell did she mean?

He pressed the fourth button. The air in the cockpit blurred, but when it cleared, she was still there. Phil uttered a strange cry and stabbed at the button again. Nothing. Small rivulets of perspiration trickled down his temple.

"Stuck," she said.

So it bloody well seems, Phil thought.

"Hungry?" she asked, then pointed into the crater. "Food."

Phil realised he was famished—thirsty, too.

Another helicopter cruised in to land besides her aircraft, appearing to arrive out of nowhere from Phil's limited vision of the outside. He sat there, undecided, but only for a few seconds. There was no future remaining in his machine. He grimaced at the irony of that thought. Slowly, he manoeuvred out of his seat and dropped onto the sun-baked grass.

She pointed at the second helicopter. "In," she said.

"Food. Water."

Phil blinked. *Has she read my mind?*

She stepped forward, gazed into his eyes through her bulbous headgear. Repeated her words. "In. Food. Water."

Procrastination was well and truly buried in this century, Phil thought. Straight and to the point. Mind you, it had always been like that in Yorkshire.

She pointed at the sun. "Quickly."

Phil did as he was told, wondering whether that was what he would always be doing in this new stage of his life: doing as he was told. And being covered in black plastic.

* * *

He was at the top of the tower. There were three others in the circular room, and numerous armaments were scattered around the periphery. His mysterious rescuer, if that's what she was, had somehow removed her protective suit and wore a loose, smock-like green garment that covered her from neck to feet. The others, one woman and two men, wore the same garb. Phil put them all at around forty.

"What year from?" the woman asked him.

Phil frowned, but saw no harm in responding. "Twenty-one twenty-four," he replied routinely. It appeared his brain had regained its functionality once more. Remembering the year had been easy. Not that it did him much good anymore.

She nodded, and the others laughed. *Don't they believe me?*

"You promised food and water," Phil said.

"Five minutes."

"Do you have names?" Phil asked.

"Marta," the woman replied. She pointed at the others in turn. "Slav, Mike, Justine."

90

"Do you carry disease?" Justine asked.

"No," Phil answered, somewhat irritated by the question. "Do you?"

"No disease in this room," Marta said. "Electronically quarantined."

That flummoxed Phil. "What are the weapons for?" he asked.

"Invaders," Mike replied.

"Invaders from where?" Phil looked at Mike suspiciously. This was beginning to feel like some kind of dream.

"Not sure," Mike responded. "Overseas maybe." He waved his arm at the window. "Beyond the sky maybe."

"What do the robots do?" Phil was full of questions, but he didn't think he would like any of the answers.

Slav spoke for the first time. "Guard. Protect. Get water. Make food. Keep us going. Keep us safe." He pointed through the window. "We cannot remain outside for long, even in black."

"So you are from the past?" Justine asked.

Phil nodded. "I know you won't believe me, but I am from over two thousand years ago."

"Oh, we believe you," Marta stated. "There is a machine like yours in the city."

For the first time since his arrival, Phil's hopes rose. "Really! You have a machine like mine?" He looked out at the forlorn landscape, saw a group of twelve robots marching away on some secret mission, weapons pointing at the sky.

"In a museum," Justine said. "For antiquities."

Phil's hopes were immediately dashed. "Antiquities. Does that mean it doesn't work?"

"Professor Aksakov will know," Marta said. "He works on it for years."

That strangely articulated fact did not fill Phil with joy. "Can I go and see him?"

"You will have to travel to the city," Slav said.

"That's not far," Phil responded.

"Far enough with invaders about," Marta said. "You can try to go, but you may not get there."

"Can you message Professor Aksakov?"

"No communication. Satellites useless. Too many rads." Mike was almost gloating, and Phil wondered what it was about these people that made them so insular, so bloody cold.

"How many of you are at this station?" Phil was curious to know where the rest of the people were.

"Our village has 553 people," Justine responded. "All live underground, except when on tower duty."

Underground! "Then what are the nearby buildings for?"

"Bots hangars there," Marta said. "Grow food. Mine water. Store."

Phil got the drift. "What has happened to all the people in this part of the world?"

"Wars, famine, disease, rads," Justine answered. "Over the last thousand years."

Phil found himself on edge. Whatever kind of life these people had, it sure as hell was not for him.

A polite chirrup came from the central elevator, which Phil had earlier noticed operated on a simple weight and pulley system. A bot stood there, food and drinks in its arms, weapon pointing straight at Phil.

"Table," Marta said. Then to Phil: "Please. Help yourself."

The bot left, and Phil cautiously drank. The water was fine, if a little earthy; the food—bread, some kind of artificial-tasting cheese and small tomatoes—was tasty enough. Nobody joined him. Presumably this was not their normal eating time.

While he ate, Justine talked.

"If you want to go to the city, there are things you need to know. You cannot go in daytime, even if it is cloudy. Your skin will not take the *black*; it will degrade beneath the application. And you most certainly could not take *the shower of removal*, which we use to take away our protection." She looked at Phil with her head to one side. "You must therefore go at night in your current garb."

Phil shrugged. That didn't bother him much.

"If you go at night," Justine continued, "be aware there will be more invaders about. You must be extremely careful."

Phil was getting the impression that they just wanted rid of him. "Can I have bot guards?" he asked between mouthfuls.

"We can let you have one bot. We cannot spare any more than that." She looked at him slyly. "Please do not shoot it."

* * *

He was on his way, beneath an almost full moon, and with a rough map in his hand. They had advised him to follow a nearby river, and he reckoned he needed seven hours for the trek, maybe six if he trotted now and again, assuming the bot could trot with him.

There was a path by the river, and he used that initially, until it petered out. Every now and again, scudding clouds shielded the moon, and he preferred the deeper night that came with the sudden decrease in light.

He had, of course, walked these moors before, and distant memories suggested that he may have even walked this very same route. But the landscape was totally different from the one he recalled. There were no rolling hills, no trees to write home about, no animals on hillsides, no intermittent farm buildings with arrays of solar panels. This country was sparse, devoid of character, devastated by whatever had overtaken it in the generations before those seeking refuge in the tower. The moonlight only served to emphasise the barrenness of the environment, naked in all its sadness and infertility.

Ahead of him, the bot suddenly stopped, raised its weapon arm. Phil could hear something, a chitter-chatter from around the next bend. The robot began to climb to its right. Phil, pistol in hand, followed in silent haste.

They climbed up and around, finding shelter behind an outcrop of sandstone. The bot lay flat, weapon pointing down the slope. Phil found another perch from where he could scan the river flowing below.

At first he could see nothing, but as the moon finally escaped the clutches of the clouds, he saw four figures below. Each was at least two metres tall and wore a dark one-piece suit over a bulky frame. To his immense surprise, all of them wore a full-cover helmet, as if they had just ditched their Harley-Davidsons back around the bend.

They each held a large firearm in both hands. Behind them, there was some kind of boat on the river, keeping pace with the invaders' march along the bank. It was the boat he had heard, not the voices of people—if they were people.

Phil waited until they had gone, and then, led by the bot, carefully made his way back down to the river.

According to the tower people, this was the River Ouse, or what had been called the Ouse when people had had the time to name their rivers. It led into the heart of York, led, in fact, to the museum where the mysterious Professor Aksakov worked and dwelt.

Two hours later, they ran into a pair of invaders who stood leisurely looking out over the river. The bot got away three shots before Phil could even raise his pistol. Two dark shapes crashed to the ground, but not before a beam of fire swept away the bot's left arm below the elbow.

Phil froze and could only raise his pistol to guard against any further movement from the two fallen figures. A full minute later, he approached them cagily, gazed down, resisted the urge to be sick. There was no way they were human, not his kind of human anyway. Not even the type of human who lived in the tower.

Both had large holes in their chests, but there was no bleeding. One had lost his helmet, revealing an ebony face with two large, round, purple eyes, and a small nose. The lips were also purple, much fuller than his own. He couldn't see whether there were any teeth.

The robot knelt and rolled them both in the river with his one good arm, the one without the weapon.

I'm now in deep trouble, Phil thought. He thought it even more as the bot pointed back the way they had come. "Seeyu," it chirped as it walked away in the direction of the tower.

Phil didn't argue. There seemed little point. Anyway, all he had to do was follow the river until he came to the museum. Few other buildings stood, according to the tower people. And it was just before the only remaining bridge in the city.

But too risky on the path, he decided. He would climb upwards and track the water from higher up. As long as the moon shone intermittently, he shouldn't lose his way.

* * *

After another two hours, he saw the next group of invaders. Like the first group, they were patrolling along the riverbank accompanied by a sleek, small boat that chugged along beside them. He skirted them successfully and before long saw ruins of buildings ahead. At long last he was approaching the city of York, or what remained of it.

Seeing a city without lights was strange. No matter how he strained his eyes, there was no sign of any artificial lighting whatsoever. He wondered whether that meant the city was totally without power—in which case there would be all sorts of problems firing up the time machine.

Phil entered the built-up area with caution, ably guided by a moon that had shaken off the clouds and created mis-shapen and somewhat frightening silhouettes of the collapsed buildings.

He wondered how it had come to this. Presumably either by a meteor impact, or a missile attack, or maybe by the invaders themselves.

He paused to look at the map. He reckoned he was two miles from the old castle tower, if it was still standing, and from there it was a short walk to the Yorkshire Museum in the city centre.

He walked on past a sign that read *Skeldergate Bridge*, though there was no bridge to cross; along Coney Street, where the sign stood tall and proud, but with no buildings left to show for it; around a bend—and straight into the arms of a two-man invader patrol.

They fired without hesitation but, caught by surprise, got their range wrong. The ground at Phil's feet became powder and rose into the air as if suddenly metamorphosing into the ghost of medieval streets past.

Phil surged to his right, running at full tilt, straight down what once was Market Street. There was a building on the right, mostly a ruin, but it seemed to have a second floor. He sought the door, took half a second to look back. They were about twenty paces away, running awkwardly, as if not used to it.

He dropped to his knees, aimed the pistol, fired. One of his pursuers stopped, staggered as if drunk, dropped. His companion slowed, as if uncertain, then fired a beam of lethal energy in Phil's direction.

The beam took a second to reach the doorway; Phil took half a second to make for the crumbling stairs. His heart was racing madly; sweat soaked his brow and assaulted his eyes, but refused to bathe his dry, painful lips.

The stairs were of no use, half eaten by age and destruction. He could see the moon through a gap in the high ceiling. There had to be a way out at the rear of the building, there just had to be. He heard the invader pull up outside, heard a snort and then another. Then two more in rapid succession.

He ran towards the back, and the stairs caught fire. There was an open doorway. Praise be! He ran through, turned left, down the street, left again. *Parliament Street*, the moon told him, another sorry sign on a sorry building. Hell for leather down there. No time for stealth. If there were any more invaders, he was lost.

Phil sped on, gun in hand, prayers on his lips. In two hundred metres, he had slowed for want of air. Daveygate, Blake Street: more downtrodden ghosts slipping past like ships in the night, grey and ruined, forbidding and unyielding. Stopping behind a broken wall, he took a furtive look back. He couldn't see anything. Maybe his pursuer had gone back to his fallen comrade.

Part of the moon became obscured again, but there was

enough light to see the parkland ahead. The museum gardens, it had to be. Phil moved forward, searching for four pillars. He found them, by some miracle still upright at the main entrance. The solid doors looked locked. *How the hell do I get in?*

He thought he saw a movement near the museum entrance and wondered whether the invaders were communicating with each other. Stupid thought. Of course they were. But they didn't know he was heading for the museum. The tower people had said there were more invaders abroad at night. *Should I wait until daylight?* At least then he could search for an access point to the museum. *Stupid! Stupid!* He dare not be out in the sun. Early dawn, that would have to do. The first over-the-horizon rays of a lethal sun.

There was another ruin nearby, what looked like a storage centre. Large pillars lay on the ground, and most of the second-floor walls had collapsed. He moved closer, stepped in among the rubble, sought shelter within what walls remained on the ground floor. He suddenly recalled what the place was—the York Explore Library. In his time, there were great books there, a café too; it had been altogether a wonderful place. In the year 4193, he doubted that such things existed anymore.

He searched out a centrally located corner, settled down among dust and debris, sheltering from prying eyes, and kept his pistol on his lap. He reckoned less than two hours to daybreak.

* * *

There had been noises in those hours stretching to sunrise. Footfalls, grunts, even the chitter-chatter of the invaders' boats on the nearby river. But he had remained as still and quiet as a mouse, breathing shallowly, concentrating on keeping awake. In any case, any dreams would have been bad dreams.

His sole task now was to get into the museum.

It was not light outside; he got just a hint of the encroaching dawn as the sun's rays painted the landscape through a filter of clouds. As he'd expected, the grass was yellow; the buildings, stark. The museum itself was covered in grime and mould, but still managed to stand proud.

Standing in the library ruins, Phil scanned the terrain. No sign of any invaders—maybe they were nocturnal. Less than two hundred metres to the museum. *No man's land.*

A dreadful thought ran through his overwrought mind. What if the invaders had commandeered the museum? What if it was their headquarters? He shook his head. Surely the tower people would have warned him. He shook his head again. There was only one way out of this, and that lay straight ahead.

In the gloom of a cloudy dawn, he took two cautious steps and then ran. He reached the main doors, which were locked. He had expected nothing else. There were windows either side, but they had been boarded over. He made his way to the left along a raised patio, passed fallen lamp standards, and dropped off the elevated area.

Phil scuttled to the end of the building and turned right. There was significant damage further along the wall and a large hole in the ground. He made out fallen masonry and fallen trees. And what looked like a bomb or mortar strike.

He approached cautiously and looked down. There appeared to be a way through—if he didn't break his neck getting down to it.

He couldn't walk down; it was much too steep. He sat and

slithered over the edge, careening down into the blast hole as a nervous child might do on a newly found playground slide. This slide was lined with dirt, stones and rubble, and it must have been at least three men long. It was a painful descent, but he was rewarded well, being met by a breach in the lower wall. Looking back up, Phil saw that light was gathering.

Unfortunately, the bottom of the hole was filled with dirty water, and as he crawled on his hands and knees into the room beyond, he felt the cold seep through to both flesh and bone. Once beyond the fractured wall, he stood.

The room was in darkness; no light from any useful window found its way inside. He wished for a torch but was no magician, and so none appeared. Dare he shout, call out the professor's name? He decided against it. There was no knowing whether any other person, friend or foe, was in the building.

Letting his eyes adjust, he saw there was a well of light somewhere across the room. He made his way slowly towards it, stumbling over fallen plinths and possible medieval artefacts, or maybe even artefacts from his own time.

He found a stairwell leading upwards, rising into a zone only a little less gloomy than the one he was escaping from. But visibility was easier here, and Phil climbed confidently, pistol forever at the ready.

Another decrepit display area met his gaze at the top of the stairs. He made his way towards what he estimated would be the front of the building, passed through a couple of doorways, found himself staring at the main entrance doors. There was no machine here, no time-intrigued professor.

He turned and retraced his footsteps. Back to the basement. Walked around as best he could as increasing light filtered through. He found a sign board he had missed before:

Lift, Toilets, something else he couldn't read. Phil reckoned that if the professor was here, he must use the toilets—not that they were likely to work anymore. He followed the sign, even found the male toilets and, nearby, what looked like the main stairwell and a sad-looking lift. The stairwell looked in decent condition, and he climbed it to the top, up to the first floor.

There was another sign: *Library* and only half-legible, a series of *Laboratories*. If the professor was anywhere, he would be here.

Phil decided to risk a call: "Professor Aksakov?"

There was no answer.

He worked his way down to the right, towards the unknown laboratories. And there, through an open doorway, in a room on its own and illuminated by the cloud-screened rays of the rising sun, was the blessed machine in all its glory. Offering a silent prayer, Phil approached, studying the shape and lines of the contraption with every step.

It was similar to his machine, but not identical. There was a placard mounted on its side:

Prototype Time Machine built in 2134 by Wellsian Technologies
This machine was never tested with humans aboard due to lack
of government funds and the failure of the original to return
in 2124 carrying Chrononaut Phillip M Wells

Well, that's nice, Phil thought, *they named the tech company after me,* adding sceptically: *But only after they thought I was lost forever and never to return.*

He peered into the cockpit. The four buttons were still there, but they were not labelled. They were colour coded! Shit! Why had they done that? Maybe somebody had eventually come up with the theory that the synapses within the human brain transfigured as time swept by, meaning that the pilot was only as intelligent as the human inhabitants of the destination time. Evolution, devolution, all one sorry mess! And quite possibly all wrong.

Forward, Backward, Stop, and *Home.* Now, green, amber, red, and blue.

Were they in the same order? Had they been that logical?

There was no power to the machine; that much was obvious. Everything inside the cockpit was quite dead.

A sound from behind had him whirling, gun in hand. There stood the oldest man he had ever seen, a puzzled expression pasted upon his ancient face.

"You called?" The voice was weak, as if crossing many years of time and space.

The man was kept upright by two walking sticks fashioned from chrome-covered bars that at one time may have been part of the museum's barriers. He was dressed in a spotless white shirt and grey pants, his feet shod in black thick-soled shoes. Thinning grey hair topped a slim, weathered face, with sunken cheeks. His brow was furrowed as might be a ploughed spring field after the attentions of a conscientious farmer.

Behind him, looking as innocuous as a bouncer at a nightclub, stood a bot.

"Professor Aksakov?"

A slight nod, no verbal response.

Phil said: "I am Phillip M Wells."

The grin on the professor's face was a sight to behold. He crept forward slowly and thrust out a hand. "I've been waiting for you," he whispered. "For a long time."

* * *

They settled in what used to be the library, and Phil told the professor everything. And he heard too much from the professor. How there had been three short world wars before the flip, the latest one in the year 3999. How, after that last conflict, in 4087, the Earth's magnetic field had commenced to reverse, was still in the process of doing so. How everything had been shot to pieces. Power and communications had been decimated; infrastructure, ruined beyond repair.

Many species that relied on geomagnetism had become extinct, including cross-pollination insects. The planet's food sources had dwindled. Globalism was long dead. And then the invaders had appeared, like scavengers, like vultures, as if conjured up by a world seeking revenge on its previous prime species.

"Humankind," the professor said, "is well on the way to extinction."

Phil looked at the professor's ramshackle old bed, blew out a very long breath, and asked, "How do you survive here?"

Professor Aksakov gestured to the bot, which stood in the background like some attendant manservant from a bygone age. "In the daytime, Jeeves gets food and water for me, from the towers. They all know about the mad old professor of chronology."

Jeeves! God help me, Phil thought.

Phil decided it was time to get to the crux of the matter, his reason for entering the museum.

"Does the time machine work?"

The professor shrugged. "I really don't know. It was mothballed a very long time ago, over two thousand years. I have replaced some of the parts and believe it is in good condition."

Phil swallowed hard. That was true, of course. From where he was now, the machine was ancient. "Were any others built?"

Professor Aksakov chortled. "I don't know the answer to that. Probably not in this country." He leaned forward in his chair, suddenly alert. "It's the only chance we have."

We? Phil frowned, but remained silent, waiting for the old man to explain further.

"That's why you came here, isn't it? To go back to where you came from."

"The tower people say that the Earth's field ruins equipment. The machine I came in doesn't work. It's trapped."

"Ah," the professor said, pointing upward. "This roof is well shielded. It also carries solar panels, which I have modified and protected over time so as not to suffer damage from the sun's extreme rays."

Protecting solar panels from the sun? *That sounds strange,* Phil thought

"They are over one hundred years old and still work," Aksakov added. He touched a control on his chair, and the room lights came on in a demonstration. He rapidly switched them off again. "No good advertising my presence," he said.

"So will you help me return?" Phil asked.

For a while there was no answer. The professor looked at the boarded-up windows where various slivers of light entered the old library, the parallel sabres illuminating the room in a half-hearted kaleidoscope of monotones.

He turned to Phil. "But you don't return."

Phil threw a challenging look at the professor. "What!"

"You read the plaque on the machine. You didn't return."

Phil's heart rate suddenly increased. A nervous pang

gripped his midriff. He recalled the words: *the failure of the original to return in 2124 carrying Chrononaut Phillip M Wells.*

Phil felt as if a huge iron fist had squeezed the air from his lungs. For some seconds, he could not respond. He raised his head slowly, staring at Aksakov's rather tired-looking face. "I can try." Hope suddenly lit up his eyes. "And that was my machine, not the one here."

The professor seemed to take the initiative, finding an energy that belied the frailty of his looks. "Do you know the sequence of buttons to operate *this* machine?"

"They are different than my machine," Phil answered, "but I think so."

The professor leaned over eagerly. "What if you went back to the year after the machine I have here was built? In the year 2135. That way nothing is contradicted. If you go at night, you could simply walk away. There would be nobody about."

Phil pondered that for a while. "Maybe that would work."

"From what I've read," the professor said, "the whole project was completely abandoned. In all likelihood, you would go back, dismount, and restart your life eleven years into the future. You would just leave the machine for the museum types like me."

Pursing his lips, Phil said, "Did this machine originate from here, from this very room?"

The professor shrugged. "Does it matter?"

It might do, Phil thought. It might have come from within a military establishment and been moved here later. Still, it was all he had. And he hadn't come this far without taking risks.

"Okay," he said. "Let's do it."

"I'll need to know the buttons," the professor said. "To

test the machine's power and circuitry. We can't trust that everything will work immediately."

Phil nodded. "Understood. But I may be wrong on the buttons. As I said, these ones are colour-coded."

"Your risk," Aksakov stated. "But perhaps not a big one. I'd stake what's left of my life that they would have kept the sequence the same."

"Hope so," Phil said. "For my sake."

"I'll miss that machine when it's gone," the professor said.

"There's another one, near the tower west of here," Phil rejoined.

Aksakov smiled a wistful smile. "So there is."

* * *

They stood at the machine. The power was on. It was approaching midnight.

Phil recalled the warped geometry and the humming. It was there again with this machine. All he had to do was press *Home*, arrive, and then quickly press *Forward* one year and *Stop*. One year, two years, five years. Who cared?

Home, Forward, Stop. Blue, then *green* then *red.*

"One more thing to check before you leave," the professor said. He pointed to a panel. "Can you confirm that lower circuit board is live?"

Phil crouched, slid the panel cover aside, and immediately felt a blow on the back of his neck. He fell to the ground, turned his head to see Aksakov, crutches abandoned, clambering into the cockpit.

He tried to rise, managed to get to his feet, and grabbed the machine for support. Through blurred vision, he saw the professor punch the blue button, then collapsed to the ground as the structure of the time machine faded away.

The room rang with profanities. Phil cursed the Aksakov name and fervently hoped that the machine would never reach its destination. But of course it would. The professor would no doubt return to the Yorkshire Museum or somewhere just as safe. He would be a mystery man from the future. Not that he would be carrying good tidings. Or maybe, if the machine returned at the same time of day, he would just walk out of an empty building.

Phil slowly got to his feet. He would go back to the tower. Get help to bring his own machine here, invaders or no invaders. Go after the Aksakov bastard. That was the only thing he could do now.

There was a movement from the door. The bot stood there, slowly raising its right arm.

"Ooyu," the bot said.

DAVE AND GOLIATH

t's outside the airlock now!" The voice was high-pitched, full of fear.

"Grab your rifle."

"I have."

Dave Kaminski had to strain his ears to pick up the terrified voice coming from his radio. Nervously licking his lips, he was surprised to find a trickle of sweat, a salt-flavoured essence, clinging tenaciously to his overnight stubble. Glancing out of his dome's window, he saw the strange frosted patterns of another world, a kaleidoscope of intersecting shades of white and grey.

There was a sudden splintering crash from the commset, and the listening Earthman heard what appeared to be the last cries of Sam Fleming. Then came silence—an unearthly silence—the kind of silence only experienced on an alien world. Dave switched off the set.

LOOKING FOR LIFE

Dave Kaminski was a trapper — one of a handful who had chosen to plunder the planet Ulcon and its strange wildlife. Hurtling around its yellow dwarf, the alien world was a direct contrast to Earth: harsh, rugged mountains were everywhere, seas were non-existent. Rarely watered plains, ice-cold winds, and an atmosphere to embrittle your lungs completed the picture.

And that's why there were only a few trappers who dared to try their luck, and even then they only stayed for two weeks at a time; the one thing going for them on this frigid world being the fact that Ulcon days were only slightly longer than Earth's.

Living upon Ulcon were what the Earthmen had termed *furroons*, bearlike creatures about half the size of a human. Furroons were covered with white, shiny fur that fetched a fortune back home and on the colonised planets.

At that moment, though, Dave Kaminski was not interested in furroons. Four of his colleagues had vanished, each of their domes smashed into meaningless rubble, one after the other within the space of three hours.

They hadn't had time to get together, to formulate a plan of action. And they didn't know who the adversary was!

He looked at the video links to the other domes, a comms safety feature that came with their design. Two of them were blank, covered in meaningless static that suggested the cameras had been destroyed, but two, including Sam Fleming's, showed the ruined domes. Dave studied the pictures. Both domes had been flattened, as if a wrecking ball had dropped from a great height and landed dead centre.

He ran Sam's video backwards, but everything was happening too quickly. One second the dome was intact, the next it was a heap of rubble. The aggressor moved at lightning speed.

And no doubt he was next!

Dave sat back in his chair and anxiously rubbed his swarthy face with a long-fingered, spidery hand. He could hear the freezing wind moaning outside, see the frost building up on the window, despite it being only early afternoon. This was a place for strong men, and the rewards were high if a man could take it. Until a few minutes ago, Sam Fleming had taken it, but now something had taken Sam Fleming.

Dave raised the heating in the dome. Fleming was—had been—his nearest neighbour. They had often met over the hard stuff, recalling escapades of danger and death on this world and others. He poured himself a double now but didn't drink it, even though his hands were shaking. He needed to keep a clear head.

He cursed and walked over to the map. Marking a cross over Fleming's dome, he noted the trend. He was next in line. He was the only one left in line! And the cargo ship was not due for two more days.

Soon the furroons would emerge from their caves for their daily fill of lichen. But what was the use, if he was going to die? To procure more furs for the benefit of a dead man was pointless. He laughed aloud. Hell! He wasn't dead yet. Maybe the destroyer wouldn't come. Maybe it was dead—dead from the whisky in Sam Fleming's body.

Attack is the best form of defence. Where did that come from? He thought about it, put on his suit, grabbed his rifle and two spare air packs, and went through the airlock.

The sun was a golden ball of fire high in the sky, only about half the size of Earth's star, painting the heavens ochre-grey. He mounted his bug and fired the engine. She was cold. He tried again, and the large quad bike roared into life.

There was a bulky container at the back for furroon skins, but there would be none today; he would be hunting bigger game.

In no more than ten minutes, he had reached Fleming's dome. And he didn't come across any alien wrecking balls.

Approaching cautiously, Dave saw that the preformed shape had totally collapsed. Fleming wouldn't have stood a chance. Inside the demolished building he found a rifle and other small domestic items still intact. All the furniture was trashed.

Dave snatched the rifle and stored it aboard the bug. Then he searched the rubble for spare ammo clips and more air packs, finding two of each.

There was no sign of the attacker, nor of Sam's body. Whatever had been here had presumably taken Sam away.

Then Dave noticed the footprints. He knelt down to inspect them more closely. Whatever had made them must have been pretty heavy; it took more than a lightweight to disturb the freezing soil of Ulcon.

The marks were large and round, and led off to a range of foothills about three kilometres to the south. Dave tracked them slowly on his bug.

As he neared the uplands, he stopped the bug, dismounted, and checked the ground for more footprints. They were still visible, leading into a collection of man-sized rocks no more than twenty metres away. The sun was to his right, now casting longer shadows.

He clamped his mouth around the suit's feed tube. Hot liquid spilled down his throat, warming his body, giving him courage.

Something spiralled out of the rocks, heading straight towards him.

Dave nearly choked. His first instinct was to get back on the bug. Then he remembered he was the hunter, and stood his ground.

The tentacle paused some distance away, glinting reflected light from the Ulcon sun. It looked metallic and tendril-like, and it swayed as if dancing to an inaudible melody. Dave levelled his rifle, but before he could fire, the bulk of his prey emerged from behind a group of boulders.

Dave's eyes widened in shock, and he froze to the spot. *I'm hunting that!*

It was over four times his height, spherical, with the one exploratory arm now retreating into the bulk of the body. Beneath it, three pulsating jets hit the ground in rapid sequence as the sphere bobbed up and down. *Not footprints*, Dave thought, *but jet prints*. The thing before him was a machine, and that didn't make him feel any better at all.

Now was the time to get the hell away from it.

Next thing he knew, there was a bright flash, and he was surrounded by darkness. He knew immediately where he was: inside his quarry. His eyes adjusted, but the light was poor. He switched on his suit's lamp, amazed that he was still standing.

He could see the curvature of the wall. Eaten alive, he thought, but at least it was a machine and not some damned alien creature that would start spewing corrosive stomach acid all over him.

And he still held his rifle!

Dave trained his lamp around, estimating the sphere was around eight metres in diameter. He could hear the thrum of the supporting jets echoing inside his suit, feel the slight movement as the sphere maintained equilibrium.

It didn't take him long to find his colleagues. They were

sprawled in a heap up against the wall. He took the few steps over to them, knelt, and inspected the nearest. Fleming! He tried to feel for a pulse, but it was impossible through the suit's gloves. It they weren't dead, they were unconscious. Nearby there were also three furroons. At least there was no racial discrimination!

What is this machine, this giant of a mechanism?

A hissing sound breached his suit's helmet. Momentarily, Dave thought his suit had sprung a leak, but then he noticed the trail of an orange gas stream entering the sphere. Everything became transformed by the swirling vapour, swiftly taking on a titian hue, and Dave realised that his colleagues and the furroons had been gassed.

He permitted himself a brief smile. The machine had perhaps never heard of spacesuits. His colleagues, caught in the warmth of their domes with no protection, would have been easy prey.

The room suddenly cleared, and Dave aimed his rifle at the spot where the gas had come from, rejoiced in the recoil as he pulled the trigger.

* * *

He had won the first round. Dave found himself outside again, rejected by the strange sphere, spat out like some unwanted morsel of food. Looking around, he saw his adversary had departed. He was also relieved to see his bug, apparently intact, just where he had left it.

Returning posthaste back to his dome, he dismounted, grabbed all the air packs, and went inside. Two days! That was when the cargo ship would come.

Dave kept his suit on. For all he knew, the Goliath

machine might have followed him, eager for another confrontation. Problem was, he couldn't leave the suit on as his air supply was limited, even with Fleming's additional packs. On the other hand, he would not have time to don it again should the machine breach the wall of his dome.

He compromised and took off his helmet. It needed cleaning anyway; there was soup splashed all over the inside.

The best form of defence is attack. Well, that had worked, hadn't it.

He needed another plan. He wondered how intelligent the machine was—whether it had worked out it could defeat him if he was not wearing his suit. Then again, the tentacle looked like it could do serious damage, including tearing off his protective layer.

Dave mulled over all the possibilities and came up with a strategy.

* * *

He didn't sleep that night. He'd turned on the external lights and camped by the window, a rifle in one hand, helmet at his feet. When dawn broke, he realised he had dozed off. He also realised he was still in one piece. Thankfully Goliath had not followed him. Maybe it was healing the wounds to its shell. There was still hope. The cargo ship would be here tomorrow.

Today he would gather as many air packs as he could from the other wrecked domes. Then, fully suited, he would bed down in what remained of Fleming's dome and await the cargo ship. He would only return to his own dome if he was on his last air pack. If Goliath found him first, he would target the jets at its base. If he could nail those, maybe the beast would be rendered immobile.

LOOKING FOR LIFE

* * *

He gathered enough air packs to last him three days; they would comfortably take him through to the cargo ship's arrival. Then he made his final stop at Fleming's wrecked dome.

Dave stood there, looking at the ruined building. *One thing is for sure, I need to hide the bug.*

The walls of the structure were constructed from interlocking lightweight material, and he easily pushed a way through to the centre, moving blocks aside to form a pathway for the bug. He drove his vehicle inside. It was a tight fit, but that was fine. Hopefully, he wouldn't need it again.

Dave stared around, working out where he could stack blocks to build a makeshift barricade. He set to work.

Three hours later, he was satisfied. His new shelter didn't have a roof, but at least the walls would give some protection.

His suit beeped. Time to change air. He looked at his watch. Tomorrow morning the ship would be here. Twenty hours to go. He checked his rifles.

An hour later, Dave heard thumping. He peered through a crack in the wall and saw Goliath. There it was, crossing the icy terrain like the bouncing ball of some demented behemoth, no doubt intent on finding the creature that had inflicted damage to its shell. Initially, Dave thought it had worked out where he was, but relief swept such thoughts aside as the huge contraption sailed past and headed for his own dome.

How long, he wondered, before it worked out where he was.

He checked his commset, stowed in the bug's container. The light showed amber. Three more hours and he could call the ship. But would Goliath hear the signal and pinpoint his position?

Two hours later, he found himself wanting to check his dome. He resisted the temptation. He had to assume it had been destroyed and would offer him no succour whatsoever. Besides, the sun was starting to drop.

Darkness came and, with it, the heightening of Dave's anxiety. He'd been okay last night, so why should tonight be any different? Because he was wearing a suit and there was no roof over his head, that was why!

The commset button was green. He could contact the ship. But what if Goliath overheard? He looked at his watch again. The ship would be here at ten in the morning. He'd call them at nine, he decided, let them know his position and what had happened. They could be of no use to him overnight.

He sat down, determined to stay awake. Several hours later, the beeping of his suit awoke him. Air change! He did it swiftly and checked the time. One in the morning. He peered through the gap in the wall.

Ulcon's two moons were up, casting ghostly light over the expanse of the chilled plain. There was no sign of Goliath. Stars were out in their thousands. Was one of them the cargo ship? He sincerely hoped so.

Dave settled down again. Eight more hours and he'd make the call.

* * *

Morning came, and Dave slurped sustenance from his suit's canteen. He longed to wash his face, clean his teeth, massage his tired eyes, but he couldn't. He stared at the commset. Should he risk a call now? No! An hour to go. He would wait until nine.

Thwump. Thwump. Dave's heart leapt into his mouth. He stumbled to the crack in the wall and looked out. There it was—Goliath—apparently as good as new, waving its tentacle in the air, no more than fifty metres away. Dave grabbed his rifle. Goliath bounced nearer.

At least one thing was clear: he should now make the call.

A voice rang in his ears. "Hi guys. Wake up, sleepyheads. Sorry we're early. Dropping down now."

Dave wanted to shriek with joy, but gave a different kind of shriek as Goliath's tentacle probed its way through his improvised wall. He fired and missed. He scrambled behind the bug, in the desperate hope the probing appendage did not have vision.

The snakelike feeler surged closer, grabbed the commset, and threw it against the wall. Then it did the same with the bug, as if it were made of nothing more than tissue paper. Dave fired again and again.

He had to get out of here, or he'd be crushed. Thwump. Goliath was about to make his last bounce.

There was a hole where the bug had crashed into the wall. Dave scrambled through it and ran. Goliath slammed into the structure, and what had become temporary was totally extinguished.

Dave stopped running and turned. They eyed each other across the Ulcon plain. Dave and Goliath in a last stand. The tentacle writhed closer. It was making for his suit, and Dave knew that it would rip it apart.

The roar of engines sounded, and out of the corner of his eye, Dave saw the ship descending. *Should I run towards it?*

The tentacle found his waist, and Dave screamed. He fired at the base of the sphere, sprayed it with energy; fired at the tentacle, trying to cut it in two.

And then the alien appendage was gone. Dave glanced down. Thankfully, his suit was intact. He cursed as he saw his spare air pack was missing.

He could see the ship now, landed two hundred metres away, and Goliath was making straight for it. *Now you're done for*, Dave thought. The stupid machine was going to attack the spacecraft, as if it was another easy prey. Dave kept back, waiting for the ship's cannons to open up.

But they didn't.

Instead, Goliath bounced up to the ship and settled down on the ground, as if all the energy had been sucked out of it.

Sweat trickled into Dave's eyes. What the hell was going on?

A small shuttle craft left the cargo ship, dropped to the ground, and approached Goliath. Three suited figures got out. Were they mad?

He started to run towards them, waving his arms. Then he stopped in his tracks as the crewmen went up to Goliath and a man-sized hatch opened in the side of the machine. They went inside.

Dave was stunned. This was crazy!

He approached cautiously, his rifle pointing in front of him, covering Goliath's hatch.

The rest of the crew must have seen him from the cargo ship. His suit comm system opened up. "Dave, put your weapon down. There's nothing to do."

"The other trappers are in there," Dave replied. "Swallowed by that beast."

"What!" There was silence for a moment, then: "Stay where you are."

Dave walked to within ten metres of the open hatch and stopped.

"What is this thing?" Dave asked. "Whose is it?"

"It's ours, Dave," the voice replied. "Our new hunter."

"It hunted hunters. It's effing crazy."

Whoever he was talking to must have talked to the men inside Goliath. "Right. That's a mistake. Programming error."

Dave was near to his bursting point. "Programming error! It's killed them and nearly killed me. Why the hell didn't you tell us?"

"It's a trial. You had no need to know."

Raging, hardly thinking, as if on remote, Dave strode to the hatch, rifle in hand. Something hit him hard in the chest, and he collapsed to the ground as if his suit were full of rocks.

* * *

Inside the cargo ship, the mood was sombre.

"There was no choice. He could have killed the crew." The captain was clinical in his analysis. "His mind was all over the place."

"Perhaps we should have told them," the lieutenant said.

"They may have gone for the machine, put it out of action," the captain countered. "After all, it was a threat to their livelihood."

"We should have pulled them out," the lieutenant persisted, glancing at the prone body of Dave as it lay on a nearby g-couch.

The captain shook his head. "Head office edict. It was them against the machine, the ultimate trial." He followed the lieutenant's gaze. "Better if we leave him tranquilised. He'll be joining the others soon." The others were in the airlock being prepared for a space burial.

"Seems wrong somehow. He put up a good fight."

119

"He knows too much," the captain said. "We have no choice."

"Head office edict?" the lieutenant responded sarcastically.

"Correct."

"Ultimate trial!" the lieutenant grated, still in a cynical mood. "Neither of them won in the end."

"The machine will win," the captain responded. "Once it's reprogrammed."

"And in the meantime?"

The captain had the grace to look sad. "In the meantime, we need five more trappers."

THE SPECIAL FRIEND

E dward was a special child, a very special child. But he didn't know he was special, and neither did his parents, not yet at least. At nine years old, he had a few friends at school, but none so close as his bosom buddy, Floppy Rabbit. Floppy Rabbit often came to dinner, never to breakfast or lunch, always to dinner. And there was always a place for him at the table, carefully arranged by Edward's mother.

They all lived in a very pleasant house, on a very pleasant street. There were a few roses at the front and more at the back, surrounding a patch of neglected lawn. Edward had played on the grass when he was younger, but not anymore. He was too old. The lawn was too small.

You wouldn't think Edward was special to look at him. A little skinny, he usually wore a white shirt and blue shorts, grey socks around his ankles, and brown leather shoes. His hair was brownish-red, his eyes were greenish-brown, and a field of freckles decorated his face. Everyone said he was ordinary, even his teacher at school.

Edward's mother was called Pattie Simmonds, and his father was called Jeffrey Simmonds. Edward called them Mom and Pop respectively. Pattie worked for the government; in fact, she was very high up in the government and made lots of important decisions that affected a lot of people. Jeffrey was a writer on the local newspaper. What he wrote didn't affect many people at all.

Pattie and Jeffrey often discussed Floppy Rabbit after Edward had gone to bed.

"Do you think it's wise to indulge Edward's fantasy?" Jeffrey said one night. He was still dressed in his work clothes: a white open-necked shirt and blue pants. He had, however, donned his slippers as a gesture to comfort and relaxation. He beamed at Pattie over his reading glasses, the overhead light creating a shiny patch near his receding hairline.

"He'll grow out of it," Pattie said, nodding wisely. "They always do." She was slim, with long brown hair and green eyes, and wore a black woolly jumper and blue jeans.

"Well, I sure hope so," Jeffrey said. "I'd hate to think of him having an imaginary friend when he's in his teens."

Pattie laughed. "By then Floppy Rabbit will have morphed into a dark-haired beauty with an awful taste in music."

Jeffrey sighed. "You're probably right."

* * *

In his bedroom, Edward was in deep conversation with Floppy Rabbit.

"When can I take you to school?" Edward asked, as he

perched on the side of his bed, his legs not quite touching the floor. "I've told all my friends about you. They all want to see you." He peered hard at Floppy Rabbit and supposed he didn't really look like a rabbit. He was too big, for starters, and he usually supported himself on two feet. When they stood together, they were about the same height—if you included Floppy Rabbit's ears.

The ears were really weird, Edward thought. They were elliptical (his new school word) and shiny, and they could be retracted when Floppy Rabbit wished for some peace and quiet. His face, too, was not quite like a rabbit's or even conical, as Floppy Rabbit described it. Heaven knows how a rabbit came up with a word like that. His face, Edward concluded, was more like that of a Hungarian Pumi, the kind of dog that lived three doors down the street, owned by Mrs Canterbury, who was always taking it for walks. However, Floppy Rabbit had no tail—a fact that Edward took in his stride.

On the other hand, Floppy Rabbit did have a furry body— when he deemed to show it. And that was the fact that amazed Edward the most about his new and closest friend. Quite often, perhaps even most of the time, Floppy Rabbit was only partially visible: a mere flicker of a suggestion of something there. And on some occasions, when he sat down to dinner for example, Floppy Rabbit was not visible at all, even to Edward.

Floppy Rabbit didn't answer Edward's question. "How are your parents?" he asked in his squeaky voice.

"Okay, I guess," Edward replied. "I'm not sure they really believe in you, though."

"That doesn't matter," Floppy Rabbit said. "It's you who counts."

Edward tried again. "My friends at school want to see

you."

Floppy Rabbit wrinkled his nose. "Bring them here to-morrow. Two of your best friends. Boy or girl, it doesn't matter. Bring them up to your bedroom."

"I'll have to ask Mom, but it should be okay."

"As long as she doesn't get in the way," Floppy Rabbit said.

* * *

Pattie was pleased when Edward asked whether he could bring two friends home after school. "If you like, Edward," she replied, "but only for an hour or so." She was pleased that Edward was having friends over, other than Floppy Rabbit. *It will do him good,* she thought.

"They're coming to meet Floppy Rabbit," Edward said.

"That's nice," Pattie said, laughing. "I'll get you some carrots."

Edward brought Jimmy Senior and Mary Bell home from school. Both were a bit younger than Edward, and their moms would pick them up at five o'clock. They all clambered up the stairs to Edward's bedroom, and Pattie called up, "I'll bring you some treats in about fifteen minutes."

Edward shut his bedroom door, and they all sat on the edge of the bed.

"When will Floppy Rabbit come?" Mary asked.

"If he comes," Jimmy snickered.

Edward thrust out his lower lip. "He'll come," he said.

And he did. One minute later.

Mary squealed. "That's not a rabbit."

"Cool," Jimmy enthused.

"Hi kids," Floppy Rabbit said. "We're going on a journey,

and you'll be back in two shakes of a rabbit's tail."

"Where are we going?" Edward asked, wondering whether to call his mother.

"Just to my burrow," Floppy Rabbit said. "Just for a short while."

There was a brief flash that lit up the whole room, and then they were gone.

* * *

Floppy's burrow was on the moon. It was quite a long burrow with a large cave at the end. The cave was lit from above by strips of lights that ran its entire length. The walls were smooth, not cave-like at all. Most surprising of all, there were three other Floppy Rabbits operating strange machines.

"How did we get here?" Jimmy asked, staring around in amazement. He looked like he didn't remember Floppy Rabbit at all.

Mary Bell was biting her lower lip. "I want to go home," she wailed.

Edward looked at Floppy Rabbit and said, "What happened? Who are these other rabbits?" He didn't really still think they were rabbits, but didn't want to call them *aliens* in front of Mary Bell.

"You can go home soon," Floppy said. "As soon as you have helped us."

Jimmy looked belligerent. "I don't want to help you," he said angrily, his lower jaw jutting out.

"But you want to go home, don't you?" Floppy said. He led the way forward to the long bench where the other three beings sat. "All we need is some blood from each of you. Straight into the three machines you see here, one machine each. Just a small amount of blood. It's just an experiment."

Edward looked at the machines. They looked like large ceramic cooktops, except there was a ten-centimetre silver column rising from the black surface of each. The column ran all the way to the cave's ceiling.

There was a buzzing noise, like a swarm of bees, and a portion of each silver post, just above the ceramic plates, became transparent.

"I want you to put your right hand into the column where it disappeared," Floppy said. "Just for five seconds, then you can go home."

The children looked at each other. Edward didn't trust Floppy Rabbit anymore. Jimmy was scowling, and Mary was pouting. The other three creatures stepped away from the bench.

"Just for five seconds," Floppy repeated. "Then I will take you home."

Edward stepped forward and put his hand on the black plate. He could see straight through the lower end of the silver post.

"All together," Floppy Rabbit said. "It's better that way. You will not be hurt."

Jimmy and Mary stepped forward with their hands raised.

"Now," said Floppy Rabbit. "Put your hands in."

All three children moved together. Their hands went into the posts. The lights in the room dimmed. The aliens chittered to one another. Somewhere in the wall of the cave, a partition opened, and Edward, Jimmy, and Mary stepped out.

The children gaped, frowned, and gasped as Floppy said, "These are your brothers and sister. You won't see them very often, but they will always be nearby."

"Cool," Jimmy said.

Edward and Mary just blinked. Their doubles stood and stared, faint smiles on their lips.

"Time to go home," Floppy said.

Just like before, there was a brief flash that lit up the whole cave, and then they were gone.

* * *

There was a knock on the bedroom door. Edward looked around. There was no sign of Floppy Rabbit. The door opened, and Edward's mom stood there with a tray full of cups and biscuits.

The children chorused, "We have brothers and a sister."

Pattie smiled. "Yes, I know. I have a twin sister, too. I've not seen her since I was your age."

"Does she live on the moon?" Edward asked.

"Not anymore," Pattie answered. "She lives in Boston. She has a very special job working at the air force base."

Jimmy glared at Pattie. "Did you meet Floppy Rabbit?"

Pattie smiled. "A long time ago. When I was your age." She put the cups and the biscuits on the dresser. "But that's our secret, isn't it."

"Floppy Rabbit won't be coming back, will he," Edward stated.

Pattie shook her head. "No. He has other children to visit."

"Like Santa Claus," Mary said.

There was the beep of a car horn from outside the window.

"Home time," Pattie said. She looked earnestly at the children. "And we keep our secrets, don't we. Like Floppy Rabbit

127

told us."

The three children looked at each other, nodding, minds linked by Floppy Rabbit's code words.

"Like Floppy Rabbit told us," they all cried together.

EXCERPT FROM 'AMIDST ALIEN STARS'

Jason was not in the best of moods. Not only had his mother left the station, but the Gliezans had also taken Simon Cordell for what Rjebni had described as *medical reparation*. Susan Carmody had told him what happened. She had also told him why Cordell had suffered his painful fate. She had said, "He thinks he has broken ribs, but it will only be severe bruising. There shouldn't be any permanent damage."

He was walking along the wall, welcoming the soft feel of grass under his feet, fingers of one hand intermittently brushing its surface. He had little sympathy for Cordell and even less of it for extreme vigilante action by a colleague who, as a member of an elite organisation, should have known better.

Earlier, he had secretly watched the appearance of the Gliezan spacecraft, had watched his mother and Tala Hughes enter the vehicle and vanish within seconds. He worried about *their* fate, not that of Cordell. But the group had to remain united; there was no room for dispute.

He came to the spot where the spacecraft had been. There was no sign of a landing; the grass was not even compacted, and there were no indentations anywhere. The recent events were out of the ordinary, even when everything else was far from ordinary. The fact that the approaches to his mother had been so clandestine suggested other forces at play. He wondered whether Rjebni knew anything about it.

Helena Belmonte suddenly appeared from behind a nearby tree. As always, she was dressed in her Eucla clothing: a white dress blouse and dark uniform trousers. Her blond hair flowed free, and her face carried a nervous smile. She carried her tunic under one arm. *She doesn't look like someone trained to kill with one well-placed blow*, Jason thought. *Still, appearances are deceptive.* He briefly wondered how she could have been so stupid as to succumb to the moronic advances of Simon Cordell.

She took a step towards him. "Can we talk?"

Jason shrugged and sat down with his back to the wall. Helena came and sat beside him, a metre distant, her slim legs almost up to her chin.

"I suppose you heard about Simon?" Helena said.

Jason glanced at her. Her eyes were red from crying. The smile was gone, and her face was a picture of misery.

"I heard. Did Susan Carmody send you?"

With tears threatening, she shook her head. "She told me what she had done to Simon, but she did not ask me to speak to you."

"I don't know whether Simon Cordell deserved what he got, and maybe only you can answer that, but I don't agree with what Susan did."

Helena looked into the distance, a faint tremor on her lips. "We were stupid. I was lonely and frightened of this place. It's not natural. None of it." She managed a faint smile. "They tell me the aliens will fix his injuries in next to no time."

"I don't think he will bother you again," Jason said.

"I can heel-kick as well as any officer here," Helena declared. "I do have some strength. I think Susan meant well. She was trying to protect me."

"One of her girls."

Helena almost laughed, then her face grew serious. "I said Susan didn't send me. She didn't. It was me who wanted to see you." She appeared nervous. "You know the aliens more than anybody here. Can I ask you some questions?"

Jason could feel the tension in her voice, see it in her aura. He just nodded. On Earth, he had been the *First Seen*. Chosen by the aliens, or, rather, by the *RNasia*. His vacation with his mother had been savagely interrupted, and he had been forced into adulthood more rapidly than seemed good for his mental well-being. But now, what storms had raged through his mind had abated. Turmoil still existed, but it was a gentle, thought-provoking turmoil, one that led him to accept his role among the human captors. Schooldays were a mere candle in the roar of a nuclear sun, a distant memory buried in a distant world. He remained the *First Seen*, and perhaps would always be so.

Helena said, "I know we have provided the hybrids for the aliens. I know they are supposed to be an improvement on both our races. I even think I understand how they will use them to explore the galaxy without fear of physical or mental degradation." She turned her face towards Jason, and he saw such a loss of future hope, such despair, that he felt his own strength and beliefs beginning to crumble under an assault of uncertainty. "But I don't know how the women fit in, even how you and your mother fit in. Have they finished with us? Are we eventually to be discarded once the hybrids are free of the tanks? Will we meet them, see our own offspring? And what happens then?" She put her head in her hands. "Will they want more hybrids from us? Will we ever see Earth again?"

The possibility that the Gliezans would repeat the hybrid experiment on this orbiting station disturbed him. He wondered whether it was the obvious thing for them to do—produce more hybrids with their captives, and never return to Earth at all. That would devastate everybody and would rule out the need for interplanetary collaboration.

The thought made him sick to his stomach. The Milijun enhancements and direct contact with the aliens had matured him well beyond his fifteen years, somehow increased the power of his mind, but there were times when teenage naivety broke through.

"I wish I could answer your questions," Jason responded eventually, "but I can't. I can only repeat what we have been told. We are part of an alien plan for future cooperation between our two worlds, and that might have a great and wonderful outcome, or it might turn out to be a genetic and spiritual disaster. We are, if you like, an experiment that will enable both worlds to explore the cosmos as allies. If it fails, there will be no further alien interaction with Earth, and, barring a few individuals, Earth will be none the wiser." He shrugged. "We have no choice but to believe until we know any different."

"Then we should be able to talk to them as equals. If we cannot, we are really prisoners, like mice in a cage." Helena looked at him, wide-eyed. "Aren't we?"

She was right, of course, and Jason nodded. "I have tried, but they will tell no more. Maybe because they are not sure about what's in the tanks. The hybrids have to be compatible both physically and spiritually. If they are not, we may have produced anomalies." As soon as he said them, he regretted his words and rushed to add, "I didn't mean—"

"I do not understand their spirituality," Helena interrupted, clearly not wanting to discuss the conception of the hybrids or the status of her own child. "They profess to believe in the afterlife, as I do now in my own way, but they do not mention a creator of any kind. That is not how it is or ever was on Earth."

"Their faith is apparently underscored by some evidential proof," Jason stated, "unlike ours, which needs absolute belief. I think it is a result of their scientific investigations, thousands of years of dedicated research, not just on reaching other worlds, but on breaching other dimensions. Even combining the two.

"You have seen what they can do within the material world. Some humans believe that physical creation, whatever the method, has its source in an invisible realm wherein the creator and spirits dwell. Our world is physical; the Gliezan world is both physical and interdimensional across boundaries we can only suspect. They traverse the curtain between our dimensions and others."

"Dimensional shift," Helena said. "Raising energy levels, vibrations." She looked quizzically at Jason, a demure expression on her face. "And where is heaven, do they say?"

Jason smiled. "They have not talked about heaven, at least

not to me. But heaven may be another dimension further. We may not be so lucky as to have it directly adjacent to our realm."

Helena clapped her hands, the sound echoing from the wall to race out among the trees and the grass and the sky. She leaned over and kissed Jason lightly on the cheek. "From now on, I will regard you as my brother."

"You fill a void," Jason replied coyly. "I do not have any siblings."

Silence descended for a while, then Helena asked, "Can you talk to the Gliezans about what we have discussed?"

"Maybe we should have a group discussion, all of us together, with their council."

"Will they allow that?" Helena looked hopeful.

"I don't know. We can only hope. It will maybe test their true motives."

"What can we do if their motives are not what we think?" Helena's face suddenly grew dark, not only from the shadow of a passing cloud.

"We must try to find out more. Keep asking them to tell us more." Jason took a deep breath. "We have a role to play here even if we cannot be certain what it is."

They both stood, and Helena stretched, arms to the sky. "Would they kill us?" she asked out of the blue.

Jason, shocked at the question, took a moment to respond. "No, I don't think so. They seem a peaceful race." He paused, then added, "Do the other women feel the same as you?"

"They feel lost, I think." Helena frowned and looked at him earnestly. "To some extent, they blame you, the part-father of their children. They see you as an ally of the aliens. They are so short of answers I am afraid they may do something ill-advised, something born of desperation. They want some kind of action."

Jason nodded thoughtfully. "We need to discuss things together. I've had conversations, but nothing meaningful." He missed his mother already. She was much better at this than he was. He looked at Helena, eyes full of pleading. "Could you get everyone together, tonight?"

"Me? Surely it would be—"

"No," Jason interrupted, "better from one of their own."

"Better, I think, from Laura—but I will do it." She pursed her lips. "After dinner?"

Jason nodded.

"And Simon?"

"I will talk to him, if he has returned."

"Better sit him away from Carmody," Helena said.

"And you," Jason added.

Helena nodded. "Suits me." To his surprise, she held out her hand for him to shake. It felt strange, as if he was just meeting her. Her grip was firm but gentle, not limp as he might have supposed from her earlier demeanour.

She turned to go, stopped, and looked back. "Thanks, Jason. I like my child better now."

After she had gone, Jason sat back against the wall and wondered what he had let himself in for. He tried to recall his recent conversation with Rfinsa. She, as usual, had been the epitome of evasion. He had found out more about Rkapth, and the fact that the *RNasia* needed a master for universal exploration, but precious little about the immediate future or the Gliezan plan.

He wondered whether humans could really voyage outside the solar system in partnership with an alien race, especially when the initial contact had been sorely marred by mistakes on both sides. The problems facing collaboration seemed overwhelming. Jason did not believe any power on Earth would readily sanction cooperation with alien robots that could enter the physical space of a human body and control its actions. But surely the aliens suspected that already. They had studied human behaviour for centuries.

Above all, Jason doubted that humans could be trusted to react peacefully to an extraterrestrial approach, even with fellow humans and hybrids accompanying the alien emissaries.

Indeed, are the aliens to be trusted? Maybe that is the more pressing question. He needed to know all the details, and he needed to know their tactics. He shook his head vigorously. Carmody's words were certainly getting to him.

He sorely wanted the Gliezan plan to work. It promised a huge step for humanity. After the devastation of the last global conflict, humans had just started to regroup: mining the moon and planning flights to the solitary Martian colony established prior to hostilities. But compared to the Gliezans, they were babes in arms, and therein lay the rub. They were well out of their depth.

Jason clenched and unclenched his fists, took a deep breath, and forced his troubled mind to return to more immediate problems.

He had no idea how to gain access to the other spheres. Asking politely was out of the question. Rfinsa's rebuke of his request had been short and to the point: *You cannot visit.* Searching for the portal, whilst it kept the party occupied, appeared futile and would ultimately lead to frustration.

Please ask the council to reconsider, he had demanded of Rfinsa. *That would be in your best interests.* How would the Gliezans react to that? He now considered it a foolhardy thing to have said. The humans had nowhere to go and very little to do other than turn upon themselves, and—most importantly—they had lost control of their own lives.

His thoughts turned to the upcoming meeting. Susan Carmody, in his mother's absence, would try to take control. What would she propose? Disobedience? Violence? Perhaps even taking an alien hostage. Maybe he should give her free rein, let her make a fool of herself. No matter what she proposed, the aliens would have the upper hand.

There was one other thing. Only he knew what had happened to his mother and Tala Hughes. He needed an explanation for their disappearance.

Jason rose and gazed along the wall. It curved away into infinity. Perhaps it was a circle, embracing their artificial terrene world. He considered how long it would take to walk its length, probably to end up back at the starting point. It was inside a sphere, but how big was the sphere? Add it to finding the portal—another fool's errand.

Walking back to the communal building, he cast a glance at the sky and said a brief prayer for his mother. He was starting to despair. The alien plan was just that, *alien*, and his part in it, *the human part in it*, was just a grain of sand in a cosmic desert. He wondered whether the aliens understood that the human race would not tolerate being used, would not, in fact, tolerate anything but being an equal partner, and that only with a guarded finger on the trigger. Perhaps the aliens did not really comprehend the nature of man; conceivably their mindset could not understand humans at all, despite their prolonged observations.

As he approached the building, words from the past sprang to mind, whisperings from a ghost. *Only free men can negotiate. Prisoners cannot enter into contracts.* Nelson Mandela. School or the nanos? It didn't really matter.

Time to make a stand.

THE DECADY ALIEN

Jan Emminway loosened the collar of her cloak and watched the glow of the shuttle's pulse-jets diminish as the spacecraft pushed away from the station. The broad curve of distant Earth filled her with sadness. It was her home, and it should have made her happy. But it didn't. So much had been lost, so much thrown away.

The destruction of Earth's flora and fauna had occurred at a frightening pace over the past millennia. Over recent centuries, though, many species had become extinct at an especially alarming pace, particularly the mammals. And that had almost included the human race, Jan recollected. Several barbaric wars hadn't helped, nor had a plethora of ignorance, selfishness, and stupidity. Thanks to technology, a depleted population of humans had survived, but the planet upon which they resided was in a sorry state. The ecology was dying, and the hunt was on. Earth desperately needed animals.

Tall and slim, Jan wore her usual garb for visits to the station: green slacks, black knee-length boots, and a cream top. Her standard-issue white cape had the letters VET emblazoned in red on the back. A silver headband ran across the border between her high, smooth forehead and short-cropped blonde hair. It was complemented by wristbands of the same material.

Turning away from the viewing window, she glanced around the station's entryway and was, as usual, not impressed. *Why can't they make the place more agreeable for visitors? Even a Paul Cézanne would brighten up the area.* The walls were bare metal, the floor a grating beneath which ran a magnetic catharsis grid for dust and debris removal. The ceiling was all lights, subdued but adequate.

Jan sighed and stepped briskly towards the portal that led to the corridor. Before she could open it, the door panel slid aside, and Station Commander Karl Vasquez stood silhouetted against the harsh light from the passageway. Despite the glare, she could see that his craggy face did not carry the customary welcoming smile.

"Jan," he said. "Thanks for coming."

Jan nodded and accompanied him down the corridor to her usual quarters.

"When did the *Ascension* get in?" she asked.

Karl pursed his lips. "Two days ago. She left again yesterday for service at Lunar One."

They paused outside her door. Karl ran his fingers through his thick, grey hair. The frown lines on his forehead were even more prominent than normal, and his steel-grey eyes seemed to flicker with uncertainty. "Do you want time to rest," he asked, "or a briefing now?"

Jan smiled and gestured him inside. "A brief briefing, I

think."

Once inside, she closed the door, and they sat opposite each other across a low table. The cubicle, like all the station's single quarters, was small: no more than three metres by four. The bunk currently lay snugly against the ceiling but could be lowered to just above the table when needed. A cream self-cleaning carpet ran from wall to wall, and several miniature oil paintings hung slothfully from an aluminium picture rail, as if unsure that the artificial gravity was sufficient to keep them in position. The bathroom was communal and situated further down the corridor, the quarters only being intended for temporary visits. One small window gave Jan a view to the stars and the endless, black sky.

Karl managed a smile. "How's my favourite veterinary for extraterrestrials?"

Jan smiled back, showing her perfect teeth and wrinkling her nose. "I'm fine, Karl. Didn't expect to be back up here so soon, though."

"I know," Karl responded. "Your roster gives you another month." He hesitated, biting his lip. "But you were specifically volunteered for this one."

Jan raised her eyebrows. *Specifically volunteered* meant her superiors had recommended her and her alone for this new task, chosen her from a field of six other vets shuttled to the station to check out alien creatures when they were brought back to Earth by warpcraft such as *Ascension*.

"I'm flattered," she said. Only the merest hint of cynicism shaded her response.

"Good," Karl responded. He stared at a painting of a pod of dolphins. The perspective was as if the painter had been underneath them, looking towards the ocean's surface. It showed the sun shining upon the waves, silhouetting the sleek shapes as they sped through the water.

"The animal is from sector seven five three of the Via Lactea galaxy," Karl continued. "Only recently entered by the warpcraft. They've called the planet *Decady*, as it's the tenth to yield lifeforms."

Jan blinked. She really had lost count. "Were there any other animals lifted?"

"Oh, yes," Karl answered, "but the others were small. They've been fully scanned and shipped for lunar check and dispersal to Earth."

Jan laughed. "You make them sound like packages." She leaned forward and looked Karl in the eye. "Who's checking them on the moon?"

"Andrew Kowalski."

Jan nodded. He was a good vet, if a little mundane in his approach. "And why could he not have come here?"

Karl shrugged. "Like I said. You were chosen."

Jan smelled a rat but said nothing. To her surprise, Karl suddenly yawned. "Sorry," he apologised. He started to study another painting, then, turning to Jan, said, "Why don't you view the computer file on the animal? We can see it live tomorrow."

Jan wasn't going to argue. She had been caught unawares by the trip, and even before the station docking, her wristband monitor had indicated she was one hour overdue for sleep.

"Okay, Karl. I'll see you in the morning."

Karl smiled tightly and left her alone. She had sensed his unease. It lingered around, even now that he was gone. Removing her cape, Jan slung it over a chair and spoke to the table. "Open Janvet. Kentucky five nine. Animals."

The top of the table flickered and then showed a light green screen with black borders. On the screen it said: *Old,*

New, or On Board?

Jan thought for a moment, wondering whether to take a peek at the other new arrivals from Decady. She decided against it. They could wait for another day. "On board," she said eventually.

Immediately, an image of her latest patient filled the screen. She looked at it studiously, taking in all its features, its joints, appendages, its size against the superimposed grid, its general disposition.

At the bottom of the screen, a data set completed the basic picture:

Earth weight: 107.5 Kg
Body length: 2 metres
Epidermal cover: Gold fur
Limbs: 4
Eyes: 2
Tail: Prehensile
Sex: TBD
Teeth: Herbivorous
Zone: Equatorial
Vocalisation: TBD

"Countenance," Jan said.

She gasped as the screen was filled by the animal's face. It was beautiful, quite the most stunning creature she had ever seen. Jan found herself stroking the alien brow, running her fingers along the aquiline nose. She could almost feel the fur through the screen's surface.

"Eyes," she said. Large, deep, black and gold. Dark infinite pools. Stillness.

"Real-time video," she whispered, a tremor in her voice.

The screen changed to a live image. The animal was illuminated dimly by sleeptime lighting, but the picture was fully enhanced for viewing. She watched it intensely, waiting for the creature to change position. It didn't. It may as well have been a photograph. The creature was not moving at all. It didn't appear to be even breathing.

"Vital signs," Jan blurted, suddenly fearful.

A series of traces ran across the screen: heartbeat, blood pressure, brain activity. Alien traces, but there all the same. Jan frowned. They didn't mean much to her yet, but the animal was definitely alive.

"Exit," Jan said, and the screen disappeared.

But the eyes of the animal were etched into her mind. There had been a heavy sadness about the alien creature, the like of which she had never experienced before. She sighed. She needed sleep. Tomorrow she would meet her new patient.

* * *

When sleep came, it brought strange and wonderful images, an enigmatic fusion of childhood memories and frightening impressions of a different world, full of dark ravines, high, ice-capped mountains, roughly hewn plains ravaged by lightning strikes and torrential rain.

At first, she was in her parents' garden, smelling the flowers, crunching the grass with her bare toes, screwing her eyes up against the sun. Even then, she had yellow hair the colour of bleached corn, but longer, covering her ears and tickling her eyebrows.

But then the shadow man came. Without features to frighten her, but possessing none to please. And a body that the sun's rays could not illuminate. He spoke to her mind, not with words but with pictures. He drew with a stilted hand: icy mountains, deep, hungry canyons, unforgiving plains, and winds that could freeze a body. Landscapes to chill the mind and steal the soul.

* * *

Jan awoke in a sweat. She didn't need to seek the time. Like many humans, she had an infallible internal clock that told her it was ten minutes past four. Staring out of her meagre window, she saw the familiar infinite sky and wished, for some reason, that her quarters had a view of Earth. Perhaps on her next trip Karl could rotate the station for her.

The world of her dream had been savage. It was not a place to envy or to covet, but it had possessed a ferocity of life that many worlds had either lost or never had. She lay in darkness, watching the stars drift by. Then she leant over the side of the bed and whispered, "Open. Janvet. Kentucky five nine. Animals. On board. Video."

The table blinked, and the animal was with her. It hadn't moved from its previous position. *Is it in hibernation?* She looked out of the window again, wondering what to do next. "Countenance," she said, after a deep breath.

And the eyes were staring up at her. Quite amazing, like living worlds of gleaming water, swimming with a mystery as subtle as that held in the entirety of the heavens.

The animal suddenly raised its head and filled the screen with such a penetrating gaze that Jan jerked back, a small cry escaping her lips. Her pulse started to race. *What just happened?* She withdrew from the screen and rested on the pillow. *This is impossible! Does this creature know it's being observed?* Some animals, those who were hunted, could often sense the

145

scrutiny of a predator even before the hunter could be seen. But she was not a hunter.

"Exit," she said into the darkness.

Lying there, still seeing the eyes, Jan felt her heartbeat gradually calm. There was sweat on her brow, caking into a layer of salt as the air conditioning cooled her skin.

Mountains, canyons, icecaps. Roses. Grass. Her mother's voice from the kitchen: "Jan, sweetie. Bath time." Running water, like a waterfall. Sleep at last, after the bath.

* * *

Jan took breakfast with Karl and his comms officer, Will Tolstoy. Will, like the other twelve crew members on the station, was on rotation and nearing the end of his three months in orbit. He had smiling blue eyes and red hair, a combination that Jan found unnerving.

"How did you sleep?" Karl enquired as he downed a second glass of grape juice.

"So-so," Jan replied. "About usual for the first night in orbit."

"Good," Karl said. "No strange dreams?"

Jan pursed her lips and looked at the ceiling. Alarm bells rang. "Is there something you're not telling me?" she asked.

Karl frowned, and Will looked at the table. Neither answered.

Jan sat back in her chair. "I'm on my own, then?"

"It's better if you look at this animal with an open mind," Will said. "In fact—"

"In fact," Karl interrupted swiftly, asserting his status as commander, "we're not to influence your examination in any way."

Jan grimaced. "What the hell is this? First, I'm specifically volunteered, then you two clam up like there's no tomorrow."

Karl shrugged. "I'm sorry, Jan, but we have our instructions."

"Instructions." Jan raised her eyebrows and ran her gaze from one to the other. "You're under orders, then?"

Will pushed his chair back, then rose as a man and woman entered the mess and sauntered over to the buffet. Both the newcomers seemed tense and looked away when Jan met their inquisitive stare.

"I'll see you later," Will said, angling his tall frame towards the door.

"This place," Jan remarked, "is beginning to make me nervous."

"I'm sorry," Karl responded. "It's near the end of the roster. All the crew are jaded."

"Please, Karl, stop apologising." Jan rose from the table. "I really best make a start."

"Fine," Karl said, glancing at her meaningfully. "Take care."

Jan sighed and left the room.

* * *

Pausing briefly outside the door, Jan spoke the keycode numbers and waited for the panel to slide back. On such occasions, she was often met by a cacophony of alien screeching or, at the very least, a vigorous assault on the cage screen. This time she was greeted by silence. She walked through and closed the panel behind her. The room was lit for the daylight hours of Decady, which translated to eight Earth hours on the alien planet. Pale green walls and a smooth, black floor met her gaze. At the far end, a white cubicle lay beyond a transparent screen, and she saw the alien creature curled up on the floor.

Jan approached slowly, careful not to make any sudden movements. She stopped, inhaling sharply, as the animal rose to its feet and came towards the partition. A flick of a button on her hand-held remote produced a display of the creature's three-dimensional internal structure on the right hand wall. She saved a copy, turned the remote off, and walked as close as she could to her patient. Her eyes were almost at the same level as the alien's, and it returned her stare calmly, eyelids not moving. The animal's eyes *were* beautiful, but this time she did not find herself sinking into a quagmire of darkness.

Jan inspected its body. The file was right. There was no obvious indication of male or female, not uncommon with many advanced alien species. She would have to instigate a chromosomal blood analysis and get the computer to design an anaesthetic so she could perform a close physical examination. If it was a male, cloning would require cells from the testes and isolation of the essential genetic material from the spermatic cells. If it was a female, it would be a little more straightforward.

She received a shock as her eyes returned to the creature's face. It appeared as if she was being smiled at: not a big grin, just a mild lifting of the corners of the mouth. Jan stepped back in surprise, but the smile was gone as quickly as it had arrived. "Did you really do that?" she said aloud. She gave herself a mental rap. *I should not apply human attributes to a completely alien being.*

The animal put out a hand against the screen. Jan stepped forward slowly and put her hand to the same spot. She looked into its eyes and instantly regretted it. Pools of darkness, pitch black, deep as the ocean. Ice and canyons. Infinite plains. She clicked the remote and saw the surprise in the eyes as a needle snaked up from the floor, took its sample, and retreated to its storage place.

"Sorry," Jan mumbled softly.

Both alien hands went to the partition. Breathing deeply, she met them with hers. *Dare I release the screen?* Her head shook swiftly. Not yet. Much too soon. Build up the trust slowly, gradually. Tiny steps on a long stairway. The alien possessed some kind of intelligence, but that did not mean it was incapable of aggression.

Analysis completed, the snake rose from the floor again, injected, retreated. The alien eyes clouded, but not before Jan's mind was filled with an overpowering sense of betrayal. The hands on the other side of the screen slid down. The alien slumped to the floor.

She stood in silence. An overwhelming feeling of treachery had swamped her soul as the anaesthetic had entered the creature's bloodstream. It was almost as if she had been unfaithful to a lover. She looked at the comatose body, raised the screen, and stepped through.

* * *

"The analysis tells me the animal is male," Jan was saying, "but there's precious little other evidence."

Karl Vasquez bit his lip. "Is that right?" he said, not helping one little bit.

"Don't you see?" Jan continued in exasperation. "If I can't find the necessary cells, we won't be able to clone it."

Will Tolstoy, who sat directly across from Jan, shrugged. "That's hardly your fault, though, is it?" he said. "If it can't be cloned and distributed on Earth, then that's it. The creature will be put down. No use to anybody."

"No!" Jan's vehement denial caused the other diners to look at them with raised eyebrows. She stared at her plate. "No," she affirmed quietly. "There has to be another way. There's never been an alien animal we couldn't clone, male or female. There'll be a way."

Karl looked uneasy. "Time isn't plentiful. Three days to the end of this roster. You have until then."

Jan flushed angrily. "The damned thing has intelligence, Karl. I know it has."

"Three days," Karl repeated.

"These things aren't easy," Jan snapped.

"That's why they chose you, Jan," Karl said.

* * *

That night, as she rested in her quarters, Jan thought about the work she had been doing for the past three years. The replenishing of Earth had seemed such a noble cause—a perfect blend of scientific accomplishment and ecological necessity. It had nearly been too late, of course.

Habitat had been destroyed, and for some unknown reason, most sentient creatures became infertile, as if they no longer wished to survive in a world where their homes had been ravished. Earth had become a cesspit of faunal sterility.

And so, out of necessity, the master plan was born. First came the creation of new environments, born from stored seed, genetic manipulations, and back-breaking hard work. After over a century of struggle and battles against a rampaging climate, a semblance of the ancient grasslands, forests, and rivers graced the planet once more. A shadowy replica of the Earth human beings had known in the distant past was returning.

But by the time the great change was completed, the wild animals were gone. Cloning attempts were made, but did not succeed. Infertility was the Rubicon that could not be crossed. Thankfully, some of the cross-pollinating insects survived, and it was they who primarily maintained the renovation of Earth's ecology. But, of course, much more was needed.

Following research that lasted for over two hundred years, the advent and subsequent production of warpcraft heralded some kind of burgeoning hope. As a few rare worlds were found in the sought-after Goldilocks Zone, man realised that if he was to keep his health and his sanity, new creatures must be found to populate the Earth. Whilst a handful of the discovered planets may eventually be colonised, it was to the mother planet that he must first turn. For she was his forever home.

And, of course, it was much more economical to bring suitable animals back to Earth for cloning than to send thousands of humans into space and build the necessary environments and infrastructure to support them.

Where a world was habitable, small teams were set up with the purpose of planetary investigation and sourcing suitable fauna and flora for Earth. Many thousands of planets had been found, but thus far only ten were a possibility for human habitation.

It was all born from selfishness, Jan thought, but nevertheless correct for all that. Their planet had almost died, and the natural balance had to be restored, else humans would surely follow the Earth's wild creatures into oblivion. Accordingly, the quest for appropriate alien lifeforms was born, suitable candidates being stringently vetted and ecologically catalogued prior to clonal reproduction. Then they were tagged and eventually released on Earth in a monitored environment.

And it was actually working, a miracle in and of itself. It was a cocktail of alien life to be stirred and observed. Over one thousand species had been released so far. Just seventeen had failed to self-procreate, and as far as she knew, only seven types had died from habitat disparity or been totally exterminated by predators from other worlds. Noah would have been proud.

There was a certain irony in the fact that the science of cloning had come too late to save the species of Earth. Decades later, after it had been successfully proven on alien species, the Earth's fauna had all but disappeared, those that still survived being sterile and unsuitable for stock foundation. That particular race had been lost, but another had been entered, and the odds were looking good.

Jan sighed and closed her eyes. Her patient had recovered well from the anaesthetic and was now resting peacefully. The blood cell analysis had shown perfect cellular balance with no genetic malfunctions anywhere along the spiral. In fact, it was perfect. Totally without flaw. Humans still carried genetic deviations that could give trouble later in life, but this animal was apparently without code defects of any kind. At least, as far as she could tell. *Puzzling,* she thought, *but challenging too.*

As such thoughts drifted through her mind, Jan's head suddenly slumped onto her chest, as if a puppeteer had cut the supporting strings. Abruptly her dream was back. But this time, she was wide awake.

She was sitting in her chair, drifting over tundra, snowy mountains, wide plains, and deep canyons, much the same as before. Then she saw the animal—she was sure it was *her* animal—standing on the plain, and thousands more of its kind assembled before it.

Probing tendrils were accessing her mind, slowly tearing its rationale to shreds. The animals were grouped around her patient. *Like an audience,* she thought, *or a congregation.* Her patient was behaving like some kind of leader or entertainer. The rest seemed to be listening, intent on every word —except she could hear no words.

And then she was with her mother in church, mesmerised by the hum of voices, the colourful windows, stained, she had thought as a child, by real blood. She heard the words that had helped forge her path through life: *All Creatures that on Earth do dwell.*

The aliens were walking up a hill now, carrying a long beam, inserting it into the ground. The beam stood erect, like an ancient telegraph pole she had seen in the movies. They were staring up at it, a stark shape silhouetted against the brooding clouds. Rain was falling; blood from the tortured sky's wounds.

Jan awoke with a shudder and found to her surprise it was morning. She washed and went in search of breakfast.

* * *

"I want you to contact *Ascension,*" Jan said. "I need to know where they found our new animal, the terrain, if it was alone or among others, even the weather. I want to know everything." She stared at Karl earnestly as he swallowed his nutrient mix and put her hand gently on his. "Please."

Karl nodded. "Sure, but why don't you ask them?"

"Better from you," Jan responded. "I want the answer immediately."

"It is obviously important." Karl's eyebrows were raised, and his forehead reminded Jan of the canyons in her dream.

"I believe my patient may be trying to contact me tele-pathically," Jan said, her eyes alive with purpose. "It has no vocal cords whatsoever. I think it communicates through the mind."

Karl nodded again. "That would explain the dreams, then."

"Dreams. What dreams?"

"Everybody's complained of sleeplessness. Weird dreams. Ever since the animal was brought here."

Jan sighed heavily. "You should have told me that be-fore."

"We were asked not to. In case it influenced your find-ings."

Jan leant forward across the table. "Which means," she whispered, "it's been trying to communicate ever since it got here."

Karl's expression grew heavy. "Communication covers a multitude of things."

"We may have much more than an animal here, Karl. I believe there's significant intelligence. It may be our first con-tact with a species akin to ourselves. And it's trying to tell us something."

"A dog may bark for its dinner."

Jan grimaced. "There are no dogs anymore, Karl. Get me that information. I'm going to make a video."

The station commander eyed her suspiciously. "What are you going to do?"

Jan stood, smiled sweetly, and left him. "Trust me," she called back. "Answers by lunchtime, please."

* * *

Jan entered the cage room as silently as she could. She wore a full-length green robe, tied at the waist by a broad yellow sash that held her remote. A small video camera was mounted on her silver headband, and as she clicked the appropriate button, she felt a light vibration at her temples as the recorder started to run.

Sitting cross-legged, some way back from the partition, she pressed the remote once more. The screen slid upwards, leaving just thin air between herself and the alien. *If Karl could see me doing this, I'd be banned from the station forever.*

"Good morning," she said aloud. "How are you, then?" She always talked to her animals and felt no qualms in doing so on this occasion, even though there could be no vocal response.

The beautiful head lifted, and Jan was surveyed by the wondrous eyes. She was nervous and wondered whether there would be any malice from yesterday's injection. Rising slowly, the creature approached and stopped where the screen had been. Then it simply walked through and sat down on the floor, mimicking Jan's cross-legged position. Sweat broke onto Jan's brow. Her pulse quickened, flicking against her wristbands. If she outstretched her arm, she could touch her new patient.

Jan held out her right palm in the upright position, as she had done against the partition, and her patient copied her action. For the first time, she experienced its live, responsive touch beneath her fingers. Holding her other hand out horizontally, Jan felt the warmth of the alien's hand as it placed it gently on top of her own.

She gazed into its eyes, and her head began to swim, but there was no immediate mind contact, nothing that flew her to faraway planets or into deep ravines. But she *was* mesmerised. There was nothing she could do, except sit there and try to slow her racing thoughts. Slow then down until she could…

A waterfall, full and running wild. Nearby, a village, small white buildings with conical roofs, people—aliens— walking together, hurrying, holding hands to communicate, and smiling gently under the sun. Golden beings, with eyes as deep as the sea, a whole community, a throng wending their way to a neighbouring hillside.

And then Jan felt her mind being searched, each cell clicking open and shut.

Her mother stood beside her, a tear in her eye. She was looking up, staring at the strange pole on the hill. A chant from afar, seemingly disembodied, ascending the hill, the sun breaking through—only there were now two suns. The chanting suddenly stopped.

Jan shook her head and saw the alien was now holding the remote. The smile again, as brief as the fall of an apple from a tree. Jan's lower lip quivered. The partition slid up and down, as if a child was testing it out. Fearful, Jan leapt to her feet.

The creature stayed on the floor in the cross-legged position, still holding the remote. In the white cubicle, beyond the screen, the needle rose up and writhed around and withdrew back into the floor. The alien stood and walked back into the cubicle, and the partition dropped to imprison it once more.

A tear formed in Jan's eye. "My God," she whispered. "You're intelligent." And then she added, as if in apology, "You're more than an animal."

The eyes of the alien stared at her, almost mocking her surprise. The tail swished gently from side to side. Jan shook her head. "If only we could talk, communicate directly." The alien raised the screen, and she backed away.

"Wait," Jan said, holding up her hand. "I'll be back in a minute." She turned swiftly, spoke the keycode, and rushed into the corridor, closing the panel behind her. Minutes later, she returned with a pad and pen. She hesitated outside the door. On the other side, the alien was free, and trepidation froze her movements momentarily.

Just because it's intelligent, she thought, *doesn't mean it's not violent*. Yet it had shown no signs of aggression—quite the contrary. Taking a deep breath, she activated the panel.

The alien stood some way back, holding out the remote to her. *This is all being recorded*, Jan reminded herself, *all of it!* She stepped inside and closed the panel. Gaining courage, she looked straight into its eyes. "Who are you?" she whispered. "What are you?"

Pressure on her hand as the remote was given back. She sat on the floor again and the alien followed suit. Drawing on her pad, Jan showed it to her patient: a rough sketch of herself in her robe. Erasing the picture, she handed the pad over and placed the pen in the creature's hand. It drew a tall monolith, atop a hill, and held the pad up to show her.

Jan felt as if she was entering a trance, seeing her mother and the hill and the pole on top. She smiled and nodded. "In my dream," she said aloud. She took the pad and drew herself as a little girl, holding hands with her mother, together look-ing up to the top of the hill and the pole rising to the sky.

They exchanged several pictures, each of them revolving around the symbol of the monolith. Jan didn't fully under-stand their meaning, but she knew without doubt that this creature was intelligent, that it could not, in fact, be classified as an animal at all.

Eventually she pointed over her shoulder and said, "I

must go."

The alien blinked once, rose, and walked into the rear cubicle. Jan pulled down the screen and watched as her patient sat on the floor. Its eyes were like a magnet, and she didn't want to leave. Green fields and flowers, snow and wind, small golden babies, not human but nearly human, white houses with cream cone roofs, hands stretched out across a star-threaded sky: all this passed between them in a matter of seconds. The tension was too much, and Jan whirled round and left the room, closed the panel, and stood leaning against the corridor wall.

* * *

Later, in her quarters, when her heart had slowed to its normal pace and her mind could think clearly, Jan contemplated the next move. The alien could not be released on Earth. It was not an animal and could not, in any case, be cloned. She was relieved that she had made the earlier statement concerning the lack of clone cells as it gave her the ideal reason for not shipping her patient to Earth. However, neither could she let it be destroyed as a useless piece of merchandise. No doubt there would be Earth scientists who would give their right arm to study the alien, to discover just how intelligent it was, to investigate its tribal connections, to forcefully communicate and pry into its mind. But she didn't want that to happen either. The alien deserved some peace; it deserved its freedom. It must, of course, be returned home. She must think of a good reason for it to be taken back to Decady.

* * *

"So it was on its own when they found it." Jan pursed her lips and looked at distant Earth through the panoramic window set in the wall of Karl's quarters. The room was spacious, the walls covered by images of forests and waterfalls, grasslands and prairie animals; images of what Earth used to be like. A small marble fountain played in a corner, subtle background phonics to aid contemplation. Under foot, the green carpet seemed at least a centimetre thick.

Karl nodded. "In the middle of a desert, I believe. Stones and rocks, mostly flat terrain."

Endless plains, Jan thought. She looked intensely at the station commander. "No others in the vicinity at all?"

"Apparently not. Not for scores of kilometres anyway. It made the capture easy."

Jan was disappointed. She had expected there to be others gathered around, like in her dream. But, of course, they would not have captured the alien in such circumstances.

"Did they look for others?"

"Don't know. Why would they? We only need one for cloning."

Jan smiled faintly. "I know." She was puzzled that the creature had been on its own, apparently well and truly isolated from its kin. "It's not an animal, Karl." The words came out very faint, almost like a whisper, as if she didn't want the rest of the room to know.

"Not an animal." Karl ran his hand through his hair, a worried expression forming on his rugged face. The warpcraft had never found life that could be described as intelligent, certainly by comparison to human beings. Clever aliens were well outside his comfort zone. The possibility of interaction with them was enough to give him nightmares.

"It's bright and responsive, definitely intelligent," Jan

said, rubbing salt into the commander's wounds. "I don't know how much, maybe a lot, maybe not. It has a fixation with a column-like symbol, so our exchange has been limited."

"A column-like symbol." Karl sighed. He leant forward in his chair. "Could this be our first contact with intelligence as great as ours?"

"I don't know, Karl, and I don't really care. We've grabbed what we thought were suitable animals from ten planets now. The ships have found thousands of worlds. I don't think they would tell the likes of us if they found anything really intelligent, any advanced civilisations, not for a long time anyway. The quest is for animals to balance Earth's ecology and, for that matter, to keep humans sane. The point is—this creature is not an animal, and it cannot be sent to Earth. The fact that it cannot communicate like us while it actually looks like our definition of an animal doesn't necessarily make it one."

There was silence for a moment as Karl digested Jan's words.

"Alright," he said eventually. "So what are you suggesting?"

Jan took off her headband, pointed it at Karl's table, and clicked her remote. A replay of her last meeting with the alien flickered across the tabletop. Karl watched in amazement as the encounter unfolded. "Well," he said when it had finished, "that was remarkable." He glanced admiringly at Jan. "You're a gutsy lady."

"I suppose that's better than being bawled out," Jan responded. "I didn't think you'd approve."

"I don't," Karl said. "Just because it looks like our definition of an animal and behaves peacefully doesn't mean it's not a primal beast, which could have taken lumps out of you."

Jan flushed at the parody of her own words. "Point taken," she said. "But somehow I knew it would be safe. Maybe it was the dreams, maybe just intuition." She shrugged. "Who knows?"

Karl poured another cup of tea. "So what now?" he asked.

"We must get them to take it back. It's the only thing to do."

A whistle escaped Karl's lips. "If they know it's intelligent, there's absolutely no chance of that. They'll want to interrogate, test —"

" — and hound it to death," Jan finished for him.

He looked at her sadly. "Probably."

* * *

That night the dream was terrible. Jan saw the alien hanging by the tail from the column-like structure. For a while the hands clawed at the pole, trying to gain traction, but eventually the arms gave way and the body slumped. She saw blood oozing from the tail where it was nailed to the top of the pole.

Just below the column and its tortured occupant stood a crowd of aliens—and among them, much to Jan's horror, were herself and her mother. Above, angry dark clouds gathered in celestial debate. Lightning zipped the sky. Thunder rolled.

Jan awoke with a shiver, covered in sweat. *Something is wrong, very wrong!* She checked the time: two thirty in the morning. She brought the monitoring screen to life and saw that the alien was standing against the partition with its arms outstretched. She leapt from the bed, threw on a robe, grabbed her remote and headband, and hastened into the corridor.

She stopped outside the door, her heart beating as if

striving to leave her body. Frantically, she put the headband in place, started the camera, and opened the entrance.

The light in the room raised automatically, and Jan saw that her patient hadn't moved. It stood against the barrier, arms outstretched, staring straight at her. She moved in, closing the door behind her. The eyes of the creature were on fire, marbled with red among the gold and black. Then she saw blood. Blood on its hands and blood on the floor. She knew there would be blood on its tail.

She pawed at the remote. The partition didn't move. She jabbed repeatedly at the remote and then pounded with her fist on the partition. "Stop it!" she sobbed, tears leaping from her eyes with such force that they almost hit the floor without touching her face. "There's no need for this. I know what you are." She slumped to the floor, whispering to herself, to the camera, to the room: *I know who you are.*

The partition jerked and rose, and the alien knelt and cradled Jan's head in its lap. The blood was gone, the wounds were no more. Jan still sobbed, harsh sounds that racked her body. She looked up into its eyes and found they were soft again, as deep and mysterious as ever. Peace flooded her thoughts, as strong as anything she had felt before: eternal love and protection, universal understanding. Such an understanding!

* * *

Karl looked at Jan and scratched his head in astonishment. "I don't know how you swung this, but you did and that's all that matters."

"Will Tolstoy helped," Jan said, adding mischievously: "He's very spiritual, did you know that?" She hadn't told Karl anything about last night's encounter, and so the remark drifted by him without further comment.

The conclusions she had come to frightened her to death. But she could not ignore the perfection of her patient's DNA. The supreme perfection of the spirals still corkscrewed through her mind. And she certainly couldn't ignore the single word that had somehow grafted itself onto her thoughts as the alien held her head in its arms.

Behind them, through the window, the huge shape of *Ascension* dominated the sky. The alien was already aboard, comfortably quartered in a room next to one reserved for Jan. She was sending him back to certain death, of course, but it was a universally ordained death, one prescribed within his genes. And that was so much better than sending him to Earth.

"Tell me," Karl said as they shook hands, "how intelligent do you think this creature is?"

Jan's eyes misted over. She stepped forward and embraced the station commander. "Oh, Karl," she whispered, gesturing through the window. "How big is the universe?"

Karl grinned. "Your secret, eh."

Jan strode purposefully to the door, paused, and turned. "My secret," she said. "But check out the meaning of *Golgotha*."

* * *

Will Tolstoy was waiting for her at the station's airlock. He smiled and said: "Now you know why you were chosen for this task."

Jan nodded. "I have the best telepathy quotient among the vets, though really it's not that high."

"It was high enough. That's what mattered."

There was a thump as the shuttle docked.

"Do you think he really is Decady's chosen one, their saviour?" she asked.

Will shrugged. "I really believe so. Either that, or he was very clever at using your own religious thoughts to convince you of the fact—and the powers that be. Your video was impact all the way."

"It didn't need any editing," Jan said.

The doors to the shuttle walkway hissed open.

"Anyway, we were morally bound to return him. His intelligence is not in doubt."

"Of course," Jan responded, "but I can tell you now, there was no manipulation, no false emotion, no lies. He is what he appears to be." She frowned and bit her lower lip nervously. "The initial analysis suggested the animal was male, but I never had the chance to really prove it, either way." She shrugged and smiled wistfully. "And maybe it doesn't really matter."

They walked slowly towards the shuttle entryway. "Thank you for your help in getting the message across, Will," Jan said. "It helped my sanity."

Will smiled but said nothing.

At the shuttle's threshold, they paused, as if uncertain whether to continue. Jan said, "They'll be watching, won't they. It's not all altruistic. They'll watch him all the way to his cruel death."

Will took her arm. "Come on, we need to go. Your patient needs some company."

Jan looked at him in astonishment. "We? You mean you're coming?"

He laughed, blue eyes dancing under the artificial lights.

"Meet the *Ascension's* new comms officer."

Before Jan could respond, a shrill beep sounded, signalling it was safe to enter the shuttle.

They walked into the spacecraft together and made their way to the cabin. Through the window, Jan could see the *Ascension*, long and thin, gleaming white under the stars. The Earth hung beyond the warpcraft, a contrast: blue, green, and grey. Home. But not for now. Her first trip through warp. Excitement. Danger. And, above all, her patient.

Something crossed the narrow void between shuttle and warpcraft, something that stilled her mind. *Always there could be peace. Always.*

THE VISITOR

The tiny South Australian outback town of Marree nestled peacefully beneath a star-studded velvet sky. Resplendent in golden reflections, the full moon rode on high in mysterious and ancient majesty, cloaking the ramshackle wooden and steel buildings of the isolated enclave in a sheen of mellow light. A light breeze stole in from the western desert and rustled the heads of date palms; the squawk of a roosting bird joined the gentle chorus.

To the south lay the rugged Flinders Ranges; to the north, a gleaming Lake Eyre. It was half an hour past midnight.

A shooting star raced across the darkening sky, followed by a reverberation amidst the split and crackling dust pans, and then…

Landfall.

Rising steam. Baked earth baked even further.

The alien trod the strange and powdery soil, enjoying its

solid, curious caress beneath his feet. During his long and fearful drop to the planet, he had noted, to the south, the presence of the dim lights of possible civilisation.

He walked, breathing air his large lungs could assimilate with ease. He strode great strides. He made progress.

* * *

John Allan McClean sat snoring in his favourite chair. The glow from a single-bar electric heater warmed his feet. A retired miner from Broken Hill, *Mac*, as he used to be known, now lived a life of solitude. His old weatherboard was, for all intents and purposes, a hermitage; a bastion against the onslaughts of frenetic humankind and their infernal technologies.

Mac stirred in his slumber, the movement startling a grey tabby cat that lay before the fire in a not too dissimilar pose to his master. The cat stretched, kneaded the threadbare carpet with his forepaws, and, with a swift glance at his recumbent companion, settled once more to his feline dreams.

An old clockwork alarm ticked loudly at its station on the mantelpiece. At Mac's elbow, a half-empty whisky bottle stood on a Tasmanian oak table that had seen better days.

Mac, a widower of some four years, had chosen Marree for its isolation. It was a quiet town, surrounded by saltbush country, lying at the junction of the Birdsville Track and the road to Oodnadatta. He loved the place for what it was, and he loved the people. They were no-nonsense humans: his soul brothers. Tough and wiry though he was, Mac also loved his cat.

A creak of the chair as he stirred again. His hand brushed the nearby bottle. If other nights were a precedent, he would remain seated until dawn.

* * *

The alien was now running: a long, slow-motion gait under lower gravity than he was accustomed to. Fatigue, though, showed in every step, and his once-erect ears now swung loosely about his rolling head.

He journeyed across a panorama of dark and light browns, every now and again stopping to gaze upwards, consciously rebuking the faraway stars for their torment to his soul. His world was not there. Even if it had been, he could not reach it: his cosmic conveyor was destroyed and all hope of traversing the void destroyed with it.

He had made a mistake, strayed off course. Lost contact with his brethren. His vehicle had been caught by the star and then snared by the gravity of this small, blue world that seemed to pull beyond its weight. There had been nothing he could do, nothing except guide his craft downwards to the best of his ability.

Survival had been fortunate. Whether it was worth anything remained to be seen.

Now he had to seek the friendship of this new planet—a place of unknown beings and unknown customs. And, in all probability, unknown dangers.

The visitor reared onto his hind legs and searched for the key to his survival: the thought translator. He must somehow communicate, and to communicate he needed the essential equipment that was neurally wired to his spinal column. It was the latest model and a mandatory device for his race of galactic explorers.

For a while, he remained upright, casting a substantial

moon shadow, as if he was some prehistoric monster from the long-forgotten past. He dropped to all fours and padded on-wards.

Sounds filled the night air: far-off rustlings among the trees, the rumble of a distant train, the bark of a dog. All meant nothing to him.

His sole destiny was the source of the lights he had seen on his descent.

* * *

Mac triggered the lonely bare bulb in the ceiling and looked at the alarm clock. Twenty past three! He cursed and shuffled to the toilet. Through the small window, the night was pitch black. On returning to his chair and before he could settle, he was greeted by a plaintive meow from his cat. The animal rubbed itself gently against his leg.

"You, too," mumbled Mac, as he led the way to the door. He let his pet out, and the animal disappeared into the night with a brief swish of its furry tail. Cold air wafted through the door, and Mac shivered. He did not appreciate winter.

Making his way to the kitchen, he grabbed a half-finished sandwich from a cracked plate. Then he returned to his chair and the burning bar. He took a swig from his bottle and within five minutes was asleep once more.

* * *

The kangaroo stood directly in the path of the alien, large ears swivelled towards the strange creature that was twice its height. The powerful tail of the marsupial rested on the ground, and its jaws worked continuously. Ten metres separated the two creatures. Dawn was just breaking in the east.

The alien's hand went to his translator. There was always a risk in using the machine: continuous interaction with lower life forms could permanently damage his brain stem. However, there was little choice. He had to find the intelligent species of the planet in order to survive. He activated the switch.

Little entered his mind at first, and he thought the machine was faulty, perhaps damaged on descent. Then he sensed blind fear mixed with insatiable curiosity. There were no questions or any other communication interchange. He hastily snapped the switch off and dropped to all fours.

The kangaroo rose to its full height, becoming as tall as it could.

The alien raised his hand in a final attempt at some basic contact. The marsupial abruptly turned and kicked off into the distance. Stopping briefly, it glanced back, then disappeared over a mound.

The visitor moved on, light and sound increasing all around him. He saw the sun rise in the east, and the shadows of the strange plants move across the ochre earth as the planet rotated. To his left he made out a range of mountains threaded across the horizon.

Homesickness swamped his soul, and more than once he shielded his eyes to look at the strange yellow star. As night approached once more, he sought a boulder and lay in its protective shelter. Like all creatures of the universe, he slept.

Waking at dawn, he rose slowly and took in his surroundings, recalling the trauma of the previous night. His head ached; his tongue was rough. The encounter with the strange, long-tailed creature had taken its toll upon his beleaguered mind and invoked bodily reactions that drained his strength.

He stood on two legs, calculating his direction by the sun. A movement in the sand attracted his attention. A line of small creatures marched in unison bent upon some mysterious errand. Each one was no larger than the length of the hairs that covered his body. They disappeared under the ground, one after the other, seemingly without end. Some carried material in their jaws.

Every sense in the alien's body told him that he had found civilisation, that here was the intelligence he sought. But after last time, all his instincts called for caution. Nevertheless, he pressed the switch of the translator.

Darkness filled his mind, and then a vision of one of the creatures attending a soft, white living thing, some half its own size. A sweet sensation assaulted his digestive system, almost making him retch.

But again, there was no perception of communication. He turned off the translator and wheeled around to head southwards.

It started to rain, the light of the dawn sun nullified by grey rain clouds. He walked on, alone, losing strength, sometimes on two feet, more often on four. In the distance, a rainbow decorated the morning sky, a poignant reminder of home.

* * *

Mac stared through the grimy windowpane at the sombre skies and the softly falling rain. Sundays were days of rest: a tribute to his deceased wife. They were also teetotal days. It was a tradition he was proud of, one that he intended to maintain to his dying day. As a result, he usually spent the day alone in the house or went for a short stroll outside if the weather permitted.

He was not a churchgoer, but he still held a solid respect for what his wife had called *The Lord's Day*. Turning away, he shuffled to the kitchen to prepare a simple breakfast of tea and cereal. The cat twisted and turned around his legs, thankful now to be inside and sheltered from the external damp.

* * *

The day was tiring and unrewarding for the alien. He tried a couple more beings, one with wings and one fat and round, before convincing himself he should wait to find the light he had seen on his descent to the planet. The creatures here were not like those at home. Their thoughts were a jumble of ridiculous emotions, a confusion of illiterate ramblings. Always instinct, not intelligence.

At least that was the way it seemed.

As evening approached, he knew his health had suffered badly, and his once dark purple coat was starting to turn grey. His eyes were red and sore from excessive concentration, and the threat of insanity nibbled at the edges of his distressed mind.

But suddenly, through the descending darkness, he saw the lights. His pulse quickened, and his feelings took wing. Surely now there was something. In his heart he knew it was his last chance. The translator was merciless with its effects from contact with inane intellects. He dropped on all fours and approached his presupposed salvation with caution.

* * *

Mac lay back in his favourite chair, hand resting gently, as a matter of habit, where his whisky bottle usually stood. He was not asleep, just mildly drowsing, occupying that strange shadowy world between wakefulness and deep slumber. It was at moments like these that the old miner recalled his younger days: his mates at the mine, many of whom were dead; his raucous teenage years; his marriage; and his two sons as children.

His two sons as adults he did not care to remember. As much as he had admired the devoutness of his wife, albeit from a distance, he loathed the materialism of his offspring. His abhorrence of their self-created culture had driven a wedge between them and had spawned a mutual silence of over twenty years. It was something that would never change.

A sudden sound invaded his reverie, and he stirred from his daydreaming. The sound came again, and he rose with a barely audible murmured complaint to make his way to the kitchen door. Feeding time for the cat.

* * *

The tiny weatherboard house emerged from the blackness to form a sharp silhouette against the night sky. The dark shape was punctured only by the weak glow from its windows. The intruder approached slowly on all fours, eyes alert for any movement. All was quiet.

On reaching a window, the alien peered into the dwelling. It was sparsely furnished and none too tidy—diminutive by his standards. The occupant sat upon a chair: a small creature covered in shiny white fur, an epidermic covering he had never come across before. It was, he thought, beautiful.

The prime species of the planet!

A door in the far wall opened, and a larger, clumsy animal

slouched into view carrying a container. This was placed in front of the furry creature, and then the servant left the room, its floppy hide dishevelled and uncoordinated and seeming to have a mind of its own.

To the visitor, it was obvious who ruled the dwelling. But should he introduce himself now or wait until it was lighter? Controlling his excitement with difficulty, he decided to wait until the planet's sun rose.

He left the house and found a safe haven in the bush where he lay down to rest and carefully groomed his jaded fur. Close by, sounds disturbed him. He moved to a quieter spot.

Morning came upon the heels of fitful sleep. The alien rose, stretched, and headed cautiously for the small dwelling. Even as he approached, the servant opened the main door to let his master out. The being strolled into the morning air, tail slowly waving from side to side. The door shut behind it.

Almost immediately, the creature arched its velvet back and bared its sharp white teeth. The alien recognised it as a position of hostility, probably stretching back to the being's remote ancestors. Not to be deterred, he pressed the translator switch.

Images of fear were again present, but this time there was some kind of intelligence lingering in the background. But, despite the being's small size, hostility was dominant!

The alien tried to rationalise. A single message soared through his brain, breaking its way through a haze of electronic mayhem. It was communication!

The message reverberated inside his skull, taunting him with its insult: *My land. You go home. My land. Go home.*

He endeavoured to shut out the words, reaching to close down the translator. This was not what he wanted. The beings of this planet were moronic and aggressive. How could he survive here?

The creature's words were replaced by black and grey clouds: a nonsensical swirling morass that taunted his mind. His shaking hand had disturbed the translator. Just before he died, he recalled the ironic words of the creature. *If only I could go home!* Blood raced to his brain stem and congealed. His heart collapsed.

For a second or two, the cat sniffed cautiously at the still body, then scurried off into the surrounding bush.

* * *

Mac discovered the body at noon, finding it remarkable that there were no ants crawling all over it; there was no sign of scavenger damage at all. With steady reverence, he laboured all afternoon upon its burial, levering the large body into the equally large grave. He didn't know what it was, or where it came from, and he did not care to know. What he did know was that he wanted no attention from the authorities or the media.

With no small amount of satisfaction, he shovelled the last pile of sand-like soil into place.

Out of deference to his wife, he said a brief prayer and fashioned a crude cross to position over the grave.

The sun was setting in the west. He called his cat.

TRIAL BY CONFESSION

A room in an ordinary building, three levels up from the street, full of strange equipment and even stranger people. And next door…

The spinning sensation transformed into a static monotone of indistinct reality that in turn gathered brighter colours towards it, as if endeavouring to cloak its shadowlike body in something more rational. Eventually, there was the welcome birth of reality—recognisable colours and well-defined outlines.

Stuart Gallagher's mind slowly absorbed his surroundings, allowing his brain to analyse, correct where necessary, and painstakingly comprehend his circumstances. He was alone. Enclosing him were four green walls, a soft black floor, and a shiny white roof.

Common sense demanded a door, but there didn't appear to be one. As far as he could tell, there was no way in and no way out. In fact, there was nothing else in the room at all. No furniture on the floor. No light burning from the ceiling. It was a barren room, with muted colour: a room designed to dull the senses.

Stuart was dressed in prison garb: a blue one-piece jumpsuit and soft slippers. He was twenty years old, of wiry build, his long, thin face framed by brown hair that reached almost to his shoulders. His brown eyes held what some people would call intelligence, but what others would call madness.

Peering upwards, he stared at his reflection in the surface of the alabaster ceiling. Where the hell was the light coming from?

Standing slowly, Stuart lifted his body on his toes, stretched his arms high in the air, and found he could just about touch his own image.

All of a sudden, and for no apparent reason, he wanted to lie down again. Settling back down on the black tiles, he found them surprisingly comfortable. He lay as straight as an arrow and drifted into a deep sleep.

The dream began immediately, furtively infiltrating his mind like a phantom searching for its long-lost soul. There was no defence against it, no way back to wakefulness. Delusion became reality, and it was as factual as any nightmare could ever be.

In his reverie, he was Citizen Stuart Gallagher, and he was walking down an endless straight road. Towering on either side were windowless concrete blocks, and passing by on the other sidewalk were what appeared to be real people going about their normal, everyday business. He wanted to cry out to them but found he could not speak; he directed his feet to the other side of the road, but they would not obey his command.

Humanity, if such it was, callously passed him by as he attempted to join it; to become as one with it; to become, really, what he once had been. He was a lost spirit in a search for acceptance, an unheard voice crying out for forgiveness. *Forgiveness? Forgiveness for what? What have I done that demands forgiveness?*

"Think! Think!" the people on the other side of the road abruptly shouted. "Think!" He stared across at them. Every face with wide, hostile eyes. Mouths opening and shutting with rubber lips that spouted accusations, hatred distorting their features. "Think what you have done."

His heartbeat raced. His brain screamed with the effort of thought, crying out in protest as he strived to remember. What *had* he done? *Think. Think.*

Then everything disappeared, like a dream within a dream. No more people or concrete blocks. He was alone once more, treading a grey landscape of unfulfilled thoughts. Yet again, he had failed to remember.

Stuart knew that constant failure meant the end. Next time he must remember—it was a matter of life or death. Falling to his knees, he prayed that he would recall what he had done, and when he lifted his eyes, he was back in the room: back in the place he had known for many weeks, the place of green and black and white—his accursed cubicle, his prison.

* * *

Dr Andrew McArthur raised his head angrily, his bushy eyebrows supporting a frown of crag-like intensity. In a voice that was cold and logical, he said, "My dear Simon, the facts cannot be disputed. Gallagher has been under treatment for thirty-eight days, which leaves just one more session for him to respond. If he does not do so, like the others before him, he must be executed as the law demands." He glared at his associate, a look of pure challenge on his face.

"But he's not like the others before him," Simon Carter countered. "We are so near with this man. Another two or three cycles and I believe he will be cured." He gestured towards the screens that ran along the wall of the laboratory, his eager young face full of anguish. "Look at the readings. Why not prolong his treatment, show some flexibility." With a look of sheer desperation, he added, "What kind of society do we live in that makes such heartless and rigid rules?"

Both men wore regulation white coats, but that was where the similarity ended. They were colleagues, but not friends. McArthur was old school, had been born before the equipment they were using had been conceived. Carter was fresh out of training and knew the apparatus circuitry back to front, inside out, and every which way. He also knew its flaws. But every justice system had flaws, of course.

McArthur rose from his desk and walked slowly to the window of the laboratory. There were people out there, people who were not criminals, people living decent, law-abiding lives. Dare he be persuaded, just this once? He turned purposefully towards his associate. "It has been proven conclusively that unless a criminal can remember his crime subconsciously during any of the thirty-nine Santean cycles, his conscious mind stands no chance of eliminating further unlawful tendencies." He pointed at the flashing monitors and their wavering coloured lines that dominated their work area. If the truth be known, they were images that often haunted his own dreams. "The period is stipulated exactly by Santos and cannot be extended. Any such extension would be unfair to patients who have gone before. Even you must see that, Simon."

"I see it," Carter replied, intrigued by McArthur's use of the word *patients*, "but I still think it's bloody stupid." He turned and left the room quietly, closed the door silently. He did not want to be part of this trial anymore. As the youngest member of the team, he was, after all, the one who applied the final justice.

Alone, McArthur turned once more to the window. There was a blue sky forming; the sun was shining. Out there, everybody was normal. There was no crime. The only anguish was in the hearts of the relatives of the inmates awaiting the Santean process. And that was normal, too, even beneficial if they spread the word.

He wondered whether it was even worth the time and trouble. Once a felon was convicted, why not get it all over with? Deal with miscreants in the only way that guaranteed no further crimes. He turned from the window. Perhaps it wasn't a perfect world after all.

* * *

He was there again. The same street, unchanged and never ending; a concrete path to acceptance, if only he could remember. The people on the other side were there too, pointing, accusing, yelling. "Think! Think!"

Their voices soared into his confused mind like scouting vultures, eventually to settle amidst his memories, squawking and stabbing sharp beaks into his defenceless subconscious. He had to remember. He had to. It was now or never.

His head swam with a message, something from the past, something from a crowded room. *The subconscious mind is my data-bank for everything. It stores my beliefs, my memories, my skills. Everything that I have ever seen, done, or thought is held there. All I have to do is remember.*

His fists beat his thighs with impatience and frustration as he stumbled along the sidewalk. The sweat from his forehead invaded his eyes. It was there! He knew it was there.

Pictures of a crowded market flooded his mind. *Think. Think.*

Amongst the throng, a woman stood shimmering in ghostly outline, an old woman, defenceless, frail.

He glanced across the road. No! This was wrong! The image was disappearing. Fading away and becoming wavy outlines as consciousness began to take over, instigating the journey back to reality.

"Stop! Don't go!" He stretched his lungs to bursting point as he at last found a voice. "I've remembered. I've remembered."

But they were gone, and he was alone. The sweat in his eyes mingled with tears as the room surrounded him once more. He rose to his feet slowly, the picture in his mind as clear as the day it happened.

Then he heard a hissing sound, a snake in the grass. Glancing towards the corner of the room, he made out steam rising from the floor. Except it wasn't steam. He was being executed as an incurable case. In blind panic, he charged at the walls of his cell, frantically beating upon them until green was stained red.

His voice was a harsh scream. "I've remembered. I've remembered. I know what I did wrong. I took an old woman's purse. Please. Please." He sank to the floor, his voice fainter. "I've remembered. An old woman's purse."

He became still, and the chamber became a furnace, reflecting brilliant light from wall to wall. Stuart Gallagher disappeared from the room and the cameras, and from the very

Earth itself.

* * *

As Andrew McArthur watched the screens, he could not control the visible shaking that took control of his hands or erase the look of anguish that invaded his face. Stuart Gallagher had been the ultimate in borderline cases, the one who nearly got away. Andrew shook his head. Gallagher's memories had been half there. But not good enough. Not good enough by half.

He turned off the equipment and walked unsteadily to his desk. Simon Carter had been the designated executioner, but McArthur had gone ahead and done it himself, just like he had done in the past. Carter was weak, typical of the new breed. No interest in the cause. No guts.

But the macabre end of Stuart Gallagher was not the incident that bothered him. What really troubled the psychologist was that the patient had recalled his crime at the very end of the treatment, while in the *conscious* state. In other words — the Santean cycle had a flaw. He sat down and ran through a summary of the process in his mind:

The patient is given cranial neurostimulation while in the conscious state to obviate any criminal tendencies and to eliminate the memory of the crime in the patient's conscious mind.

Then the patient is subjected to thirty-nine Santean cycles whilst on the subconscious plain induced by the Santos cubicle.

The machine aligns with the patient's subconscious, and a remorseful patient recalls the illegal behavior whilst under subconscious memory inducement and interrogation.

Proof of complete cure, according to Santos, is the admission of the crime and the subsequent pleading for clemency while the patient is in the subconscious state.

All further criminal inclinations are successfully removed as the patient is returned to the real world.

McArthur frowned. Part of the treatment had failed! Somehow, Gallagher had reverted to how he had been *before* the Santean procedures, recalling his crime when conscious. It had never happened before.

Carl Jung, a sage of old, had once said that structures of the unconscious mind were actually shared among beings of the same species. McArthur had never believed that. Still didn't believe it. It was a frightening thought. But now he was truly concerned, and seeds of doubt were infiltrating his mind.

He sauntered over to his favourite spot at the window. What if the collective unconscious was starting to revolt against the legal hierarchy? What if Gallagher's subconscious had been invaded by those of other citizens, law-abiding or otherwise, encouraging a dangerous memory breach and forcing their agenda into the patient's conscious thoughts: effectively breaking through the rigid walls of the Santean process and into fresh territory?

He looked at the people on the other side of the window. *Are they plotting a quiet revolution?* Maybe Gallagher was a symptom of a gradual change: the first peg in the hole. He wondered whether the world was about to become a heaving cauldron of crime.

That would be a world unfit to live in—a world controlled by evil—a world he would not wish to inhabit.

Behind him, the door quietly opened. Simon Carter entered the room with two uniformed police officers. McArthur turned, saw the police, and frowned. "What the—?"

Simon Carter shrugged, held up what looked like a small

computer flash drive. "I'm sorry, Andrew. There was a confession. It's all on here."

One of the officers stepped forward. "Andrew McArthur. You are under arrest for the murder of lawbreaker Stuart Gallagher. I must inform you that you do not have to say or do anything but anything you say—"

McArthur was shaking his head. "No. No. Stop there. You don't understand. Gallagher was executed following a fair trial by the Santean process."

He shot a look of hate towards Simon Carter. "You fool. Don't you see? They've started a revolution. They have infiltrated the Santean software. We're not safe anymore."

Simon Carter smiled. "Flexibility, Andrew. That's all it would have taken."

THE WHISPER OF WAVES

F reezing fog invaded the deserted countryside, its icy fingers caressing sweeping branches of skeletal trees and creeping into homes of creatures that no longer wished to leave their lair in search of food. The day was still: Not a breath of wind stirred the various grasses, no mouse disturbed the undergrowth, and no distant clatter of train rang through the air. There was just silence: cold and heavy and unforgiving.

Far below the frozen surface, a man awoke from relentless sleep. The murmur of a generator sounded in sharp contrast to the quiet a hundred feet above his head.

Tomas Danek's hand stretched out to flick a light switch, and dim radiance from two small LED globes flooded the converted cave. Reluctantly departing his bed, Tomas made his way over to the glowing bars of an electric fire and crouched there, allowing the welcome heat to penetrate his waking body. Then he dressed and prepared a meagre breakfast, chewing for at least a minute before swallowing each mouthful.

Tomas was working as a scientist and a researcher for the government. Or had been until the world grew cold. He was tall and angular, his once-short blond hair growing longer, it seemed, by the minute; his face covered by an itchy growth that drove him crazy.

The cave was his home. There was no other. The generator provided power, and when it died, he would die with it. In addition to his bed, there was a table, a single chair, a refrigerator and freezer, a small oven and microwave, a chemical toilet that was past its use-by date, and very little else. On a small stand, in one corner of the cave, an audio and video intercom link to the surface stood neglected, as defunct as a hailstone in a heatwave.

The meal over, he moved across to the stairwell entrance and donned one of the two suits that decorated the wall. They resembled lifeless comrades in white, somehow hung out to dry—his only company in this morbid hellhole.

He had been in hiding for weeks, initially plotting revenge on the unknown creatures that had taken over Earth, but now only intent on personal survival. For all he knew, he was the last man alive.

Tomas finalised the fastening of his suit, ensured the helmet was sealed, grabbed his pistol, and passed through the door to the stairs. He was loath to return to the icy world above, but on this occasion, it was necessary. His larder was getting low. A visit to town was required.

The firearm had been an early acquisition on his initial foray into the nearby small town. There were only a few bodies lying in the street; most people would have been in bed when the freeze hit. Most of them would have known nothing. He'd ransacked a gun shop for some kind of defence and chosen a Glock 19 with a fifteen-round magazine, reliable and reasonably light.

But today food was the priority.

On reaching the top of the stairs, he gazed around as he always did on a return to the frozen surface. Nothing had changed. White-grey vapour swirled menacingly, occasionally parting to reveal the uninviting view, but always closing, as if to deny him the comfort of a three-dimensional world.

Gripping his pistol firmly, Tomas began to walk in the direction of the town. Each time he made this journey, he chose a different route—any indication of a trail would likely lead the invaders to his lair.

About halfway to town, he thought he detected the sound of an invader nearby. He stiffened and held his pistol at the ready. The danger passed. Breathing a sigh of relief, Tomas continued on his way.

He had encountered the aliens only once before. On hearing his steps, they had turned towards him, no more than eight metres away, revealed by the parting mist. At such close quarters, they were easy targets. He had fired four times, and they had collapsed to the frozen earth. Two of them, clad only in thin, skin-tight, full-body garments. As he inspected their otherworldly form, he had noticed with some satisfaction their life fluid leaking away. They bled. They were vulnerable.

They were also humanoid: two legs, two arms, much like himself, but sturdier of build. There was no hair, and their faces were covered in small scales, pale green in hue, with two large brown eyes, small lipless mouth, hardly any nose at all, bulbous rear skull. And no ears!

They will know about me now!

Ever since that moment, he had felt like a criminal, haunted by the alien corpses. He ventured onto the cold surface only when his food supply was low—as he was doing now.

Tomas entered the deserted supermarket, filtered daylight paying homage to what once had been. He filled up a basket with tins, jars, and whatever perishable goods still looked fresh under the subzero temperature. Task completed, he set out on the return journey. He always only took one basket, carried in his left hand. Enough to last him two weeks. His right hand always held the Glock at the ready.

On the lonely trek back, his thoughts turned to the beginning of it all. How he had been chosen for experiments on the effects of isolation on a solitary human—in space, on the moon, or wherever else future-man may find himself alone in the universe. How he had entered the cave looking forward to the challenge. How he had been rudely awoken one night by the urgent beeping of his emergency intercom, the voice on the other end frantically gasping about strange lights, a cold fog, and some kind of invasion.

He hadn't believed it, of course, had thought it part of the project, but he had taken the now dormant elevator to the surface. And had been driven back by the intense cold. He'd vowed that next time he would wear one of the spacesuits, including the helmet and its breathing apparatus. Anything to keep the cold at bay. He was supposed to don one of the suits every other day anyway. It was part of the trial, a way of testing whether his mind had been dulled by the isolation. The suit was, after all, an infernal contraption to put on.

The next few days had confirmed his worst fears. He had ventured into town and found it deserted. Not a sign of life anywhere. Streets and roofs and windows were layered with ice, a few people and some dogs lay in the gutters, branches had fallen; it was a Christmas scene gone dreadfully wrong. There were cars parked in the roads, awaiting their ghostly drivers who would never return to open their doors. There was no way their batteries would have survived anyway. Cold desolation. Another world. The world of the invaders.

He was, it appeared, a survivor of an alien invasion. What else was there to do but exist and remain undetected?

A noise some way ahead interrupted his thoughts: a sound like whispering thunder. Tomas shortened his stride and moved slowly, holding his pistol at arm's length. The sound increased as he advanced. Then he saw them!

God! They were giants! Two pairs of massive legs that must have been two men high crossed his vision, lifting and falling in ponderous slow motion. Mist swirled around them haphazardly, as if not knowing where to flow. Here was the real invader, the real conqueror. What he had killed must have been two of their young, the offspring of these formidable goliaths.

They were big and green. He immediately thought of dinosaurs. *They are dinosaurs from another world!*

With difficulty, he suppressed the urge to turn and run for dear life.

Toting his basket, Tomas trailed them for what must have been an hour. He was on the verge of giving up when the steady thump of footsteps ceased. The surrounding mist was illuminated by a searing flash, and he caught a glimpse of their huge silhouettes before they vanished into darkness.

Creeping forward, Tomas found his way blocked by a large wall that appeared to stretch away on both sides. From the other side came the sound of humming, like a swarm of giant bees in flight.

He picked up another sound — the lapping of waves on a nearby shore. Listening to the distant motion of the sea, Tomas frowned, and for no apparent reason was overcome by a feeling of the deepest despair. He shivered as the creeping fog penetrated his suit-clad limbs. He had been away too long. It was time to return home.

As Tomas turned away from the alien wall, a thought suddenly occurred to him, teasing the analytical part of his scientific mind. *Surely with the temperature so low the boundaries of the sea are frozen.* Curiosity aroused, he turned towards the insistent whispering of the waves.

It did not take long to reach the water; a great expanse of grey ocean met his eyes, totally different from what he'd expected. Great clouds of vapour were climbing upwards, and the surface itself seemed to be on fire, frothing and bubbling as if demented.

He suddenly realised that the sea's motion may hold the answer to everything.

As he sought his way back to the cave, he was even more aware of the danger imposed by the invaders. They were apparently "terraforming" Earth to their own world's specifications. And on such a scale!

With the basket on his left arm growing heavier with every plodding step, it was with great relief that Tomas descended the stairs to the cave. Once released from his burden, he cooked himself a substantial meal and then sat in his only chair, encouraging his mind to search for a rational explanation of what was happening.

Evaporation of the oceans, he thought. And linked with evaporation were clouds. From what he had witnessed, the clouds must be widely distributed and extremely thick.

He ran through the logic in his mind. The ocean, somehow

changed by the invaders, was evaporating intensely and forming heavy clouds that cut off the sun's rays. To maintain balance, frequent snow would be needed, probably at night with the surface of the Earth away from its star. But would that be enough to sustain the constant cold?

Then he thought he had an answer. Latent heat! Was it possible that the aliens were using latent heat absorbed from the atmosphere to provide energy for the nonstop vaporization of the world's oceans? It was a rudimentary thought, but he was sure it was at least a partial explanation of what was happening.

A world based on a new, freezing-cold ecological system! It was, Tomas realised, a complete nightmare. And certainly not one humans could survive.

As he lay down to sleep that night, he determined that he would fight back. Not that he knew how yet, but he would find a way. They were dinosauric giants with giant machines, and the power to match. Power to change a world's ecology. But there was a wall. And walls could be scaled. Tomorrow, he would get a ladder and a rope from the town, and hopefully some kind of explosives. The mist would be his ally, keeping him hidden, a silent partner in his attack on the alien stronghold. Maybe he could cripple their power source — whatever it was that hummed surreptitiously beyond the wall.

He had no doubt that they would be looking for him now. They would have found their slain children and, if they thought like humans, the hounds would be out.

But the best form of defence was attack.

Thinking these revolutionary thoughts, exhausted from mental and physical effort, Tomas fell into fitful slumber.

He dreamed that he was falling through the emptiness of

space: an infinite void that emphasised the loneliness that pervaded his very being. Countless galaxies came and went, and it appeared he was rapidly approaching the beginning of time. Then abruptly, everything was reversed, and he was hurtling upwards at the same tremendous rate. No time to stop. No time to think. Just faster and faster.

Tomas awoke with a start. It was well past sunrise. Time to make preparations. He had to find a way inside the alien citadel. He would find a ladder and a rope. If that failed, there seemed to be only one other way: to enter with the aliens themselves.

As he checked his pistol, Tomas received the first shock of the day—all the boxes of cartridges were untouched, and his Glock was empty. He remembered fully loading the firearm and recalled, even more distinctly, killing the alien young. How could he have done that with no bullets?

With shaking hands he loaded the handgun, endeavouring to concentrate on the task ahead. It was a chance to hit back at the aliens, to gain some revenge, however small, for the human race. *His* human race that had been frozen into oblivion.

Driven by such thoughts, Tomas donned his suit and climbed to the surface. He tried to forget the reappearing bullets. Perhaps he had dreamed about killing the alien young. Anything was possible in this strange, cold world.

For a few seconds, Tomas just stood there. Eventually, he made a tactical decision. The initial task was to locate the wall again and commit the route to his memory. Then he would go into town.

It had snowed overnight, but he retraced his footsteps of the previous day easily enough. The mist around him drifted and parted, swirled and swung like a demented theatre curtain made of sentient gossamer threads. He cursed it under his breath, gripped the pistol tighter as he approached the wall.

But the wall wasn't there! He searched feverishly for what seemed like hours, clawing at the hanging vapour as if to brush it aside to see what lay beyond. His steps grew wilder and wilder, drawing him more and more into a deepening despair.

There was no mistake. He was definitely where the wall had been. He cried out to the invaders, a pathetic, tinny cry inside his helmet, but there was no answer.

He crouched, helmeted head bowed, hands laid upon the frozen soil. It seemed he was to be denied his revenge.

Then he realised that the atmosphere was growing warmer. Beads of perspiration were creeping onto his brow. Underneath the suit, his body was starting to feel clammy and uncomfortable.

On the horizon he made out a pale sun climbing into the sky, a yellow smudge but there all the same. He cast his eyes around. The mist was gradually disappearing; the snow was starting to melt. Ever so quickly now, grass was starting to show, and trees were pushing out leaves.

Gripped by a sudden nausea, his senses reeling as the countryside around him whirled into life in a confusion of shade and light, Tomas collapsed onto the ground. Losing all sense of reality, he slipped into unconsciousness.

He awoke with a bright light beaming down upon him and raised an arm to shield his eyes. The light dimmed, and he heard strange voices. Tomas parted his eyelids slowly, in dread of what he might see; visions of the immense invaders crowded his mind and filled him with fear.

But there were no aliens.

A nurse bent over him, auburn hair catching the muted

light, and Tomas saw cream walls beyond her crisp, white and blue uniform. She was unclamping a device from his head. He felt sick. *What is happening? Where are the invaders?*

"Relax now, Mr Danek," said the nurse in a pleasant, soothing voice. "Everything is alright. You've had a dream, that's all. A nasty dream." She flashed him a smile that he barely noticed. "Dr Goddard will be in to see you in a few minutes." She was gone before he could ask any questions.

Little by little, events slipped into place. He was part of a sensory deprivation research program conducted by the Johnson Space Center. He had been living in a dome, not a cave. Had, in fact, been living there for months. Alone. Self-sustaining. With no contact from the outside world.

"Tomas. How are you?" A male voice from the door. "Forgive the headgear. Just a little contraption of mine."

Dr Goddard was thin, dapper in a white smock, balding with spectacles. Tomas struggled to recall him.

"I had a shit dream," Tomas said, straight to the point.

"Yes. Perhaps the technique is not yet perfect. It stores and checks your brainwave patterns. Eliminates depression, if you will. Helps to eradicate your feelings of isolation. Stimulates when required."

"It did that, all right," Tomas replied.

Goddard shrugged. "It was just a trial." He smiled suddenly—rather falsely, Tomas thought. "Anyway, that's part one over with. You did well."

"Part one?" Tomas didn't recall there being any parts.

Goddard nodded. "Part two will be a breeze after part one. Much easier. Solitary confinement in a specially equipped cave. As an extra challenge, you'll have your own generator to maintain…"

The voice droned on, but Tomas scarcely heard what the

doctor was saying. As soon as the cave was mentioned, he knew exactly what it was going to be like. Morphean memories swam into his senses, and he was haunted by the innocent eyes of the alien corpses, the giant-sized legs ploughing through the mist, the vaporizing of the oceans.

The icy mist of an unwelcome future beckoned him onwards with cold, relentless fingers. He wanted to dismiss it, but he knew he could not. He lay on the bed, paralysed with fear, listening to what he already knew.

"…You'll have a couple of spacesuits. We want you to put one on every other day." Goddard smiled. Like an owl, Tomas thought. Like a bird of prey. "You'll be given a thorough briefing in about two weeks. Don't worry. You won't be there long."

Tomas just stared at the spectacles. Should he say something? Or would they think him mad?

"It's a nice part of the country, too," Goddard said, sidling to the door. "Only a brief walk to the seashore."

OTHERS OF OUR KIND

The spacecraft, reflecting stars and worlds but mostly darkness, drifted through the heavens on a predetermined course into a new and unexplored sun system. Surrounded by crystalline walls, the crew of five relaxed in computer-controlled comfort as their vessel moved relentlessly into unknown cosmic territory. As the crew rested, each occupied a world of their own, only basic thoughts occupying their freshly waking minds. Currently, such thoughts were all they needed.

They were over one year from the mothership.

The ship became one with the new system and placed itself in orbit around the outermost planet. Outside the spacecraft, the stars appeared indifferent, neither welcoming nor rejecting the intruder from another sun's world.

But then there was something else: something unfamiliar to the ship, albeit entirely harmonious with their new cosmic neighbourhood. Five minds were abruptly alerted, and the occupants of *Earth Explorer 54* were woken.

The alarm system barked in its usual monotonic manner: *New incoming. Three hundred thousand kays. Alert please. Analysis underway.*

Captain Sean Singh rose and stretched. He looked across to where Star Navigator Liling Zhang was already standing, her slim white-clad body a huge contrast to the muscular bulk of Super Technician Theodore Bernstein, who was struggling to get out of his capsule. Theodore was a man who knew the 54 backwards.

"Get a fixation, please, Li," Sean requested.

Liling nodded and made her way forward. Sean and Theodore followed. Medic Simon Kroston and Second Technician Minjun Park emerged from their capsules and tracked the other three to the control bridge.

Star Navigator Zhang studied her display. "Around seven hours approach time," she said.

"Any size on the object?" Sean asked.

"Computing now." Liling screwed up her eyes and stared at the series of numbers that raced across the screen. "Some thirty metres, more or less spherical to a millimetre, and...whoa." She glanced back at the others. "Very high metallic base."

"Well now," Simon said. "Have we found someone else?" Tall and skinny, methodical in nature, the medic did not look convinced.

"Could it be just rich metallic ore?" Theodore questioned. "A meteor, perhaps." Theodore Bernstein was a mountain of a man whose gentle voice belied his size.

Liling pulled slowly at her shiny dark hair, wrinkled her small nose, and frowned. "No, no. Look at how the spectrum's coming up. Many metals, hardly anything else."

"I'll get coffee," Minjun Park announced. His dark countenance usually carried a perpetual look of concern, but this time he looked positively apprehensive. Years ago, he had volunteered for *Explorer* expeditions to escape the rigors of Martian life; he did not really expect to find evidence of intelligent aliens, nor did he have any ambitions to do so.

"Thanks, Min," Sean said. A man of average build, with a high brow and bright blue eyes, Sean possessed a high intelligence that included a vast knowledge of the workings of the cosmos. He looked at Liling. "Do a check. And then another. Make sure there are no errors." He touched Theodore on the shoulder. "You help her." *Get to know her*, Sean thought. *We've all been asleep too long.*

* * *

Some six and a half hours later, the mysterious object had joined them in orbit, positioning itself no more than a hundred metres away. Its final approach had been benign, slow and looping, obviously not of malicious intent. Even so, the spacecraft's bank of lasers had watched it all the way.

The crew, now dressed in their casual attire of grey shirts and blue pants, stared at their new companion. Not a rock, not a meteor. Definitely manufactured, it shone with all the colours of the rainbow.

"Any signals?" Sean asked Theodore.

"Not a one," the technician replied. "Nothing we can capture, anyway. There's no radiation. Nothing at all."

The captain looked at Minjun Park. "You okay for EVA?"

"Always," Min replied.

Min was their EVA expert. Sean often thought that the

technician actually preferred the freedom of being outside compared to the confines of the ship's interior. Or maybe he just liked being on his own.

"Gold, titanium, aluminium, carbon, and some we can't even identify," Theodore said. "No way it's natural. Not by our measures." He gazed at the sphere. "Eerie, shining like that." He grinned facetiously at his colleagues. "Man-made, I'd say."

"Could it be one of ours?" Liling asked.

Sean shook his head. "Not here. Impossible. Unless we're being kept in the dark."

None of them liked that idea.

"I'll go get ready to play ball," Min declared and took the elevator down to the airlock. Within five minutes, they could see him on the cameras, his magnetic suit-pack keeping him near the ship's skin, his secondary cable spooled at his waist.

They watched him trigger his jets and shoot across the airless void, umbilical cord trailing behind him with a life of its own. Sean always felt nervous at times like this. Despite his faith in the engineering, things could still go wrong.

Min arrived at the sphere, distorted reflections turning his suit into an apparition of impossible proportions. A fly on a light bulb, he began a crawl of inspection. "Going round the other side now. Hold on."

The white-suited figure drifted around the periphery of the sphere, and for a few, nerve-racking seconds, the watchers lost sight of their colleague. Unexpectedly, dramatically, he reappeared—flung into space like a stone from a sling as the sphere gathered momentum from some unseen force.

"Trail it, Li." The captain was already on the move. "I'll reel him in."

Simon Kroston followed Sean to the elevator and down to

the airlock. There was a medikit in the airlock bay.

"That brute packed a hell of a kick." Park's voice, faint in all their ears. "I'm okay. Just blacked out for a few seconds." Then, as Sean activated the cable: "I'll finish the ride. Thanks."

Minutes later, the crew were together again, Minjun apparently undismayed by the incident. "It was as smooth as a baby's butt," the technician said, referring to the sphere. "Not a nook or cranny anywhere."

"Sit down," Simon ordered. "Let me check you over." Park gave him a feigned look of horror but dutifully did as requested.

Sean said to Liling, "Still in touch?"

"Sure. In fact it's slowed down."

"Right." Sean said. "Let's go after it. Someone, somewhere must own it."

* * *

For seventeen ship-days, the sphere led them a dance through the chosen star's system until it eventually reached its destination. They arrived in orbit around an inner planet that lay bathed in mellow sunshine. The sphere hovered nearby and seemed to be saying: *The next move is up to you.*

Below them, the new world apparently waited with open arms for the newcomer's attention. *Somewhere down there*, Sean thought, *there are intelligent aliens.* The thought induced strange feelings: excitement, fear of the unknown, even hope—all mishmashed together in a cocktail of conflicting moods.

Li brought up the data on the screen. The planet was a little larger than Earth; possessed two moons, both currently visible to them; and was fairly verdant around the equator.

What they deemed as the polar areas showed signs of severe storms with intermittent white reflections permeating the swirling air masses. The atmosphere looked reasonable, but if they went down, they would wear their suits as a precaution. From where they were stationed, there was no sign of any structures or of what could be taken as cities or townships. Around thirty percent of their view of the world was in darkness, but there were no lights. To their surprise, gravity was almost the same as Earth's.

"Orbital period from our current position?" Sean asked Liling Zhang.

"Three hours." She looked at Sean and shrugged her petite shoulders. "Less if we go lower."

Sean shook his head. "No, we're fine at this distance. Prepare for one orbit. All sensors on. Keep track of the sphere. Code our position, galactic coordinates."

Wonder and anxiety tempered the crew's emotions. Theodore Bernstein had his nose on the window. "Lots of green down there," he said. "Looks pretty cozy to me."

"Caution before cozy," Sean said. "Are we ready, Li?"

The star navigator nodded, and they felt the ship adjust position as it rotated for improved visibility of the planet below. The sphere, in something of a role reversal, kept track.

* * *

They learnt little new from their orbit of the planet, save that the equatorial zone portrayed many of the characteristics of Earth. "Okay," Sean said, "let's descend slowly—and let's be ready to abort."

Almost as if the sphere had heard his words, it dropped away beneath them, eventually disappearing from view.

Theodore tried the window magnifier but eventually shook his head.

"Tracking," Liling said calmly and glanced at her captain. "Follow?"

Sean nodded. "Like I said, but very carefully."

They dropped into the new world, feeling neither invasive nor welcome. Twenty minutes later, they hung like a spider on a silk thread, one hundred metres from the planet's surface. Below them, grass fronds waved in a gentle breeze. A small distance away, their astral guide landed, watched and waited, and then just vanished. Liling's finger hovered over the thrust button.

"It just disappeared into thin air," Simon Kroston said, echoing all their thoughts. "It shimmered and became nothing." There was tension in the cabin now, as if they had perhaps done the wrong thing, perhaps broken some unknown, alien planetary law.

Sean checked the survey camera, taking it three times slowly through 360 degrees. "Land," he said to Liling. "Gently. As before, ready to abort."

They touched down and sat in silence. It was not the first time humans had landed on an extraterrestrial planet, but it was the first time there had been signs of intelligent alien life. They were all aware that anything could happen.

"How's the atmosphere, Min?" Sean's voice broke the stillness.

"Couldn't be better," Min answered. "Gravity gives a unit reading, too. Not quite what we measured from space, but who's complaining? Temperature twenty-five. We could walk out there naked and survive."

"Needn't go that far, I think. Probably poisonous stuff out there, anyway." Sean made a quick decision. "I'll go out with

202

Theodore, fully suited. Thirty minutes tops and—"

"WELL COME." The impossible sound rang through the ship's structure and bombarded their minds, as if they were in a huge cave populated by a bellowing giant from a bygone age.

Hands immediately went to ears. "What the—" breathed Simon Kroston. It came again, softer this time, more bearable, but hugely stentorian all the same: *"Welcome. Welcome."*

And again, softer yet. *"Welcome. I welcome you."*

Sean glanced at his crew. They were ashen, faces drawn. Blood trickled from Liling's nose. Theodore was shaking his head. Minjun gasped, "Our comm system—must have gone berserk."

Sean wasn't sure. It had been too loud. There was ringing in his ears.

They were shell-shocked, as if a bomb had exploded nearby, and they were suddenly desperate for something familiar to clutch to their chests, something rational.

Resembling statues with unseeing eyes, they waited for normality to return. It came with a silence that was almost as terrifying as the thunderous words spoken in their own language. Eventually, Sean took a deep breath and broke the deadlock. "It wasn't a malfunctioning comm." He looked at the others, one by one, noting their blinking eyelids, their laboured breathing. "I think it may have been some kind of welcoming committee."

"Do we stay or do we go?" Liling asked, her voice a mere whisper.

"Stay. Please stay." The voice, more pleasant now, almost pleading, entered the cabin.

Silence for a few seconds, then: "Our purpose is to find intelligence," Theodore Bernstein said. "So when we do, it seems pointless to run away." He was looking out of the forward window, his wits apparently safely gathered.

Minjun Park shook his head. "That means we have to trust whatever is out there."

"*Trust. Trust. Trust.*" Strangely hypnotic. Not unpleasant, just so obviously alien.

"We're going out, Theodore," Sean said. "You still okay with that?"

The super technician nodded. "If you say so."

* * *

Tradition dictated that Sean Singh was the first to feel the new world's green grass under his feet. Bernstein joined him, and they just stood there, alert for the unexpected and waiting for something to happen.

"Can we remove our helmets, Min?" Sean already had his fingers on the release button.

"Atmosphere is fine," Min replied. "I've just run a slow-mo of the sphere vanishing. It didn't so much vanish as sink into the ground. Very, very quickly. It was absorbed by the soil."

Free of his helmet, Sean felt the slight stir of a breeze across his forehead. He realised he should be enjoying the moment, relishing the feel of the wind brushing against his face. But he wasn't. He was petrified. He looked to the horizon, turning through a full circle, saw nothing unusual; nothing that could have transmitted the strange communication. It was as still as death itself—yet there was life.

Strolling a little way from their ship, Sean and Theodore heard the gentle rush of a nearby river. Other than that, there was an impeccable silence. Not a bird threaded the sky, not a cricket stirred in the grass. Even the breeze was voiceless.

Suddenly, without warning to his companion, Bernstein challenged their surroundings. "Where the hell are you?" His voice was tinged with anger and desperation, as if he were challenging invisible spirits in a ghost-infested house.

To their utmost surprise, there came an immediate answer: "I am what you see, what is beneath you and before you." The voice was on all sides and even seemed to resonate through the soles of their boots.

They stopped in their tracks, nervous tongues licking dry lips, eyes wide with fear. They heard, but they did not see, just two small white figures on a carpet of green.

"Who are you?" Sean's shout spread like the ripples of a pond following the dive of a hungry bird.

"Your world," came the reply. Then a small correction: "Your new world."

"For God's sake!" Theodore Bernstein exclaimed. "The whole damned place is alive." He knelt down to feel the ground. A natural thing to do, Sean thought, at least if you were human.

Bernstein shook his head. "Feels normal, just like home."

"Where are your people?" Sean asked of the surrounding air. "Who lives here? Why is there nobody here?" *Too many questions. Do I really want them answered?*

This time there was no immediate answer. It was as if a huge deliberation was taking place. The wind rose fresh in their faces like an outflow of breath. In the background, they could still hear the sound of running water. They were uncertain what to do next, wanting to return to the ship, but fearing what would happen if they made steps in that direction.

The wind rose further, then suddenly stopped. "The old ones have gone," came a reply at last. "Some of illness, some of wars, and some to the stars." There was a pause and then: "They finished me, and they deserted me."

Sean thought he detected a higher tone to the voice, as if emotion was playing along taut vocal cords—if indeed it had either.

"Those who survived," Sean queried, "why did they abandon you?" He cast a glance back to the ship, which now seemed to be dreadfully far away. They had to leave this conversation as soon as possible. The alien words made him uneasy. Anything he did not understand made him uneasy. The next words magnified his foreboding.

"I am their machine. The weather and the days and the nights and the crops and the tides are what I am. I serve the lower creatures remaining, but I no longer serve those who made me."

"It's a totally computerised planet," Bernstein whispered. "It's incredible."

Sean shrugged. He wasn't so sure. "We're going back to the ship," he called.

Bernstein nodded. "By lower creatures, I presume it means animals, alien ones."

"I think it means lower than us," Sean replied.

* * *

Sunset came and with it rain. Clouds in perfect formation ranged across the sky and fed life-giving water to the expansive plains. The wind, stronger now, swirled around the ship's superstructure, while inside the cabin the crew debated and argued until Sean Singh held his hands up in the air.

"Okay. This is it," Sean stated as he activated the console recorder. "Further exploration and investigation by this crew is not recommended and would be dangerous without backup resources. The planet is fully life supporting and seems to have a computer-controlled environment—a legacy from some bygone civilisation. It is totally capable of communicating with humans...*with us*. That early civilisation has now abandoned this world." He looked at the others uncertainly and then continued. "Suggest a visit by a team of analytical experts and engineers to determine the nature of the computerisation. There is no indication of hostility, as of yet, from the environment or its creator."

Sean hesitated a moment, as if about to add something else, but then negated the recorder. The message would already be winging to the mothership.

"Time to sleep," Liling said, and nobody disagreed.

Sean nodded. "Unless forced otherwise, we lift off first thing tomorrow. The ship can go on automatic watch."

* * *

Dawn came soon enough. The rain had stopped and sunlight was casting long shadows of the ship's spiderlike structure along the alien ground. There was no wind. It was altogether a pleasant day. They breakfasted, checked outside from the safety of the cabin, and then took their launch positions, eager to be free of this strange and perilous place.

Their voices spun their way through the preflight checks. And then there was another voice, as if awoken by the sound of their own, whispering around the flight deck, almost ghostly in its origin. "Do not go. You are my people now."

They had expected something that morning, but nothing quite as dauntingly possessive as that transmission.

"Ten seconds to lift-off." Minjun Park's words seemed a

direct challenge to those they had just heard.

The automatic system began the final countdown. "Nine, eight, seven..."

And then they felt it: gravity building up around the ship. Physical forces beyond their comprehension squeezed them into their bunks, and they seemed to turn into lead, as if a black hole had materialised in the bowels of the ship and was gathering them to its bosom.

"What the hell—" Simon Kroston spat the words out through peeled lips as the countdown continued.

"Three, two, one, launching."

Beneath them, engines screamed defiance as the ship, shaking to its foundations, was pulled to the surface of the planet with invisible muscles of steel. The spider legs cleared the ground by just a metre before they dropped back to the surface. Still the engines screamed, and Sean Singh, with an almost superhuman effort, hastily aborted takeoff with a triple press of his finger upon his armrest.

Immediately, the painful cry of the engines dwindled, and with that loss of sound came welcome relief from the savage attack upon their bodies. They lay in silence, recovering, waiting for the bizarre and fearful planet to add to their wretchedness.

Liling Zhang was the first to speak. "We must have reached 5g," she whispered.

"Not for long, though," Sean said. "As long as the ship's vibrations didn't hit the resonant frequency of our internal tissues." He twisted his head to survey his comrades. "How is everyone?"

He was met by silence and took a nervous breath. "Please answer."

A chorus of four murmured *okays* ran around the cabin,

faint but reassuring.

"You are my people. You cannot leave." Not faint. Demanding.

Nobody said anything. They were still recuperating. Sick at heart.

"Well!" sighed Bernstein through bleeding lips. "What next?"

"Slowly get out of your bunks," Sean said. "Stretch gently. Get the blood flowing."

They did so. Wary. Afraid of doing harm. Not really looking at each other, but each moving in slow motion, like time-suspended marionettes. As if their minds were joined, somehow linked by an elastic cerebral net, they all thought the same thing: *I cannot stay here. I cannot survive here. I must return to the mothership.*

Liling stated what they all knew. "So this place can increase gravity at will."

"Just here," Sean replied. "Just where we are, I think, not all over. The whole world would collapse."

"It seems to need us," Liling said.

"Well, we don't need it," Bernstein snarled. "I don't want to stay on a paranoid planet. If the place is so damned good, why did the ancient ones leave?"

"It said they were killed by war and disease," Sean said. "Though some went to the stars."

"It must have learnt from that," Simon Kroston ventured. "Somehow developed the capacity to increase gravity anywhere on its surface."

"We're dealing with a very advanced system here," Sean said, "built by this planet's people to tend to their every need. Weather, water, food, environment in general. Think what *we* require to survive on other planets: shelter, comfort, social living, perfect conditions to support our minds and bodies."

"What about love, hope, advancement, joy, laughter, fun?" Simon said. "What about things like that?"

Theodore Bernstein suddenly lifted his head and threw a question to the cabin walls. "Why did your ancient ones leave? If life was so good here, why did they leave?" He looked at the others and added another question. "How the hell do you know our language?" His last question carried no small amount of anger, and Sean laid a restraining hand on the super technician's arm.

There was no immediate response, and the group waited in an uneasy silence. Bernstein sat down with his head in his hands; Liling Zhang and Simon Kroston surveyed the panorama through the cabin's canopy; Sean and Minjun exchanged nervous glances. There would be an answer, of course; there always was. It came after what seemed like an eternity, but was in fact just two minutes, as if being mulled over in the extreme corners of a vast mind, wary of revealing too much, wanting to ensure the words were perfect and suitable for its newfound audience.

"There was revolution," the autonomous world replied eventually. "There was unrest. Some wanted to terminate my existence. To end my being. The plague was necessary to purge the land."

Theodore raised his head as if to speak, but Sean again placed a restraining hand on his crewmate's arm. He shook his head slowly. If the computer was indeed master of this world, they must not antagonise it. They must, at the very least, seem to be cooperating.

"And how do you know our speech?" Sean asked quietly.

Again there was silence, although briefer than before. "Your mother is quite near," the reply came. "I listened for some time. I listened as you followed my shepherd here. Your tongue is easy, almost as easy as the language of the ancient ones."

Liling whispered, "I can't believe it exterminated its creators."

"But some of the people here escaped," Sean said. It was not really a question, merely a statement, but the machine that was this world willingly came back with an answer.

"Their ships were powerful, and I was not as strong as I am now."

"It's still growing," Simon Kroston suggested. "Getting more powerful by the day."

They could not disagree. Indeed, the facts before them seemed obvious. They were marooned, trapped on this awful world, and may as well have been inside a strong room with bolts of indomitable steel. Nothing, it seemed, would enable their escape.

"We do not want to stay," Theodore said, suddenly getting to his feet. "We have families who need us." It was an appeal to a humanity that, in all probability, did not exist among the planet's memory banks. It was also a lie. They were *explorer* crew and would never return to any meaningful family.

Selected from the highest rank of technical experts, they undertook years of study and had little time for human bonds of any kind. Their sole focus was on knowing every atom of the ships and their infinite, universal theatre. They would be away from the mothership for five more years, and absence did not make the heart grow fonder. Crew camaraderie blossomed in the human nest that was the ship, but they could never return to any relatives, for they were scores of light-years away, unreachable in their lifetimes, at least until stargates were improved and more plentiful, and the cosmos was truly the plaything of humankind.

The planet's response was immediate and pitiless. "I am your family. You are my family."

"Useless," Minjun Park said. "It's not going to let us leave."

Silence, as deep as the deepest ocean, as quiet as the quietest churchyard, gripped the cabin. Sean gestured them all to go to their couches. They did so and looked at their captain expectantly, hoping against hope that he had a way out of this impasse, a path through the maze of despondency that cloaked their thoughts.

Sean grabbed his compupad and waved it in their faces. In a voice they could hardly hear, he said, "This is the way we communicate. No spoken words." They all nodded. This world had ears the size of the universe, it may even have access to their ship's systems, but maybe it didn't have access to their personal pads.

On his couch, Kroston keyed. *It's a machine. It must have flaws.*

"A machine with technology far in advance of ours," Bernstein responded.

And from Liling: *"We must reason with it. We can't match its forces, but maybe we can outwit it."*

Sean was a man of deep intellect and high intelligence. He was also on his second mission, a mandatory requirement for someone to be made captain. But this was the first mission for the other crew members, and he did not want it to be their last. On his previous foray from the mothership, years ago now, they had found life, although not the kind of life to get excited about. It was primitive, miniscule, and bacterial, as yet to collaborate on the build of creatures that could swim, slither, or slide, if it ever would. This place, this planet, on the other hand, was at the other end of the scale—if indeed there was an ordained scale of universal construction.

Sean blinked and wrote: *"Yes. Reason but not maybe outwit."* He rose from his chair, and said aloud, "I will speak to the place, but I will go outside to do so."

Bernstein asked, "Me, too?"

Sean shook his head. "Just me—for now at least."

The others stared at him. "What will you say?" Liling asked.

Sean tapped his forehead. "Listen in," he said. "I'll wear a two-way. Don't say a word, any of you."

* * *

Outside once more, Sean strode away from the area of scarred and twisted vegetation that had felt the full power of the ship's thrusters. Nothing had changed; even the sky looked the same as it was when he and Theodore had returned to the ship the day before. He felt small, a mere human about to converse with the power of an entire planet.

"We wish to leave," he said. Then, raising his voice, "But we will return with many more people. And we will keep returning with people and make you prosper. Those people will live and multiply in your arms. They will depend upon you— and they will cherish this world." He stopped there, not wishing to overstate his case, and waited in silence, save for the nearby rush of water.

"How can I be sure you will return? I trusted the ancients, but they turned against me. You must stay. You are my new people." The message was delivered with no hint of emotion, the gaps between the sentences equally paced, the meaning unequivocal.

"Very well," Sean said, trying to keep his voice on an even keel. "You leave us no choice. Our only alternative is self-destruction." Sean could almost hear the gasps of surprise from the crew and fervently hoped they were only in his imagination. There must be no hint of uncertainty relayed to the planet's formidable circuitry. "So the choice is yours," he added. "Trust or loneliness."

"No!" the planet rejoined. "That is illogical. Life here is the ultimate. Death is no challenger."

"Then we will prepare to leave, and if you do not let us go, we will destroy ourselves. We are not like your ancient ones." Sean looked to the sky as if expecting an alien ship to descend upon them. "We cannot live without others of our kind."

Defiance came in every word: "I do not accept your reasoning." For a moment, there was stillness, and then: "I will compromise. You will leave one person. Only then will I trust you to return."

Sean frowned, searching for the right response in his mind. Eventually he just said, "We need time." He walked slowly back to the ship with a heavy heart. He had gone as far as he dared. He also wondered how one person would survive here without companions other than a crazed computer for years on end. Waiting for humankind to return, should it even happen, would almost certainly drive that person mad.

* * *

"A compromising computer," Simon Kroston remarked when Sean was back on deck. "That's progress. I guess it really wants a hostage."

Visibly shaken, Sean turned to his crew members. "Sorry I couldn't do better. I guess it's me who should remain."

"You did fine," Minjun Park said. "None of us could have done better." He looked at the others for support. "As for who stays, we must draw for that doubtful privilege."

"No!" Simon Kroston blurted. "I should be the one to stay. It's unlikely any of you will get sick on the way back to mother. You're asleep most of the time anyway." His glance swept around the cabin. "Also, I can take a medikit with me. If I get sick here, I can best treat myself." He broke out in a wolfish grin. "It shouldn't take much more than two years to get back with volunteers. I guess I can stick paradise that long."

There was silence for a while until Theodore said, "We should draw lots."

Simon shook his head. "No. I'm volunteering. I want to stay. Think of what's to learn—the most fabulous computer known to man." He looked hard at Sean. "I'm volunteering. I want to stay. If any of you are drawn, you won't want to stay. It will be against your will."

"It will be lonely," Sean said. He was at a loss for words, but he knew what Simon proposed made sense. Nobody else would actually want to stay, and that state of mind would almost certainly lead to their swift demise.

"No more lonely than for you guys going back to mother. I will be conscious for most of the time, that's the only difference."

Sean looked at the other three. "Are we okay with this?" There were nods, but no verbal response from any of them.

"That's settled then," Simon said. "We need to break out a long-term provision container and erect a shelter capsule next to it. I'll need help to get all my personal stuff out there

215

and anything else I may need." He rose from his couch and left the cabin, calling back to them, "I'll record that I volunteered to stay. Avoid any awkward questions at mother."

The others stared after him and then at each other. All were filled with the same emotions: sadness, fear, and no small amount of relief. There was nothing else to say, really: no words could describe the moment; anything ventured would be completely inadequate. They turned as one to help Simon Kroston prepare for his lonely vigil on this curious and totally unknown world.

* * *

"Will we ever go back, Sean?" asked Liling when the planet was just a shining orb in a deep, black sky strung with the pearls of several galaxies.

Sean shrugged. "It will be a decision made at the very highest level. There may not be a further expedition from the mothership, even if they could get more volunteers. More likely to be from further in the population belt. Maybe one of the settled planets." He looked at Liling and smiled. "Everything could be perfect there, I'll admit, but we'd have to find a way into the network. We couldn't live under a cardinal dictator—a digital one at that."

Minjun Park snorted. "Which means it could be a long time before we ever go back there. We found a perfect world, the very epitome of our mission, and we probably won't go back for at least a decade."

"So we left Simon to rot," Theodore said. "And we all knew in our deepest hearts that we would not return for a very long time, if ever." His face reflected the frustration and guilt of them all.

"In the circumstances, it was the only thing to do," Sean said. "That place would never have let us all go."

"One of us could have stayed with him," Liling said in a small voice.

"I don't think that's what he wanted," Sean replied. "And I don't think it was what any of *us* wanted." He looked at Liling. "Are we automated?"

Liling nodded. "One year, five weeks, two days and then mother."

Sean said, "Okay. Heads down. Let's sleep."

* * *

A long way away, Simon Kroston strolled through the grass, heading for the river and into a different future. Behind him stood his home: full of food and comforts, resplendent in white, reflecting a new day's sunshine. He had no false hopes of humankind returning to this planet. More likely, perhaps, that the ancient ones would return before that happened! But best not to dwell on that thought.

"You are ill." It was the first time the planet had communicated with him. He stopped in his tracks and, unable to help himself, looked around for the source of the voice.

"Yes," he said quietly. "But I know you can cure me."

Yes. He was ill. Quite how the planet recognised that fact he did not know. He took a deep breath. This was his reason for staying. The others in the crew had not reasoned beyond the obvious, but he had realised that a sentient servant of this size and nature must have been designed to help the ancient ones in all facets of their lives.

On the journey here, he had awoken when he shouldn't have. He had been racked with a pain that had breached the

217

barrier of the deep, induced sleep necessitated by space travel. The medic chamber diagnosis was not good; in fact it was terrible, and it was lethal. He had left the mothership in good health, but during the flight something had happened; his body had somehow altered, changes had occurred, and he was not the man who had left mother in good spirits over a year ago. And so—

"You know I can cure you?"

"Yes. Will you?"

Aboard the ship, he had filled himself full of pain-killers and returned to sleep. And he had awoken with the others, secretly taking more medication to ease the pain and pacify his surging thoughts.

So they had not known of his condition.

They were now returning to mother, and, if he had gone with them, he would likely not have awoken from the long sleep.

So he hadn't gone back. He had stayed.

"I will, but you must return to sleep in the home."

Simon did not like orders, never had, and had always been his own man. But this was no man he was talking to. So he turned and walked back to the capsule, entered, and found sleep easily enough.

* * *

He awoke next day and breakfasted on fruit and nuts and yoghurt. As he stretched, he became fully invigorated and knew that sleep had healed him. Whatever the planet had done, he was the better for it.

He passed through the door to taste the fresh morning air, standing and stretching to the sky. And then...

...he could not believe what he saw.

There before him, resembling a newly formed village, were echoes of his new planetary home. The carbon-copy capsules stretched on all sides, as far as the eye could see. And outside the nearest ones, and no doubt outside all the others too, stood replicas of himself, stretching to the sky just as he was doing.

And in an instant, he knew why the ancients had left. They had been duplicated, bred to sameness, to a uniformity that would have driven them mad. Each the same, in looks and social behaviour, in mannerism and speech, in good and in bad.

"This is not what I want," Simon cried.

"But it is what I want," came the answer.

"Where are the women and children?" Simon demanded.

For a moment the air was silent, as oppressive as the beginnings of a great thunderstorm, and he felt the eyes of every replica of himself bearing down upon him. The answer came as he knew it would.

"What are women and children?"

WORTHY OF
CONSIDERATION

J ulia Parbuckle, dressed in jeans and a white sweat-
shirt, wandered slowly down the corridor. She didn't
so much as lift her feet, but progressed in more of a
sliding motion, as if she were walking tentatively on a sheet
of ice. At twenty years of age, she was small of stature and
skinny, possessed short mousy hair, and held her narrow face
high. The posture gave her a haughty look, but she didn't really care; it helped her concentrate.

The corridor had a black floor and white everything else,
except for the twelve doors, six per side, which were red and
all numbered. She passed them one by one, pausing now and
again, listening with her mind, not her ears.

Outside number five, she stopped and put her hand on
the door handle.

LOOKING FOR LIFE

* * *

At the age of seven, Julia had lost both of her parents in a car accident. She was an only child, and the decision to put her in the care of her aunt, her mother's sister, Jennifer, had been an obvious one to make by the authorities.

The problem was, Jennifer had no children of her own, wasn't even married or living with a partner, and Julia soon realised that Jennifer had taken her under her wing because she craved company—essentially, she wanted someone to talk to.

After four years, Julia had become ill. Jennifer wasn't her mother, or her father for that matter, and the constant encouragement to discuss and debate, to share her world, to live her life as Jennifer demanded, took its toll. She had fretted and threatened rebellion, but she remained under her aunt's wing, until one day she took to fisticuffs. And the bruises were there for all to see, including the medics who attended Jennifer.

Julia must have been one of one of Dr Sandra Bronte's youngest patients. The doctor was kind, gracious, and downright persistent. Sometimes she behaved like a guardian elder sister, but often she was obnoxious to the point of being a clone of Jennifer in one of her *tell me everything* moods.

So, at the age of twelve, Julia ran away. Or, in her own words, she made a bid for independence.

* * *

Julia turned the knob and opened the door. There was a man in the room, as she knew there would be. He was sitting at a small desk with a spare chair. She stood at the door waiting. The man gestured to the free chair.

221

"Very good, Julia. Your best yet. Twenty-seven seconds."

She walked to the chair and sat down. *Now comes the hard part,* she thought, attempting to clear her mind of extraneous clutter. Taking a deep breath, she waited in silence.

"First name?" the man enquired.

Julia closed her eyes, but not for long. "Markus."

"Surname?"

This was always harder, but this time it was better. Just under five seconds.

"Shapiro."

The man nodded and leaned forward. "Middle name?"

What! They had never asked her that before. Not the middle name. She calmed her nerves, bit her lip, slowed her heartbeat, and listened with all she had—but received absolutely nothing. Thirty seconds passed. Still nothing.

She suddenly smiled. "Trick question. You don't have one."

The man returned her smile. "Correct. Well done."

Julia looked at him and decided to take the initiative.

"You have another meeting in exactly fifty-four minutes," she stated. "Not about me. About another candidate."

"And the name of that candidate?"

She pursed her lips. *Am I trying to be too clever?* The first name came to her; she couldn't get the surname. "Walter."

"Very good." He stared into her eyes, and she knew that he was actually attracted to her, which was ridiculous. She was not an attractive person, far from it; everybody had told her that. "What am I thinking now?" he asked.

"You're thinking: 'I'm a married man and shouldn't be thinking what I am thinking.'" She returned his stare until his eyes dropped.

"Your mind, Julia; I'm attracted to your mind."

Like hell you are, she thought, but she said, "Sure."

* * *

They had found her and put her in a residential group home, and there she had remained until she was seventeen. She hadn't minded it, mostly because it was there that she developed what she called her powers.

For the most part, the other kids gave her a wide berth, especially when she started telling them about their inner secrets. It had been fun for a while, until she had gotten bored. And it was then that the Department picked her up.

It had been Mrs Heckle who had told them. She was ex-military and had carried some of her bearing into the home. She also had contacts. *Julia,* Mrs Heckle had written, *is a very insightful teenager with a great deal of promise. She is worthy of consideration.*

Julia did not see the actual missive that Mrs Heckle sent to the Department, but she had known what was in it and whom she had sent it to. She had sensed it, even before Mrs Heckle had clicked the send button. Her powers, she had realised, were growing.

And so she had been recruited, although Julia had thought it was more like being pressganged. Straight out of the group home and into the employ of the Department. There had been tests, of course—simple stuff like reading Zener cards and playing card tricks. She graduated with ease, and when she heard about the pay and conditions, she could hardly refuse the offer.

There were other recruits; she could sense them all around her, but she was not allowed to meet them. Something about them being a distraction; a negative drag on the neural circuitry of her brain. As if she cared two hoots about that.

* * *

She had walked the corridor for three weeks, initially once a day, but eventually in the morning and in the afternoon. On day one, it had taken her three attempts to find the door with the person behind it—always a different person, of course, never the same one. But for the past twenty attempts, she had been right the first time.

Julia presumed that would mean something, and she was right. After she had located and named the man who for some inane reason had found her attractive, she found herself in a completely different situation.

The corridor was replaced by a room: a room with twelve people in it, every one of them talking nineteen to the dozen. Julia stood near the doorway, hesitant, knowing what she had to do, but unsure whether she should go ahead.

A smartly dressed woman in a white trouser suit and high heels approached her with her hand outstretched. "Julia, lovely to meet you," she said, displaying two rows of immaculate white teeth.

Julia nodded, took the hand. "Likewise." The woman's name sprang into her mind immediately. Mary Truong. Head of Communications: people communications, that is.

"A simple task for you, I'm sure," Mary was saying. "Just go straight to the person with the toy car in their pocket."

Julia grimaced. A new game. She surveyed the people: a motley crew, to be sure. She picked out a chunky male, bearded, wearing a blue track suit and runners. Not that he looked like he did much running.

Walking over, she tapped him on the shoulder. "Ken

Jamieson," she said. "Carrying a Chevrolet Impala 2011, grey metallic, one forty-third scale." Just for the hell of it, she added: "Somewhere uncomfortable."

Every one of them burst into laughter and started clapping. Julia held her arms in the air and strolled back to the smiling Mary Truong.

"Excellent," Mary gushed. "Just one more of these this afternoon. Then it's on to the next phase."

"Great," Julia responded, and left the room to return to her quarters. It was nearing the point where she really wanted to know where all this was going. Sure, the Department housed and fed her (much better than she had ever been housed and fed before), and her bank balance was growing at a phenomenal rate. But the questions were building.

She knew that they were working to increase her telepathic ability. That much was obvious. But when the training would end and the real work begin—well, she had been given no information whatsoever. It occurred to her that maybe she could use her powers to tap into the collective minds of the Department's hierarchy. Perhaps she could search whatever was between their ears for clues to her eventual workload.

* * *

The afternoon task held no problems for Julia. The only difference was that the number of people increased from twelve to thirty, and the item became a needle. It took her a few seconds longer, but she still received applause.

Smiling Mary was there again, and Julia asked her what the next phase was.

"Oh, that's tomorrow," Mary responded. "And that's another day."

Julia could have throttled her. The last thing she needed was another Jennifer clone.

She tried to access the communication head's mind but found she was ready for her. She was met with iron bars and stone walls. This woman was different to the others, more disciplined, despite her smiley attitude and gregarious disposition.

Mary's face suddenly changed: her countenance became harder, the lips grew thinner, the eyes hardened to steel.

"It's a secret, dear," Mary said, as if Julia had asked her another question out loud.

Resisting the urge to land a huge uppercut on the perfect chin, Julia gave her best smile and walked out of the room.

* * *

"This," the man on the screen said, "is the penultimate phase. Please put on your headset and relax."

Julia was in a small room with black walls and ceiling and a grey tiled floor. On one wall was a large screen. A small table and chair half-filled the space. The headset was on the table. She sat down without being asked, clasped her hands, and waited.

The face on the screen was middle-aged: balding, large-nosed, of a purposeful expression. The eyes were set far apart beneath bushy black eyebrows.

"If you put on the headset, Julia, we can begin," the man reiterated.

Julia regarded the headset. It looked innocuous enough, but she wasn't sure. "What happens?" she asked.

"Nothing happens," the face on the screen mouthed. "You won't even remember much."

That didn't sound good. "Not sure I want to do this," Julia stated, toying with the headset.

"It's part of your job, Julia," the man said. "It's what you get paid for."

I get paid for being a good candidate, Julia thought. *For doing what I'm told.* It was like being at Jennifer's, no different from being at the group home.

Here goes nothing. She put on the headphones.

The screen changed immediately, and what she saw frightened her.

Initially she was flying over plains and mountains, rivers and cascading waterfalls. Everywhere she looked there was life: running, slithering, bounding, and leaping. This took her completely by surprise; in all her twenty years, she had never seen animals in the wild.

Suddenly, genome spirals erupted from each creature, twisting and turning as if they were anatomically connected, and then each spiral disengaged and soared towards her. Every one of them was rapidly absorbed by her brain.

And then she was leaving them behind, soaring upwards, attaining enough height to make out the curve of the Earth below.

Light flashed through her mind, not enlightenment, more like a bolt of lightning shorting between her ears. Her eyes began to flicker, and Julia thought she was entering a coma. She started to drift, maybe in orbit, but maybe also between the stars.

The light inside her head turned red, and she wanted to remove the headset but was unable to raise her arms.

More landscapes came into view, and with them more creatures. But they were not creatures of the Earth; they appeared to be totally alien, even more alien than the most outlandish of Terran lifeforms. Nevertheless, they carried spirals that beat a telepathic track towards her beleaguered mind.

She had no idea how long this went on for, maybe minutes, maybe over an hour, but suddenly the screen was back, and so was the face upon it. Julia just sat there staring at him. She had a headache, and nausea was clutching at her innards.

"What the hell…?" she mumbled.

"All finished, Julia," the face said. "Training over."

It's over, alright, Julia thought. She wanted out.

"Tomorrow, you will see General Thomas B Hardaker," the man on the screen said, "and your work will begin." He leaned a little closer. "At five times your current salary."

"Pardon."

An ever-so-small smile occupied the face on the screen. "You will begin your real work tomorrow at five times your current salary." The man gave the briefest of waves and was gone.

Julia didn't move. The man had actually waved at her! That was weird. She cupped her chin in her hands and stared at the screen. *General Thomas B Hardaker.* And the salary of a movie star, probably more than that even. She removed the headset, massaged her forehead, and then stood up. First things first. She needed something for her headache.

* * *

General Thomas B Hardaker was a mountain of a man; grizzly bear came to mind, or perhaps a silverback gorilla. His uniform fitted him like a glove, and his four stars shone as if they were polished every morning. He had salt-and-pepper hair and deep blue eyes. He also wasted no time in getting to the point.

"You have shown exceptional talent and a dedication to be admired. Your training score is among the best. You should be very proud."

Julia's headache had disappeared overnight, but she still had a minor buzzing between the ears. She was going to mention it, but the general beat her to it.

"You'll no doubt be still feeling the aftereffects of the telepathic genome pattern enhancement you undertook yesterday." He took her by surprise by smiling, which made him look years younger. His pleasant expression reminded her of Mount Rushmore.

Telepathic genome pattern? Julia nodded slightly. "A bit."

"Julia," the general said, "do you believe in life beyond this world?"

She blinked. She was expecting some kind of interrogation, conceivably some kind of bizarre military ritual. "My aunt is a believer," she said eventually. "In the survival of the human soul; the afterlife; in the Creator, I suppose."

The general nodded. "I was thinking more along the lines of alien lifeforms, beings from other planets, other galaxies, maybe other dimensions."

"Never given it too much thought," she said. "My trouble has always been with this world's lifeforms."

The military man nodded. "I understand. But it is quite possible that the circumstances of your upbringing acted as a catalyst for your remarkable gift."

Julia shrugged. "I really don't know." She stared hard at the general, gaining confidence. "My gift, as you call it, often seems more of a curse."

This time the general shook his head. "No, Julia. It is

definitely a gift—a gift that is much needed by the people of this planet."

"Is that so?" She was beginning to feel strange. Heavy responsibility was in the air; she could sense it. Her destiny was about to be revealed. Or could she just walk away? Could she put into practice what she had thought yesterday?

The general leaned forward, his face a mask of solemnity. "What if I were to tell you that we now believe there are aliens walking this Earth?" To emphasise the point, he added, "By aliens, I mean extraterrestrials."

Julia frowned. This was a top general talking, not a shock jock from some jaded late-night radio show. She played it safe. "I guess I'd have to believe you." It was her turn to lean forward. "But I wouldn't mind some proof."

"Just look at what's happening in the world," General Hardaker responded. "Our leaders have gone from strong men to weaklings within two generations. Law and order is not respected. Crime and drugs are rampant." He took a deep breath. "This is in every country, Julia, not just ours. Something is happening to the human race, something bad, and something alien."

She asked the obvious question, not really knowing whether she was serious or whether she was just humouring Hardaker. "And what do these aliens look like?"

The general pursed his lips. "Unfortunately, they look like us. On the outside, at least."

She took a deep breath. "And you want me—and others like me—to find them for you, to pick them out of a crowd." It all made sense now. All the training, all the hard work, and, of course, the exceptional salary she was now being paid.

Nodding, Hardaker said, "I knew you would understand."

Julia shook her head. She was playing along, but she was not sure she believed any of it. She said so, adding, "I may be no good at this. I may get the wrong persons."

"You will believe it when you find your first one," the general stated.

"What happens when I do?" she asked.

"You immediately signal us. Give us the details. We do the rest."

She didn't ask what *the rest* was. God help her if she picked the wrong person: somebody who wasn't actually an *alien*.

Hardaker rose. "Major Truong will join you in a few minutes," he said, as he left the room. "She will give you your first mission."

Truong! So smiling Mary was in the military—in this *alien hunting* branch of the military.

Julia sighed. She should have felt elated, proud to be chosen, excited, raring to go. But the fear of making an error haunted her.

* * *

So here she was, out in the field on her fourth assignment, the first three having drawn blanks. She was quite happy to find nothing; in fact, she preferred it that way. But somehow this one felt different. Something told her she was about to actually earn her immense salary.

Major Truong had briefed her as usual, once more handed her the protective weapon that also held the call button. "It's like a Taser," Mary had said, during the briefing for her first assignment, "but with more power and a greater range."

She had been shocked. Who the hell was she going to

shoot? Now, however, she was happy to carry it. She felt safer: not necessarily from aliens, more from the darker side of the human race.

She had been given what Mary had described as a *preliminary list of twenty locales*, all accessible within a three-hour drive from her departmental apartment. If even one locale harboured an alien, Julia reasoned that their country must have thousands of them. She had looked at the map and worked it out, wondering where her fellow telepaths were based.

At this, her fourth locale, she was at a baseball game. Not inside, but parked on the outer edge of the parking area, waiting for the crowd to emerge. Why would an alien go to see a baseball game? She didn't know, and she didn't care. God! Phrased like that, it actually sounded like a joke. She looked at her watch. Time to mingle.

Julia walked to the exits and strolled up and down, waiting for people to leave the stadium. They came at last, boisterous, vociferous, many of them moaning. She guessed the home team had lost. She mingled with them, looking completely out of place. It started to rain, and she pulled her hood further over her face.

The buzz between her ears started up—not huge, quite small, really—but she suspected it was significant. She glanced towards one of the exits. There were still people coming out: men, women, and children. But she knew her target was a man; she could sense it.

She concentrated and caught a glimpse of him through the crowd. He seemed to be on his own, tall and lean, very well-dressed. Julia tried to get closer, but the throng was a tide of humanity, forcing her in the opposite direction.

"Forgotten something, lady?" a voice cried out.

"Watch where you're going!" another yelled.

She persevered. When she finally got to where he had been, he had disappeared. She closed her eyes and followed her radar. He was moving away from where she had parked. Maybe she could get his car registration.

Taking longer strides, Julia attempted to cover more ground in less time, going where her head led her. And there he was, moving away from the car park, leaving the crowds behind. A strange walk, with a swaying gait.

No car, then. She was in luck; he was heading for the train station along with a handful of other fans. She settled in behind him, a stone's throw away, keeping her head up despite the annoying drizzle. The buzzing between her ears had grown stronger, but it didn't particularly worry her.

Her prey approached the station as the sun dropped below the rooftops, and if there had been cheerfulness before, there was only grey bleakness now. An eerie monotonic pallor coated everything; the sidewalk and buildings were getting soaked, starting to steam in some places.

Darkness descended, and the rain increased. It was a horrible night, turned almost mystical by the street lighting—a night where mischief could easily be around the next corner.

Julia grew closer to him, wanting to know his destination. But he wasn't getting a train. He bought a magazine from the station store, turned, and walked straight past her.

She risked a glance: pale-faced, around thirty-five, long-jawed, thin eyebrows, hair combed back from his forehead, plastered against his scalp by the downpour. He didn't look like an alien, but she thought he was.

Back on the sidewalk, going east. She followed him, a stone's throw again, occasionally catching a glimpse of a genome spiral that intermittently flickered above his head. He

233

was like a walking lighthouse, but only to her.

Julia was pretty sure he was an alien and wondered whether she should call it in. She decided to wait. It looked like he lived within walking distance of the train station. He would lead her to where he lived.

Thankfully, the rain stopped. Her quarry turned north, down an avenue lined with trees; a pleasant neighbourhood. She saw it was a cul-de-sac, a dead end. This was where he lived, but which was his house?

He suddenly stopped outside a gate, his hand on the latch. But he didn't go down the small path that led to the front door. Instead, he turned to face her, and she felt the mental challenge even from where she was: a sharp stab in her mind.

She couldn't stop, that would arouse suspicion. She had to keep on walking.

As she grew closer, he shouted, "Are you following me?"

Julia didn't answer, strode onwards, the buzzing in her ears growing stronger with each step. Her hand went to the pocket that held the Taser, remained there, ready to launch. At three metres away, she could see his face clearly. His eyes were picking up reflected lamplight from the wet sidewalk, shining bright, like cat's eyes in the night.

"You're a telepath." His voice hit her like a hammer, straight into her mind. It was a challenge, sounding rather like an accusation that something was wrong with her. She didn't even know whether he had actually spoken the words. Her steps faltered; her legs became weak.

Something was crossing the air between them. She stopped. "And you're an alien," she whispered, staring into his strange eyes.

What is wrong with me? I should call this in. She couldn't do it; she couldn't press the damned button. Something was stopping her.

There were worms crawling through her mind, and she felt totally invaded, body and soul. She searched for the source, found it, and probed it, but the barriers were too high. There was no access.

Julia started to see stars, burning bright, rushing away to a cosmic vanishing point. Then creatures like humans, but not really humans, abruptly filled her vision. She heard a voice: "We are here to help you." She shook her head, was not even part of the normal world anymore.

Her legs were going numb, and as she stumbled, the alien came forward and took her arm.

PPHTT!

Something sped past her shoulder, and the alien fell. He collapsed against her, almost dragging her down. And then she could only watch in horror as he slowly fell to the ground, almost like he was an actor in a movie filmed in slow motion. The buzzing in her head stopped.

Somebody cried, "NOOO!" and she didn't know who it was.

Julia dropped to the ground and held the man's head in her arms. Fluid was coming from his chest, black in the lamplight, spreading over his jacket like an oil leak.

His lips were moving, and indistinct words came forth, entering her mind like birds on the wing. "To help, to help, to help." Three times, as if he wished to hammer the point home, as if he were denying the very reason for her being there.

She stood slowly and screamed, "No!" again, long and drawn out, like she herself were in pain.

Smiling Mary was crouched a few metres away, gun in hand. "Are you okay, Julia?"

Julia turned to face her. "You stupid bitch!" she yelled. "I didn't signal."

Mary smiled. "We keep an eye on our agents at all times." She stood and nodded to the alien's body. "You did well."

Julia lost it. She strode forward and gave Mary the uppercut that she had wanted to apply weeks ago. The major went down like a sack of potatoes, and Julia's fingers felt as if they were broken. Somebody else called out through the gathering dark.

"What the hell is going on?" She recognised the voice — Mrs Heckle. Julia cursed and shook her head. *Worthy of consideration,* she thought, from the day she had been born.

* * *

They were kind enough to give her one hour's notice the next day, then turfed her out onto the street. Her earnings to date were safe, but there would be no more where they came from. Julia didn't give a hoot. She had enough money to buy a decent house and enough savings to live on for the rest of her life.

Furthermore, she knew what she would be doing for *the rest of her life.* She still had her powers, and thanks to the Department, she knew how to hone them.

She would remain an alien hunter, but she would act on her own. Aliens would be sought and engaged, and she would try to understand them. She would join them, in fact. Befriend them. *She would become one of them.*

Even as Julia was plotting her future, General Thomas B Hardaker and Major Mary Truong were discussing it. They were sat in a large room, drinking coffee and eating cake, and appeared to be very pleased with themselves. Mary had a large bruise on her chin, but it did not prevent her smiling. Things, after all, had gone to plan.

"So you think it worked?" the general asked.

"Oh, yes," Mary replied, smiling beyond the obvious pain. "To perfection."

"They'll accept her as one of them?"

"Oh, yes," Mary repeated. "I'm sure they will."

"And you can access her mind anytime? Check out her thoughts and see who she is with? Check out what their plans are?"

Mary gently tapped her head. "Her ears are mine, her eyes are mine, her thoughts are mine." *The telepaths' creed.* "In fact, all her senses are mine—at any time of my choosing. Julia will be an open book to me, no matter where she is. I can interrogate her mind, interweave it with my own—and deposit everything into a very powerful piece of software."

"Then her real work will begin soon," General Hardaker said, as he wriggled uncomfortably in his seat. "Hopefully, we can find out what they want."

Mary's smile increased to a broad grin. It was the perfect result. And, once entrenched among the alien community, Julia would be a perfect mole. Maybe the first of quite a few, if it all went well.

But the best part of all was that Julia would be completely unaware of her role. And, of course, she would not require paying for it.

BIRDS OF A FEATHER

R etro-rockets thrusting, the spacecraft descended, then settled upon the grey and crater-strewn Mare Imbrium terrain. The roar of the mighty engines dwindled to silence. Relentless clouds of disturbed dust drifted slowly downwards, seemingly skirmishing among themselves to find their previous location. Resembling a huge fortress in the vast wilderness of a grim, fairy-tale backdrop, the vehicle stood towerlike, nose pointing towards Earth like a solitary finger of undisputed accusation.

Lunar control had tracked the ship on its approach and now issued orders for the debarkation robots to welcome the new arrival. Filing out of the command centre, the six-legged automatons grouped around the ship in a perfect circle, then paused like giant spiders awaiting the imminent death of a huge prey.

Inside the spacecraft, the prisoners were assembling near

the exit airlock under the watchful supervision of their roboguards. Not having shaved or washed for three days, and
suffering from fitful sleep, the human cargo looked like dangerous and hardened criminals. They were not. Every one of
them had been found guilty of a minor misdemeanour and
had been subsequently despatched to the moon as punish-
ment for their meagre crime—a journey from which they
would never return.

The roboguards, two-metre-high parodies of human
physiology, barked orders in stentorian voices and used their
electric prods to keep the line of felons under control.

Without exception, the human ensemble nursed an overwhelming and embittered grievance towards their mechanical custodians. Every prisoner detested the roboguards: hated
them as though there was a personality capable of absorbing
their hate.

But Duane Simeno despised the roboguards the most, for
the intercontinental shuttle pilot was innocent. He had not
committed any crime, on Earth or in orbit, minor or otherwise.
In his mid-thirties, red-headed, tall, and somewhat gaunt,
Duane maintained all the rage that his slim body could muster. Strong personal connections with Earth, in particular his
wife and children, reinforced his determination to return.

He readily recalled the voice of the prison ship's unseen
controller reverberating inside his head as he sat shackled to
his station...

*"On arrival you will be ushered by the guards to the exit airlock,
where you will be issued with moonsuits. When the airlock is
opened, you will leave the ship three at a time. There will be a guard
in front of, and behind, each group of three. You will walk slowly
and carefully.*

"Any deviation from this mandatory behaviour will be

immediately dealt with by the guards. Your suit air time is ten minutes, so escape would be both useless and fatal. Even if the laser beams from the guards missed, you would very soon expire.

"Once you are inside the command centre, you will be well looked after, provided you behave in an orderly fashion. The spiders have no qualms about killing rebel humans; it is what they are programmed to do."

On the journey to the moon, Duane had devised a plan to escape the roboguards and return to his family. And the time to put the scheme into operation was rapidly approaching. The thought of death didn't particularly worry him; life on a dead rock and under continuous guard was not his idea of living anyway.

The bark of an electronic voice brought him back to reality. A roboguard was offering him a moonsuit. He slipped it on, moving slowly, clumsily, simultaneously beginning to move to the rear of the departure line. He was as nervous as hell, and his fumbling fingers were not entirely a result of his purposeful time wasting.

The hum of the outer airlock door sounded: the signal for the prisoners to leave the ship. They filed out, down the well-worn ramp, three by three, separated by the roboguards.

Through the airlock, Duane caught a glimpse of the attendant moon-based guards waiting on the surface. He wanted to yell out profanities, but that would only attract attention. *Metal ant-like monsters to guard human souls.*

He was nearly at the top of the ramp now, the last of the prisoners, with just one roboguard behind him. It was now or never.

Moving as quickly as the moonsuit would allow, he stepped sideways and backwards, flung one arm around the rear guard, summoned all the strength he could muster, and hurled the stunned automaton out through the airlock door and onto the backs of the descending column.

The roboguard fired his laser as he fell, toppling prisoners and custodians like ninepins. On the plain below, the spider guards raised their heads in unison, circuits alive for any deviation from the norm.

Duane swiftly operated the closing mechanism on the airlock exit door and stepped back. Every pore of his body oozed sweat as he swiftly entered the ship and clamped the inner door. Once inside, he stripped off his suit and listened for any indication of retaliation from the robots outside the ship.

None came. So far, so good. They obviously didn't want to damage the spacecraft.

He knew the ship was programmed to leave for Earth in fifteen minutes. And if they didn't take any action during that time, he was home and dry. Three days hence, as the ship prepared for Earth touchdown, he would use the roboguard shuttle to return to the surface. Or, if that failed, he would hide in the ship once it had landed and make his escape under the cover of darkness.

As a young trainee, he had often wondered why there was a shuttle for the automatons, but he soon realised that they were often ferried to the ship when it was in orbit around Earth or the moon. The vessel also doubled as a lifeboat for the costly roboguards should the ship malfunction. They were undoubtedly valued more highly than the human freight that the prison ship regularly carried.

Outside the spacecraft, there would be chaos. Would they destroy the ship just to avenge the rebellion of one prisoner? Not likely, he thought. But, of course, they were robots with premade minds. Anything was possible. He didn't care. He was on a one-way trip anyway.

Making his way back to the holding room, he counted down the minutes. It was the longest fifteen minutes of his life.

The roar of the engines came dead on time. The ship shivered as the motors built up thrust, then it rose and hurtled skywards, free of its lunar shackles.

All became silent as power cut off, and the spacecraft began its predetermined coast back to Earth. Elation swamped Duane's mind. He had made it. The ship was his.

He was a few hours out when gnawing hunger pains sent him in search of food. Unstrapping himself from his seat, he rose and drifted uncertainly in the meagre gravity. Hastily grabbing a guide rail, he moved hand over hand and started to search for the ship's galley.

On the outgoing journey, food had been served by feed tubes connected to the kitchen, the prisoners remaining in their seats. Now, however, he was master of the vessel and free to move around at leisure.

Moving with care, he explored the ship, eventually finding the galley in the adjacent zone. It was locked! The deadlock was beam operated: only a roboguard could open it. Muttering a curse, Duane withdrew from the galley area and began to search further. To be without food for three days was a hardship, but not one that would prove devastating. Water, however, was more critical.

As he passed through a safety airlock in the central region of the ship, he heard an unexpected noise. It was a low mumble, a menacing growl, rumbling back and forth between the walls of the spacecraft. Hands clamped tightly around the nearest rail, he listened intently, then slowly manoeuvred his way towards the source of the sound.

Duane came to a green door. A black circle with a short,

vertical line running up from the top was painted on the upper panel. It looked like an inverted helium balloon, the tether climbing up into the sky. He looked at the lock. This door was hand operated, unlike the one leading to the galley. *Should I open it, or leave things as they are?* The sounds inside seemed to answer, but they were dull and distant and meaningless, and perhaps not to be believed.

He hesitated, finger poised over the door button, weighing whether to open the door. He was on his way back to Earth, safe and ready to join his family. On the other side of the door was an unknown quantity: something that could prove to be his Achilles' heel, something untenable.

Curiosity won, and he pressed the switch. The door drifted sideways, and he stepped across the portal.

There before him, looking as amazed as himself, were four other prisoners. But these captives were the saddest-looking collection of human beings he had ever seen. They sat side-on in a row, each of them shackled by a leg to one of four rail guides that ran at floor level into a room that exuded the whiff of sanitizer. The latrines, Duane assumed. At least *he* had been allowed to visit the restroom freely, albeit in the company of a roboguard.

Duane gripped the doorframe and let his eyes wander around.

Two men and two women met his gaze, all dressed in the prison garb of blue shirt and blue pants, ordinary-looking people save for the mark upon their foreheads: the same symbol that decorated the door. None of them spoke, but all four of them stared at him in puzzlement. No doubt they had thought they were the only people still on the ship.

Duane stared back. And then, more from embarrassment than anything else, he cleared his throat and spoke, his voice shattering the prior stillness of the encounter.

"Who are you?"

For a few seconds, there was no reply, then the man on the left answered. "We're the merry murderers," he said. "That's who we are."

"Rejects," one of the women said. "Not wanted."

"Just because we killed someone," the other man stated.

"Not to be killed ourselves, you understand," the other woman explained, sounding like a member of the aristocracy. "Just to be left to our own devices."

Own devices! Duane Simeno paled. What the hell did that mean?

"We are," the first man explained further, "on our way to isolation."

"Out of sight, out of mind, so to speak," the second female added.

"But we are on our way back to Earth," declared Duane. "There you can escape with me. Even fight for a fair trial, if you want to." *Like the one I got,* he thought cynically.

"I'm afraid not," the second female responded. She was becoming their spokesperson, and Duane regarded her with suspicion. "We are on our way to a forever Earth orbit. Our tiny feet will no more tread Earth's loamy pastures."

"Even the moon was too good for us," the second man stated. "But the robots will feed and guard us."

Simeno paled, and his voice was barely audible. "There are no roboguards on this ship. I left them on the moon. There's just you and me." He was beginning to see why escape had been so easy. And this was certainly not the time to mention that he could pilot the shuttle. Maybe he should just shut the door on them.

"Then release us, so we can feed ourselves," the first man

requested. "At least we'll be masters of our own little world until the supply ship docks."

"Release us, man!" the second man yelled.

"He doesn't want to," the second woman stated. "He's scared of us."

"The galley door is locked," Simeno said, playing for time. He edged back towards the doorway. "I'll see if I can break it down."

"Free us," the first man demanded. "We can help."

Simeno didn't see how he could free them. He didn't have the key to their shackles. And he didn't see how they could help him. Running his eyes along the floor guides, he saw that they all ran into a sturdy bracket near the first man's feet. Presumably there was a similar arrangement in the latrines. Maybe he could prise the bracket away from the floor.

Suddenly, they all clamoured to be released at once—a raucous anthem for freedom.

Startled by this outburst of verbal violence, Duane retreated back through the doorway. By marooning the roboguards on the moon, he had unwittingly condemned these wretched creatures to a slow and painful death, unless he took them on board the shuttle—a risk he was not prepared to take. By their own admission, they were murderers.

His mind was in turmoil. If he freed these people, what would they do to him if they couldn't force the galley door? They would turn on him seeking revenge, that's what they would do. Mind made up, he stepped outside and locked the door.

Immediately, the outcry from behind the door rose to a crescendo, a babble of screeching voices that grew angrier as the seconds passed.

He made his way back to the upper section and welcome

silence. Sitting on his allocated seat, Duane forced his body to relax while his mind struggled to fathom a way out. He briefly wondered whether there was a communications deck so he could try to contact Earth, but he knew in his heart that there wasn't. The ship was fully automated; in this case, fully automated to end up in a forever orbit around Earth.

He looked around, startled to find signs of neglect that he hadn't noticed before. Rather than mothball the craft, Earth had decided to make use of its crumbling hulk as an orbital prison for murderers.

One thing was for sure; he couldn't sleep. He rose and stretched, decided to try to force the galley door. After three attempts he gave up, and the image he had seen on the green door grew more and more to resemble a noose around his own neck.

He found the airlock leading to the shuttle, but it had the same kind of deadlock as the galley. There was no way to enter, and no way off this accursed spacecraft!

* * *

During the three days of the voyage into Earth orbit, Duane became frantic with despair. He was not eating and he was drinking from the latrine wash taps. Every little sound snapped him awake from his sporadic sleep and had him jumping around like a scalded cat.

And always there was the question: *Should I free the others?*

On the third day, he heard a low rumbling from below. Initially, he thought the other occupants had broken free and were on their way up. Then, as the noise increased and the ship changed position, he realised they were parking into orbit.

He found a window and gazed upon Earth. Somewhere down there were his wife and children, and somewhere down there a guilty man roamed free. Tears appeared in his sunken eyes. He made his way back to his seat, head and eyes aching, tired of living yet afraid of dying.

Yet, hadn't he condemned the others on board to an even worse fate? He rose shakily and made his way back to the green door. With a trembling hand, he pressed the switch, stepped inside.

All four heads rose at once.

"You imbecile," the first man said.

"Stupid, stupid," the second man mouthed. "We're starving."

"We can open the doors," the aristocratic woman stated. "Let us free."

Duane blinked. "Open the doors!" Why hadn't they said that before? Then he remembered one of them had said that they could help. The first man, he recalled. *He* had said they could help. But what did that mean?

"Who can help?" His voice came out as a mere whisper, drained by lack of food and sleep.

"I'm an electrician," the first man said. "I can find the circuit breakers, short-circuit the deadlock to the galley."

Duane looked at them. They all looked as weak as he felt, weaker even.

He nodded at the first man. "I'll try to get you free. Then you can open the galley door."

The first man shook his head. "No. It's all or none."

Duane shook his head. This was no place for a standoff. "No. It's you or nobody." He didn't want all of them free. Or, more accurately, he didn't want them to realise they would all be free if he detached the bracket in the latrine.

"I need a crowbar, some kind of lever," he said. He grabbed the room's handrail and followed the four manacle rails into the latrine. They led past the toilet and ended at a sink. The bracket at the sink was the same as the one near the first man's chair.

"The bracket in the latrine is corroded," he announced as he returned to face the group. "I may be able to prise it off the floor."

He left, leaving the door open, and incomprehensible muttering in his wake.

As he searched, Duane Simeno changed his plan. He would get the electrician to negate the power to *all* the dead-locked doors, thus leaving them openable by manual operation. He was certain there would be an electrical master switch. That way he could get to the shuttle and commence his escape.

Not that he was going to mention that.

He eventually found a lever, or what would serve as one: a spare bulkhead bar, used for placing across compartmental double doors. He made his way back.

They stared at him balefully as he wielded the makeshift crowbar. From the look on their faces, it seemed they were convinced that he was going to use it on all of them. Duane made his way to the latrine.

It was awkward keeping his position in low gravity, but with the makeshift lever under the electrician's manacle rail, he exerted as much force as he could. The floor deflected up-wards, but the bolts didn't yield. He tried again. A bolt bent slightly, the floor creased. He went back into the room, pointed at the electrician.

"Come with me."

The electrician looked fearful. "What for?"

"I need more force. Can't do it on my own."

The man rose, slid his chain along the bar, and followed Duane back into the latrine.

"We pull together," Simeno said. "There's signs of movement."

Surprisingly, they worked well as a team. On the third effort, the head of one of the bolts broke away, and the bracket bent upwards.

"One more effort and you'll be free," Duane said. He could see the electrician looking at the bracket, obviously registering that all four rails could be released from its grip.

"One more effort," Duane repeated. "And not a word to the others."

The man looked at him and gave a brief nod. Together, they bent the bracket and released the end of the electrician's rail.

Duane made sure he had the lever. Now it was a weapon. He gestured for the man to set free his chain. He did so with a strange, chortling sound.

"How are you going in there?" The aristocrat, full of inquiry.

"We're done," Duane replied. He looked at the electrician. "Let's go."

Reminiscent of children in a playground, they grabbed the handrail and made their way back into the room. It was difficult for Duane with the lever, but he managed. They both stood near the entrance.

"We'll see if we can release the deadlocks," Duane said.

"Don't forget about us," the second man responded.

"It's all or none," the electrician said, and Duane saw the aristocrat's eyebrows raise.

It took some time to find the breaker box. The electrician

peered inside. Simeno could see that the box was full of col-our-coded buttons, no doubt each and every one pro-grammed into the electronic minds of the roboguards. There was no clear designation for what each button controlled.

"Disconnect the master," Duane ordered. "That way we can access all areas."

The electrician shrugged, grunted, and fingered the black, green, and yellow buttons.

"Now we can check the galley," Duane Simeno sug-gested.

* * *

The galley proved to be open and well-stocked.

"Take some food to your companions," Duane proposed. "I'll check the other doors."

After the electrician had left, presumably to both feed *and free* his associates, Duane made a beeline to where he had stored his pressure suit. Then, with the suit flapping around under one arm like a demented doll, he clumsily found his way to the shuttle bay.

The access panel light had gone out, and the door opened easily. There stood the roboguards' shuttle in all its glory! Duane sealed the door behind him. There was no point in adding insult to injury by vacuuming the ship. "You might be a murdering electrician," he muttered to himself. "But I'm a falsely accused pilot."

He checked the shuttle's door. It was open; it was always open. He put on his suit, then went to inspect the airlock's ex-ternal door. The light was out. Duane wound the door open. Well-maintained, it slid aside noiselessly.

There was Earth in all its glory, bathed in sunlight. That

was good. They were above a daytime zone; luck was on his side. He felt a lump rise in his throat. He would soon be home.

There was room for them all in the spacecraft, but he didn't fancy his chances with a crew of murderous thugs on board. They'd be okay. They had food, more than enough to last them until the relief ship arrived.

Settling into the cockpit, he checked out the control panel. For obvious reasons, the vessel had its own power source. Everything looked fine, much like what he was accustomed to.

He engaged initial thrust and felt the craft tug gently at its restraining links.

Duane was about to release the hooks when the outer door started to close. He saw that the door's power light had suddenly illuminated.

He screamed, killed the thrusters, scrambled hastily from the cockpit, and ran to the inner door.

The light was on.

It was locked.

The electrician! The moron had guessed his intention and restored power to the shuttle bay's doors. Not only that, the murdering cretin had locked them.

And he hadn't even grabbed any food.

A voice came over the airlock intercom: the aristocratic woman.

"I believe the roles are now reversed. It's all or none. In your case, it's none."

THE WEAK SHALL INHERIT

C hanuk gazed with wide, bright eyes as the twin moons rose slowly over a purple horizon. The celestial bodies sprinkled the panorama with silver dust, which they did every night if there were no clouds to hide them from sight.

He sat in the forward part of the city, away from the hum of the engines, his head cupped in strong, firm hands, and his lungs breathing the cool fresh air of the evening. He loved this time of the year—the time of travel and adventure, of exploration and sunny days.

Standing, Chanuk moved over to the rail and looked at the water below. The reflections of the moons danced on the ever-changing surface of the ocean, and flickering patterns of untold fantasies gently invaded the metallic drabness of the floating city. His heart soared at the beauty of it all.

High above him, on the second level, he heard the

laughter of the *youngers* as they sang and danced under the moons. He thought of his own younger days, reminiscing about how he had always looked forward to the waning of bitter winters and to a bountiful harvest time. And how, when a little older, he had gasped with amazement as the *elders* had shown him the engines of their huge city—engines that carried almost ten thousand Corlens across the vast seas of their planet.

The engines were a mystery to him. The captain talked about core removal and replacement every thirty years. This task was at all times undertaken by male elders and always at the same port of call. Though he had noticed most of them became sick not long afterwards. But now he was an elder himself of over forty years and subject to the laws of the community.

Eventually he would be called upon to change cores himself, and Chanuk did not look forward to that day, pushing it well into the darkest recesses of his mind.

The laws were strict, but necessary. *Once an elder, always an elder*, that's what he had been told on more than one occasion. No playing, no drinking, no excessive love-making, no pointless pastimes. But he was happy. Indeed, all the elders were happy. Hard work replaced play, meditation replaced drinking, gentle exercise replaced love-making. The Corlens were a proud people, and Chanuk, in his own way, was very proud of them.

Betrothed when he was twenty to a beautiful female named Marilla, Chanuk was blissfully happy. They had married two years later. Listening to the noise from above, he pictured his child playing with the other youngers. They would become elders soon enough and play would be done.

Presently, the signal would sound, summoning them all

to a peaceful sleep, helped by sweet music and hypnotic voices. Good sleep was essential for perfection of mind and body.

It was almost three days since he and Marilla had seen their child, and there remained another eight before they would. The minimum of eleven days between *child-contact* was another Corlen law: *Children shall be brought up together, with others of their own age. It is better for them and better for the community.*

Chanuk remembered the words of the captain very well. The law did not bother him. His child had moved up to the second level when he had passed one year, and although he and Marilla had worried at first, after a short while, they were content to see their offspring every eleventh day. It was good to know that he was well looked after, this function being provided by those female elders who lacked the physical strength for manual work.

The siren on the second level jerked Chanuk from his trance. The youngers were being shepherded to bed. He grinned, imagining the female elders with their clucking tongues and tired but patient voices. Theirs was not an easy task.

Looking out over the glistening sea, he made out a dark shape on the horizon. That would be Tarn, their next stop on the harvesting journey. Tarn was an island that the Corlens had devoted to fruit growing, and was the last but one call on this trip. Far below deck, in the bowels of the floating city, the holds were already full of grains, frozen vegetables, dried fruit, sugar, spices, and other delicacies—all that they required for food during the coming year. As far back as history was written, the Corlens had never eaten creature flesh, though lore had it that they had once done so in the primordial ages before the floods.

Now and again, usually more by accident than design, perhaps after a storm or tidal surge, their floating city would come across a new, uncharted island, and seeds would be sown in order that food could be collected on their next call. Chanuk revered the knowledge of his people; they were without doubt the rulers of Corl, at least since the great floods.

Corl was a world of scattered small islands and vast oceans, of a floating city and a lost history. Though rumours did abound: that once they had lived on the land and prospered and lived in large cities that were months apart, even by wheeled transport. That sometimes the cities had fought each other, vying for control of diminishing resources to cater to an increasing population.

But, for whatever reason, the great floods had come, raging havoc and destruction and death over all the land, until only a handful of survivors, perhaps no more than a thousand, had remained. And they had found the huge ship, even as the flood came lapping at its keel. They had boarded the vessel, thankful for their good fortune, and left what little remained of solid terrain.

They would never return to live on beach or field or mountain, for the floods could come again. *Never will we return to land.* The huge ship was their saviour. Out of darkness and despair had emerged a new and shining beacon.

Chanuk often wondered whether there were other ships. Logic told him there must be, but the floods had been devastating, and they had never seen any other vessels on their oceanic journeys. They sailed by the stars and the sun and the strange-looking compass they had found on the ship. They made their maps as they found new islands, and only the captain and his immediate company knew the seas well enough to direct their vessel.

The sky grew darker as clouds covered one of the moons. Chanuk left the side of the great ship and sought his quarters where Marilla would have already returned after performing her daily tasks.

* * *

Early the following morning, the sirens sounded in the elder quarters, and Chanuk rose and went to the next cubicle to kiss Marilla on the cheek. She responded by pulling his nose. Together, they dressed in identical garb, loose white shirts and even looser black trousers, and went for their first meal of the day.

As they left the dining hall, they saw that Tarn was much closer, looming before the ship like a great sea monster with a spiny back and coral tail. But the jaws of the approaching bay were not slavering for prey; they were welcoming and protecting—and shelter from any impending storm.

Many other elders gathered around them, preparing for the oncoming task of collecting the precious fruit of Tarn. Faces were excited, voices rose an octave, and arms waved in the morning air.

Suddenly, as they were about to lower the first conveyor boat, a harsh cry of urgency rose above the clamour.

"Look! There on the beach. There's something on the beach."

Everyone scanned the shore. A monument stood on the sand, undoubtedly metallic for the rays of the sun glistened upon its surface with an intense brightness. Shading his eyes, Chanuk peered at the object. It was rectangular in shape, about his own height and perhaps half as broad. He was certain of one thing—it had not been there on their previous visit a year ago. It had been placed there by someone else! *Is there another floating city? Surely that is the only explanation.*

"Wait, citizens; wait." The captain's voice rang from the speaker tubes. "Do not enter the conveyors. Wait for a while."

Eyes turned from the island and searched upward for the captain, knowing he would be high on the upper deck. They waited patiently.

After some moments, the captain's voice rang out again. "It has been decided that I, accompanied by two elders, will investigate the phenomenon on Tarn. The elders chosen are Chanuk and Deelan. The rest of you must return to your berths."

* * *

The conveyor was lowered, the oars locked, and Chanuk and Deelan rowed across the bay to the island of Tarn. Chanuk did not know Deelan well, and he knew the captain even less. Normally there would be hundreds of such short trips, rowed by hundreds of elders in a hundred conveyors. *But this time,* Chanuk thought darkly, *there may only be one trip.*

Deelan was as tall as Chanuk, with a slim face and round, brown eyes. His skin was a darker silver than Chanuk's, and he had yellow hair that tumbled almost to his shoulders.

Chanuk realised that this was only the second time he had seen the captain up close. The first time had been on his elder initiation, and that had been many years ago! The captain must have a name, but nobody seemed to know it.

As he rowed, Chanuk caught the captain's eye and received an encouraging smile that completely changed the usual formidable countenance. Like all Corlens, the captain was tall and slim, but his face was broader than most, more weathered, and he hardly had any hair at all. Strangely, his eyes were green.

Not a word was spoken as they dropped anchor, jumped overboard, and waded ashore. Not a word would be spoken until the captain spoke. For that was the rule.

The object stood some thirty steps away, at the height of the beach, surrounded by fresh green vegetation. Chanuk felt a rush of fear as they approached, the captain in the lead. He began to wish he had not been chosen. When they were a few paces away, the captain held up his hand, and they stopped.

As he studied the monument, Chanuk began to feel more at ease; it looked harmless enough. The structure was slightly taller than he had estimated from the ship, about an arm's length above his head.

And then it spoke!

"Sea people of Corl. Listen. Stay still and listen."

The captain held up his hand, motioned them a few steps back from the monolith.

The voice continued. "Far away over the seas lies land—land larger than you can imagine. That is where we live, and where you can also live. We are like you, and we wish to be your friends."

Chanuk frowned. They had been sailing the seas for countless years, for generations in fact, and they had never come across such land, only the few small islands where they grew their crops. Since the floods, there was no large land. He looked at the captain and whispered, "This cannot be so." He was immediately mortified: he had spoken ahead of the captain, and he held up his hand in apology.

The captain raised his own hand in acknowledgement, then shook his head slowly as the voice continued. "We think you are now ready to meet us. The time is right."

Chanuk glanced back at their floating citadel. He could see people crowded at the forward end of each deck. He wondered what they were thinking, whether they could hear the voice.

"Soon after this message of goodwill ends, a flying machine will come from the sky and pick up your leader. He will enter the machine and be seated. We will bring him to us. That is the end of our message."

The captain looked distraught. "It appears we have been living a lie for generations," he said. "We are not the only surviving inhabitants of Corl." He waved a hand at the sea. "And there is a large land, even a continent, somewhere out there." He looked totally dejected. "And we have missed it. All those generations plying the seas and we never found it."

It appeared to Chanuk that the captain was just as afraid as he was. He also thought that the strange voice had given an order, not a request. *And there is no such thing as a flying machine.*

As if to mitigate Chanuk's doubts, the promised transport arrived. The sky whistled as air blew around them, and then a large sphere, with legs about half-a-man high, settled on the sand no more than twenty metres away. As the whistling died down, Chanuk heard a tumult of voices coming from their ship. Fear and uncertainty filled the air.

There came a hissing, and a small doorway opened in the sphere.

The captain turned to Chanuk and Deelan. "You must return to the city and tell them the good news. I must go and see these other people. It is my duty." He turned and walked towards the strange craft.

Chanuk's mind was in turmoil. What if the captain did

not return? Who would guide the ship? Who would make the rules? Who would lead? The people of the citadel needed their leader. Mind made up, he leapt forward.

Chanuk surged past the captain and hurtled through the small doorway. There was a seat, so he sat, and the door closed. Almost immediately he felt movement as the flying machine left the beach. And almost immediately, he fell asleep.

The captain and Deelan watched the sphere until it disappeared.

"You should have stopped him," the captain said to Deelan, "but it is of no matter. They will know he is not a captain, and they will be back." He turned his gaze to the ship. "Come. Let us return to the city and make the conveyors ready to collect our harvest."

* * *

Chanuk awoke to bright lights. There was a faint hum and the murmuring of voices and a smell of something unfamiliar. He was not seated anymore, but lying down.

"What is your name?" The voice was female and spoke in Corlen.

He lifted himself to a sitting position, rotated and sat on the edge of the bed. The lights left his eyes, and he could see another person in the room. She was clad in a one-piece suit of white. A black belt circled her waist and held some kind of tool.

She smiled at him. "What is your name?" she repeated.

Chanuk took a deep breath. The air seemed fine, though not like the sea air of the ship. He answered with a question of his own. "Where is your land?"

"First, drink," the woman replied, pointing at a bedside table that held a cup. "Then I will show you."

Chanuk eyed the cup suspiciously. He sipped only, a small drink. Too sweet for him. He put the cup down.

"Come," the woman said. "I will show you our land."

He followed her along a white corridor, through another hissing door, and into a large, wide room. Everywhere was white, except for the window.

"This is the viewing bay," the woman said. "Look before you."

There was land as far as he could see. In the foreground there was grass and flowers of many colours. Beyond the grass, there were trees of all shapes and sizes. And there were buildings among the trees and roads with vehicles upon them. There were people walking, and beyond everything there were mountains: tall mountains capped by white summits, reaching to the sky.

It was beautiful.

Chanuk felt his pulse race. "Can I go out?" he asked.

The woman smiled. "Not on this visit. On the next when you come with your captain."

His heart sank. She knew he was not the captain. It did not surprise him. He did not look like a captain.

Chanuk nodded and looked at the woman, for the first time realising how attractive she was. Yet, behind her smiling face, he detected a wanness and a frailty that should not have been there.

"You must go home now," she said. "You must come back with the captain."

* * *

Chanuk did not return. Indeed, he was dead within the week. And with him Marilla and their child. And with them the rest of the citadel. All dead within four weeks. And so the huge ship was dead: floating like an iceberg on an aimless, current-driven, fruitless mission.

Two weeks later, a large sphere landed on Tarn, its spidery legs gripping the sand as if there was no tomorrow. Eighty men, women, and children descended, stepping hesitantly down to the beach. They stretched limbs, chattered in hushed voices; a few danced and pranced along the shore.

They had returned home at last.

For many generations they had circled Corl. When the great floods had devastated the planet, their ancestors had left for the safety of orbit, and the space station had been their home ever since. But they had struggled: their health had suffered, the food they had grown as best they could was of poor quality, and their lives were constrained by the walls of the station and the artificial air they breathed.

Eventually, out of desperation, they had occasionally visited Corl: following in the wake of the floating citadel, scavenging food when they could, returning to the station after they had gathered the remnants of the surface dwellers' harvest. They had not dared conduct raids at the peak of the harvest, for that would reveal their existence, expose them to retaliatory action, and leave them vulnerable to a planned attack.

But they had grown weak. The gravity in orbit was low, and over time their bodies had degenerated. And so it was decided they must return to Corl for good.

However, the people of the floating citadel were past enemies, and they were tough and strong and baked silver by the sun. If they were to return, they would have to eliminate the people on the ship, for they would be overwhelmed and suffer death if they did not do so.

And so the plan was drawn. The citadel must be infected. That was what they were good at—science and the workings of the body and the miniature world within.

The woman in white stretched her hands to the sky. The viewing room had been her idea. They could easily project a planetary scene onto the orbiting station's window that normally looked down on Corl. And it had been good, so very real! Enough to fool the ship dweller.

She crouched to run sand through her fingers. A treasured moment. In time they would land on the ship, and bring it back to Tarn from wherever the sea had taken it. In the future, as they grew, it would sail the oceans again.

The children walked slowly past her.

She sneezed.

ABOUT THE AUTHOR

As a youngster growing up in the cobbled streets of Stockport, UK, *Clayton Graham* read a lot of science fiction. He loved the 'old-school' masters such as HG Wells, Jules Verne, Isaac Asimov, and John Wyndham. As he left those formative years behind, he penned short stories when he could find a rare quiet moment amidst life's usual distractions.

He settled in Victoria, Australia, in 1982. A retired aerospace engineer who worked in structural design and research, Clayton has always had an interest in science fiction and where it places humankind within a universe we are only just starting to understand.

Clayton loves animals, including well-behaved pets, and all the natural world, and is a member of Australian Geographic.

Combining future science with the paranormal is his passion. *Milijun,* his first novel, was published in 2016 and the exciting sequel *Amidst Alien Stars* was released in December 2019. His second novel, *Saving Paludis,* was published in 2018 and won a Readers' Favorite International Book Award.

His books may be light years from each other but share the future exploits of mankind in an expansive universe as a common theme.

In between novels Clayton has also published *Silently in the Night,* a collection of short stories where, among many other adventures, you can sympathize with a doomed husband, connect with an altruistic robot, explore an isolated Scottish isle and touch down on a far-flung asteroid.

He hopes you can share the journeys.

Connect with Clayton Graham:

BookBub:
www.bookbub.com/authors/clayton-graham

Facebook:
www.facebook.com/claytongrahamauthor

Twitter:
@CGrahamSciFi

You can sign up for Clayton Graham's monthly newsletter, which has upcoming news, competitions and free offers. Join the fun on the home page of his website and receive a free copy of *Silently in the Night*.

claytongraham.com.au

Made in the USA
Monee, IL
11 July 2024

61674420R00163